How to Be a "Wicked" Woman

How to Be a "Wicked" Woman

MaryJanice Davidson
Jamie Denton
Susanna Carr

BRAVA

KENSINGTON PUBLISHING CORP.

http://www.kensingtonbooks.com

BRAVA BOOKS are published by

Kensington Publishing Corp.
850 Third Avenue
New York, NY 10022

All Kensington titles, imprints and distributed lines are available at special quantity discounts for bulk purchases for sales promotion, premiums, fund-raising, educational or institutional use.

Special book excerpts or customized printings can also be created to fit specific needs. For details, write or phone the office of the Kensington Special Sales Manager: Kensington Publishing Corp., 850 Third Avenue, New York, NY, 10022. Attn. Special Sales Department. Phone: 1-800-221-2647.

ISBN 0-7582-0707-7

First Kensington Trade Paperback Printing: August 2004
10 9 8 7 6 5 4

Printed in the United States of America

CONTENTS

The Wicked Witch of the West Side

MaryJanice Davidson

*For Kate Duffy and Cindy Hwang,
who have nothing in common with Jeannie
except her workload.*

"I'll get you, my pretty, and your little dog, too."
—Wicked Witch of the West

"I'm not bad, I'm just drawn that way."
—Jessica Rabbit

One

"You bitch! You've ruined my life!"

Jeannie Desjardin blinked in surprise, then glanced at her watch. Huh. How 'bout that. It was Tuesday, just before nine in the morning. She usually didn't get a bitch-you-ruined-my-life call until Wednesday afternoon.

"You're evil," the voice on the other end of the phone continued. "You're despicable; you're a wretched, horrible, nasty, awful *cow*. You'll pay for this one!"

She yawned and wrote THIS SUCKS on page forty-seven of the manuscript she was reading. "Is this the waiter at Lutece? Because I told you last night, I wanted my tuna steak medium rare, and you brought me a plate of sashimi. It's—"

"This isn't the waiter," the voice snarled.

"Oh. Then is this my dry cleaner? Because I'm not picking up the jacket, and I'm not paying for it, either. I'm *not*. I dropped it off with a quarter-sized mustard stain on the left lapel, dumbass, and now the whole thing is piss yellow. And where can I wear a piss yellow jacket? *Nowhere*."

"This is Earl," the voice hissed.

"Earl? I don't know any—"

"*In the art department! I work four offices away from you!*"

"Oh, Sucky McSuck! Sorry; didn't recognize your voice."

"I've told you a thousand times not to call me that," Sucky snapped.

"And I've told *you* to go back to art school. But I bet neither one of us is getting our way, what do you think? What's on your tiny little mind, Sucky?"

"I'm not redoing the cover for *Love's Snarling Fury.* It's fine the way it is."

"Oh." She shifted the phone to her other ear and put a pencil in her mouth, pretending it was a cigarette. "Well, if by 'fine' you mean 'unbelievably awful,' then we're on the same page."

"You hate all my covers," Sucky wailed.

"That's true," Jeannie agreed. "I do. If only you weren't so attached to orange and puce."

"I'm taking this one to The Big Guy," Sucky promised.

"God?"

"No, your boss."

"Oh," she said, bored. "Bob."

"Right! As in, the owner of the publishing house? As in, the guy who could fire your evil ass?"

"Don't tease, Sucky."

"You'll pay for this one, Desjardin!"

"It's pronounced 'duh JAR din.' Stop saying my name with a French accent, it drives me crazy."

She chomped on the pencil and heard Sucky hiss, "Stop breathing, it drives *me* crazy."

"You got anything else? Because I'm trying to have a career here."

He slammed the phone down for an answer.

She hung up and pulled her newest Palm Pilot out of its cradle. The last one had blown up when she'd put her schedule into it, but the sales geek guaranteed her this new model was up for the challenge.

She called up her schedule for the morning, then deleted:
9:00 A.M. meeting with Art Director.

Well! That was easy.

Two

Bob Anderson put his suit jacket on, though it was quite warm. The hottest summer New York had seen in ten years, and that was saying something. Still, it didn't matter. He had a meeting with *her*, and it would be best if she couldn't see him shivering while he laid down the law.

His office door rattled—Jeannie's way of "knocking" was to kick the door—and then there she was, standing in the doorway, scowling at him.

He opened his mouth to say thanks for coming, or good morning, or some other normal person greeting, when she launched.

"Don't even think about it."

"Now, Jeannie—"

"I'm swamped as it is, Jocko."

"My name is Bob."

"Swamped. Buried. Squashed. Loaded down. Over-worked. Underpaid and underlaid."

"Thanks for sharing."

"If you dump any more authors on me, I'm going to puke. Are you hearing me, Jocko? I'm going to pee-yuke."

"Well, tough," he said, thankful for the suit jacket. "We're all swamped, Jeannie. When you drove two of our best editors to nervous breakdowns—"

"Those two retards didn't know Tolstoy from Tolkien."

"—the rest of us, and by us, I mean you editors, had to divide up their workload. Besides, I'm only giving you one."

Her flinty eyes narrowed. Her sallow complexion reddened. Her wild, curly black hair seemed to bristle like a hedgehog facing down a predator. Really, it was ridiculous that she was great looking.

She shouldn't have been. If you took any one of her features—the wide, mobile mouth, the long nose, the ice-colored eyes, the out-of-control hair, the lanky body utterly without curves—and examined it, it wasn't pretty. But the package as a whole worked. Men couldn't take their eyes off her. Of course, that was because usually she was—

"—to fucking resign, Jocko! How about *that?*"

"Would you?" he asked gratefully. "That'd be great. Effective when?"

"No you don't," she backpedaled instantly. She was stuck with him, and vice versa. She wouldn't last a week at Pocket or Warner . . . the H.R. department would write her up and run her out. "You don't get rid of me that easily. And you *definitely* aren't dumping Hope Desiree on me."

He didn't say anything, just looked at her. She stomped around his office, and he observed her black panty hose had sprouted a run, almost as if she'd ruined them through sheer rage. "You are insane! That cow and I can't work together, we'll *eat* each other!"

"Resist the urge," he said. "Hope is practically our entire winter list."

"I give a shit! So now she's slacking and you're gonna dump her on me?"

"Dumped," he said. "Past tense."

Her bony hands snapped into fists. Dressed as she was—black turtleneck, black leather miniskirt, black hose, black pumps—and skinny as she was—one-forty, tops—it was like being menaced by a profanity-spewing streetlight.

"You suck," she gurgled. It was all she could manage, given her red-faced rage. He would have feared for her blood pressure, except the bitch was insanely healthy. He couldn't recall her ever getting sick, and he'd known her for fifteen years. "You . . . just . . . suck."

"And while I've got you in here," he continued, cold sweat trickling down his back, "I just got a call from our now-hysterical Art Director—"

She stopped in mid-gurgle. "Who?"

"Earl."

Instantly, her rage surged in a new direction. Psychotic *and* afflicted with ADHD. *Lovely*, he groaned inwardly as she went off.

"What, you hired a new guy? In *this* economy? Would it kill you to send me a memo? Goddammit!"

"You never read them anyway. Sucky McSuck."

"Oh. Oh, him! Sure, I know him. You should fire his ass. Have you *seen* his latest?"

Unfortunately, he had. Even more unfortunate, Jeannie was right—it was a terrible cover (a pea green background? What had the man been thinking?). Earl would have to try again. That was, undoubtedly, Jeannie's most aggravating quality: she was usually right.

A riddle: what do you get when you mix a near-genius I.Q. with poor social skills, a volatile temper, and no conscience?

Answer: If you own the publishing house she works for, you get an ulcer.

"I'll talk to Earl. But, Jeannie, once again, if you could try to be a little more tac—"

"Blah, blah, blah." She twirled her fingers—the nails chewed to the quick—in a "whatever" gesture. "What, you're asking favors now, after wrecking my week?"

"I'm not sure asking you to indulge in decent human behavior counts as a 'favor'—"

She made an impatient gesture. "So, what? I gotta, what? Tell Hope the Idiot she's gotta make deadline no matter what? Seriously?"

It was amazing. She was one of the best editors in the business, and she could barely speak English. A transcript of her speech would be incomprehensible. He sighed and said, "It's a little more complicated than that, as you know. Hope can be . . . temperamental."

"I don't have time for that shit!" she screeched, in the searing irony of the century.

"Make time," he suggested, using every ounce of his control to keep the satisfaction out of his voice. "In fact, I suggest you visit our number one author and do whatever you need to in order to get that manuscript in here on time."

She ranted for another six minutes by his clock, but they both knew it was done. Jeannie might hate reality, but she *was* a realist. A publishing house wasn't much of a house without books. Hope was the star of the winter list. Hope's editor, a fine woman who disliked confrontations, had excelled at babying her favorite author. Now that editor was gone. Fled, some said. Killed and devoured, others said.

"And don't forget about the Rack!" he called after her as she stormed out. The R.A.C.—Romance Authors' Conference—was the biggest such convention of the year. It was also two days away.

Bob Anderson looked at the clock and decided to start drinking his lunch early today. He'd earned it.

Three

The cab, which smelled weirdly of noodles, pulled up outside a handsome Manhattan brownstone. Jeannie hopped out, gave the driver a twenty, then waited a toe-tapping ninety seconds for change (she sure as shit wasn't tipping the guy for taking the long way and running three red lights) and a receipt. Bob Anderson wanted to send her to chat with Hope Desiree? Fine. He could pay for it, too. And he could pay for the bottle of Advil she'd need for the drive home.

She got her change (a pitiful three bucks! for a sixteen block cab ride!) and her receipt, and the cab drove away with an insulting blat of exhaust which left her coughing on the sidewalk. Like most New Yorkers, she shrugged it off as the cost of living in the greatest city in the world and clomped up the steps of the brownstone.

Beneath her left arm was the formidable Hope Desiree file. Four inches thick, it was bulging with interoffice memos, a cover questionnaire (like all prima donna writers, Hope did not bother to fill out her questionnaire . . . and look what it got her!), contract copies, flap copy notes, and the partial manuscript of Hope's latest, *Love's Snarling Fury.*

Love's Snarling Fury? Jeannie wondered, buzzing to be let in. *Who the hell thought up that abortion?*

The doorman gave her the old hairy eyeball and rang her up. Ah. Good. Ole Hopie was in the mood for company. Well, that wouldn't last long. *Probably thought Bob sent me in for a wheedle,* she thought. *Ha!*

"Are those Marlboros?" she asked the doorman as she waited for the elevator. She indicated the bulge in his coat pocket.

"Yeah. You want one?" He started fishing for the pack, but stopped when she shook her head.

"Not now. Maybe later."

"Oh. Well, seeya."

She grunted in reply and stepped into the elevator, tapping her heel and examining the toe of her shoe during the interminable ride. When Jeannie was in a mood to chew ass, she disliked waiting for the opportunity. Her third—fourth?—shrink had pointed this out, like it was *profound* or something.

She jumped out of the elevator—into an entryway. Oh ho. Hopie was doing nice for herself . . . on Anderson and Son publishing dollars, thank you very much! Jeannie, used to the ridiculous amount of money successful romance novelists raked in, was still amazed: Hope lived on the entire top floor of some pretty choice Manhattan real estate. How much did *that* cost?

She heard padding footsteps. Then the door at the end of the entryway opened, and a yummilicious fella was walking toward her. Shirtless! And sockless. And shirtless!

"Hi," he said in a pleasant baritone. "You must be Jeannie Desjardin."

Even though she had nothing to say to Mr. Hardbody, she couldn't resist correcting him. "It's not French, pal. It's pronounced duh-JAR-din."

"Oh." He stuck out his hand. She stared at it. Then, remembering long-ago prompting by her fourth—fifth?—etiquette teacher, she stuck her own hand out and shook his. His hand was warm and dry. His fingers swallowed her paw.

And he was at least a head taller, which was weird . . . she was five ten and didn't often run into men so big. Not even during the cover model shoots—those boys were pretty, but *short*.

This guy wasn't short. In fact, he was kind of breathtaking, if you liked them with broad swimmer's shoulders, a flat stomach, long legs, and dark brown hair with red glints in it.

She shut down her drooling before it could really get started—who had the time?—and said, "I'm here to see Hope Desiree."

"Uh-huh." He let go of her hand.

She blinked and tried again. Of course! He was so pretty, it was not surprising he was dumb. God's way of keeping things fair. "Hope. Desiree. I. Need. To see. Her."

"I know. I'm. Steven. McCord."

"We. Could. Do this. All. Day. You're. Fuckin'. Hilarious. Where's. Hope."

He grinned at her—gorgeous, *gorgeous* smile, damn, who was his dentist?—and his blue eyes twinkled. Twinkled! They were the exact same shade as the faded jeans, which clung so lovingly to his long, long legs.

You have no time for a crush, she reminded herself sternly. *Also, men hate you when they find out you've got bigger balls. To business!*

"What are you smirking at?" she snapped, waiting for the smile to fade and the shuffling away to begin.

If anything, his insolent grin widened. "Oh, nothing. I'm just surprised Bob didn't tell you."

"Bob—I assume you mean Bob Anderson, the CEO— doesn't tell me shit if he can help it. Which works out great for both of us, because we don't get along."

"Uh-huh. I'm Hope Desiree. I mean, I'm Steven, too, but Hope's my pen name."

"No, it isn't."

"Yeah. It is."

"Nuh-uh!" She was as close to panic as she ever came. It

couldn't be! Word would have gotten out, Hope's old editor would have mentioned it, *Bob* would have mentioned it, he wouldn't have sent her in blind like this, he—

Oh, he absolutely would.

"Goddammit!"

"It's probably somewhere in that big file," he said, indicating the bulging manila folder which she had slammed on the floor and was now kicking. "Uh. Don't slip."

"I skimmed in the taxi," she admitted breathlessly. She forced herself to relax. When she stood on the file, she could almost look "Hope" in the eye. "It's not that big a deal, y'know. I mean, I keep my head down at the office. I'm there to work. Not investigate the gender of all our authors."

"Fine."

"Fine. Okay. Hope. Steven. Whatever the hell. We gotta talk."

"Well, I'm kind of in the middle—"

"I don't care if you're in the middle of a blood transfusion. *Now.*"

He shrugged and turned away. "Okay. Follow me."

She stepped down and chased after him. Damn! Hope Desiree had an ass that wouldn't quit. She wondered if he'd had implants. Was it possible to have a butt implant? In this city, she'd believe anything.

Four

"So," he said, indicating an overstuffed chair near the window, which she ignored. Polished hardwood floors! She could practically see her reflection. "Something to drink? Coffee?"

"No. Listen up. You're seventeen days late with your manuscript. We need it. Get back to work."

He raised his eyebrows. "You're a little different than my last editor. Shouldn't you be telling me I'm a creative genius and you understand writer's block and to do the best I can?"

"Maybe you noticed I don't use Preparation H for lip gloss."

He burst out laughing. She frowned. He laughed harder. Her frown deepened. "If I hadn't before," he said at last, gasping for breath, "I would now. You're a pistol, aren't you?"

"Pistol, ball-buster, demon from hell, whatever. So. Work now."

"Well, I can't."

"I've got an advance check here," she said, flipping through the file, then giving up—the fucking thing was too big—"that says you can."

"Oh, right. That."

"Yeah. That. Six figures of that. Which you cashed ages ago and which is now probably long gone. Work now."

"I guess I'm a little confused," he admitted.

"What a large fucking surprise."

"No need to be rude. And I'm afraid I don't see what the big deal is. My last editor never minded when I was a little late—"

"Pal—do you see your last editor anywhere around?"

"I'm assuming you killed her and have dangled the body from your web. Also, writing isn't my only job," he continued doggedly. "I actually have a couple other ones, and sometimes those commitments have to come first."

"Not this time. Look, your book is the lead in our winter list. We need it, like, last month. You've gotta finish it."

He sat down and watched her pace. "Suppose I told you I had writer's block?"

"You'd also have to suppose I give a ripe shit."

"That's true," he said. "I *would* have to suppose that."

"Writer's block!" She snorted. "Did you ever hear of a doctor saying, 'So sorry, can't operate on you today, I have surgeon's block'?"

"Well, no," he admitted, grinning again—he was like a Cheshire Cat with six-pack abs. "So you're equating writing with surgery? Nice to see you've got some respect for the process."

"Fine, did you ever hear of a plumber saying he couldn't fix your sink because he had plumber's block?"

"A plumber in this city probably makes what I make."

"That's true, but we're getting off the subject. The cure for writer's block, my friend, is to get your ass in the seat and write."

"You know, you're kind of cute when you're not making faces and your forehead isn't all laddered down with frown wrinkles."

"Blow me. Now will you get to work?"

"First of all, it's physically impossible for me to blow you—although I'm tempted to try—"

"Oh, sexual repartee," she said, pretending to be bored. "I'm all tingly."

"—second, I've never in my life had a woman say that to me, and third, why don't I just give your boss a call, tell him I need an extension? That way you won't get into trouble—"

She laughed.

"—Okay, so you obviously don't care if you get into trouble, which is admirable, if slightly scary, but anyway, I'll give Bob Anderson a call and—"

"Who do you think *sent* me? He wants the book, Hope. He needs it. Which reminds me, I was looking through your manuscript on the way over, and I'm gonna need some major rewrites, too."

"This is turning into a fun day," he commented. He leaned forward, rested his elbows on his knees and looked glum. "I'm so glad I got out of bed."

"Serves you right for not turning in your best work," she said triumphantly. "What were you thinking? That's not rhetorical, by the way, I really want to know: What the *hell* were you thinking? What was going through that tiny little mind of yours, Hope?"

"Stop that. And how do you know that's not my best work?" he snapped. "You've been my editor for, what? Five minutes?"

"Hope, in case you missed the news flash, I'm a fuckin' great editor—one of the best you're ever gonna get to work with."

" 'Get' to work with? Oh, lucky, lucky me."

She ignored the sarcasm. "You and I both know that manuscript isn't your best. I could pick something better out of the slush pile."

"Now you're just being mean." He pouted.

"I don't know if you were too busy lifting weights or drinking protein shakes and just ran out of time, or if your other jobs took priority, and I don't much care. I'm gonna tell you how to fix it, you'll fix it, you'll *finish* it, I can go away, you can go back to posing for Mr. Hardbody calendars, Bob can get your book on the shelves, readers can buy it, and everybody's happy."

"Maybe I should try another publishing house," he suggested. "Since Anderson and Son is getting difficult to work with. I could find an editor that can appreciate—"

"Oh, fucking spare me, all right?" she burst out. This was why she hated, *hated*, working with big name authors. You tell them you know they're phoning it in and they get huffy. You point out plot holes and they threaten to walk. You *edit*, and they can't fucking take it. She'd rather work with a newbie than a lister any damn day—the newbies at least *tried*. "Take it like a man, for Christ's sake. If you don't want the best book possible on the shelves, then shame on you."

His dark brows arched. "An aesthetic, huh? I couldn't tell with all the swearing."

"Look, pal—"

"Steve."

"I don't care. Let me tell you something about Anderson and Son. Bob Anderson has more money than J.K. Rowling. This little publishing house is one of the last independents in the country, and it's his baby. He could take a loss every year and still pay off his mortgage and your mortgage and the mortgage of everyone you know. So he doesn't much care about best-sellers—though we were all pleasantly surprised when your last book went to number two for seventeen days—"

"Eighteen."

"—he cares about the product. It's one of the few reasons I can bring myself to walk into that building every day. Anderson and Son is known for *quality romance,* get it? Not bodice rippers, not 'trash,' not politically correct heroines who live in the eighteenth century and talk like they're in the twenty-first. You want to phone it in and cash the checks, not a chance."

"That was a wonderful speech."

"Shut up. Now for the last time, *why aren't you writing?*"

"I have a commitment I need to keep," he said. "Not for the money, before you accuse me of being greedy on top of everything else. I'm a volunteer. Tell you what—you come with me and I'll bring my laptop."

"I'll do better than that—whatever it is, *I'll* do it, and you'll bring your laptop."

"Uh, I don't think you'd want to—"

"Why? Are you performing surgery? Jumping off a building? Doing geometric theorems?"

"Nothing like that, but I definitely think you won't want—"

"Steve-o, are you going to sit around with your thumb up your ass or are you going to get your laptop?"

"Okay. Fine. I'll take you up on your offer. No fair crying to me about it later, though."

"I haven't cried in twenty-eight years."

"So that's how you keep your complexion dewy fresh. Lemmee go get a shirt. I'll be right back."

Dewy fresh? she thought, watching him leave. Who *was* this guy?

Five

Steven McCord kept trying to look at his new editor out of the corner of his eye, and cursing himself for a kid with a crush as he did so.

She was just so—different. Different? Yeah, that was it. Great looking, a little thin for his taste—he'd see if he could get some steaks into her—but that mass of dark curls and the bee-stung mouth were really something. And the way that bee-stung mouth was constantly open and hectoring him was something, too. He didn't think any*one*, never mind any woman, had ever talked to him like that.

She had impressed him, and she had shamed him, too. When he started in this business, he'd had the exact same mindset she did: Put out your best work, always. Get your shit done on time, always. But modest fame and fabulous royalty checks had lulled him, and he was embarrassed (yes, tell the truth and shame the devil) and a little glad to be caught at last.

It—she—was curiously refreshing. After his years on the N.Y.P.D., he'd gotten so he could tell a lot about a person in a short time. It was like street instincts; they just showed up one day, product of all the input of your other five senses, and never left. Anyway, right now his people sense gave him the strong impression that you always knew exactly where you stood with Jeannie Desjardin. No mind games, no overly coy flirtations, no "her eyes say yes but her lips say no," none of that stuff.

That alone made him interested in knowing her a little better.

Right now she was staring into Room 187, where Drawing and Modern Interpretation was being taught.

"This was your big commitment?"

"Yup." He smiled—he couldn't help it—and waited for her to bail. He certainly didn't expect her to—

"Fire up that laptop," she said, only she said it over her shoulder as she strode into the room and kicked off her shoes, and there went her blouse. And now she was squirming her way out of her skirt. Next she was wriggling out of her black panty hose (which were fit only for the trashcan now; he'd spotted two runs while she was yelling at him in his apartment), and there went her black bra and her black panties.

Nude, she hopped up on the modeling table and struck a pose.

"Nice tattoo," he managed.

"Draw," she ordered the gaping class. "Write," she told the gaping Steven.

They did.

"Well. That was really—"

"Pedestrian," she yawned. She was fully clothed—except for her tights, they'd gone straight to the trashcan, goddamned cheap things!—and on the street again. "Standing in one spot for forty minutes—bllurgh! Next time remind me to bring a paperback."

"Next time?" Steven gasped.

"Yeah, *next time,* as in, the time after this one. We had an agreement, pal. You bring your laptop and write, I take this commitment off your hands. And maybe, just maybe, we'll get your book out only a week late instead of two months late."

His mouth kept opening and closing, she observed dispassionately, like a goldfish. "Jeannie, I never expected you to—"

"Your idea, pal. Too late to whine about it now."

She watched him shut his mouth with a snap, looking—weird!—furious. Too bad, so sad. Another man astonished to run across a woman who kept her promises.

They waited at the corner for the light to change.

"You're very—uh—you don't have a vitamin deficiency or anything, do you? You're so thin," he finished lamely.

She yawned, and wondered if the deli across the street was any better since it reopened last month. "Nope," she replied comfortably. "Just bony. You should see pictures of me as a kid. I was a stick with braids. Not a pretty sight."

"Well, I thought it was really—really something. What you did back there."

She stared at him, puzzled. "I said, didn't I?"

"Well, yeah." He smiled at her. Not a wiseass grin, not a got-you-over-a-barrel-don't-I? smirk. A real smile. He had a gorgeous smile. The big goober. "I just didn't expect you to go through with it. The professor really liked you."

She leered. "I'll bet."

"Not like *that*; jeez, Jeannie, the guy's got grandchildren your age. He said you had great bone structure."

"Guess he was tired of your bone structure—dammit!"

"What?" he asked, but he asked the air, because she was already charging across the street—luckily the light had finally turned—and stomping up to a tall, thin homeless man leaning on the steps to his brownstone. "Aw, Jeannie, leave him alone!" he hollered after her. "The poor guy doesn't mean any harm!"

What does he think, she wondered, charging up to Sammy. *That I'll eat the guy?*

"Sammy!"

" 'Lo, Jane."

"For the billionth time, it's Jeannie, and what the hell are you doing on the street?"

"Shelter's no good," Sammy replied calmly.

"What are you talking about, no good? It's one of the nicest ones around!"

Sammy shrugged. He was dressed—sort of—in tattered khakis and a brown T-shirt. The loafers on his feet were Bill Blass; New York was a wonderful city to live in because rich people threw great stuff away. His gray hair was shoulder-length and pulled back in a ponytail. His eyes were a fathomless brown; they had seen everything. "The rules. Didn't want to stay."

"Dammit, Sammy!" Her finger jabbed him in the middle of his scrawny chest. He raised shaggy eyebrows at her but didn't move. "I busted my ass finding you a bed in that place!"

"Nice of you," Sammy allowed, "but I didn't ask."

"Fuck that!"

"Now, Jane. I'm going to think you aren't a lady if you keep talking like a sailor. Having been one," he confided to Steven as he rushed up, panting, "I would know."

"A sailor," Steve asked, panting lightly from the sprint, "or a lady?"

"Son of a bitch!"

"When I was a drinking man," Sammy continued, "which is to say, lunchtime, I thought that was my other name, because she used it so often."

"Don't blame me for your DT-inspired fantasies. Listen, I'm going to call the shelter again, and this time I want you to—"

"Never mind, Jane."

She refused to let her shoulders slump, although that's what they wanted to do. "Come *on*, Sammy. It's not safe for you out here."

"Weather's nice," he replied, his gaze shifting from her to Steven, then back to her. "And I like being outside."

"That's fine for summer, but how about when the wind-chill is ten below and there's a foot of snow on the ground?"

"Well." Sammy looked into space for a long, thoughtful second, then brightened. "I figure I'll worry about that then."

"Dammit!"

"Now, if you want to talk about my book idea . . ."

"Sammy, I already told you—you're a better thinker than writer. And the world really doesn't need another Princess Di conspiracy book."

"Then," Sammy said, raising himself to his full height, which was considerable, "we got nothing to talk about."

"Like hell!" She started to reach for him, but Steven grabbed her and pulled her back.

"What are you going to do, Jeannie?" he said, trying to sound reasonable while she kicked and flailed. "Drag him to a homeless shelter?"

"Ayuh," Sammy replied, watching them with old, amused eyes. "That's what she was going to do. Thanks for your help, son. Bye, Jane."

"Go back to the shelter!" she hollered after him, and got a laconic wave in return. "Son of a *bitch!*"

He turned, halfway up the block. "And don't forget our bet, Jane."

"Fuck that!"

Sammy shook his grizzled head. "That's too bad, Jane. Sorry to hear you won't keep your word."

"Dammit! All right, all right, but it's a stupid bet!"

"Ayuh," he replied, and continued up the street. "Goodbye, Jane."

Steven was practically running to keep up with her. "So, you torture writers, you torture Bob Anderson, but you're nice to homeless people—after rejecting their book ideas—and place bets with them?"

"Change the subject, Hope-alicious."

"All right, are you going to the R.A.C.?"

"Yes."

"Well, maybe we could travel together."

"What? What?" She gave Steve her full attention. "You're not going. You're not going! Are you going?"

"Sure; this is the year I'm being 'outed.' "

"Outed?"

"Huh. You really don't read any of the memos, do you? This is the year a zillion romance writers expecting a middle-aged woman are gonna get *me.*"

"Oh, great," she groaned. "A circus."

"Awww." He punched her shoulder. "It'll be swell."

Six

Steve walked into the lobby of Anderson and Son and found . . . nothing. A few people going to and fro, a busy receptionist, but nothing else. His old editor used to wait breathlessly for him in the lobby, but apparently Jeannie wasn't about to do anything to make his ego any bigger.

If he wasn't careful, he'd fall in love.

"Steve McCord," he told the receptionist, who, with her mane of red curly hair and big glasses, looked like a disturbingly sexy Orphan Annie. "I'm here to see Jeannie Desjardin."

Orphan Annie (Brigitte Flanagan, her desk plate proclaimed, and if that wasn't a name for a romance heroine, he didn't know his shit) pointed her pen at the bank of elevators. "Sixth floor," she said pleasantly.

"Thanks."

"Um," she replied, in the manner of polite-but-distant New York receptionists everywhere.

The elevator whisked him to the sixth floor, and he found himself, to his dismay, as excited as a kid on prom night. He hadn't been able to get that loudmouthed nut out of his head all evening. So he'd stayed up working on the revisions she suggested—okay, demanded—and around four o'clock in the morning it occurred to him that she had been right: it was just what the book needed.

He wasn't sure if that made him want to choke her, or strangle her.

The doors slid open, and Bob Anderson was waiting for him. The old guy was positively dapper in a charcoal gray suit, spotless white shirt, and . . . tennis shoes? "Steve! What brings you downtown?"

He held up a disc with one hand and shook Bob's hand with the other. "I thought I'd drop off the revisions Jeannie and I talked about."

"Well, thanks for stopping by." Bob looked pleased, the poor dummy. As if Steve had taken a cab and braved lunch traffic to see *him.* "You could have e-mailed it, you know."

Steve shrugged.

"Let's see, you haven't been here for awhile, have you? Well, let me give you the nickel tour. This is the editorial floor, where—"

"Get that fucking thing away from me, I'm not going to tell you again!"

She was here! Steve shouldered Bob aside so hard the older man nearly went sprawling into the open conference room. From his vantage point, there was just a sea of cubes . . . where was she?

"C'mon, Jeannie," some unseen person was pleading. The poor idiot. "Everybody else signed it."

"Connie, you know what'll happen if I do."

Steve rounded a corner and there she was, nose to nose with a woman who was quailing before the wrath of Desjardin, but still holding her ground. "It's the nice thing to do."

"The nice thing—hello, Connie," she said impatiently, "it's me, Jeannie Desjardin. Have we met?"

"It'll look bad," Connie said stubbornly, while leaning as far from Jeannie as she could get and still stay on her feet, "if you're the only one in the department who doesn't sign it."

"Ohhh nooo! It'll *look* bad!" Jeannie threw up her hands. Connie flinched. "Whatever will I do? Because I really give a shit for how things *look.*"

"Sign it," a gravelly voice said from behind them both. They turned, and Steve craned his neck. A dumpy, sixtyish woman with dyed black hair and the longest fake lashes he'd ever seen was sitting in front of a frosted door that was lettered, ROBERT ANDERSON, CEO. At first Steve didn't recognize the white stick that was jutting out of her mouth—it had been years since he'd seen someone smoking inside a building.

"Sign it," the woman—obviously Bob's executive assistant—said again. "It'll be good for a laugh."

Incredibly, Jeannie obeyed. She snatched the card—so that's what they were yakking about—from Connie, who looked simultaneously crushed, relieved, and horrified, signed in a rapid scrawl, and practically threw the card back at her.

"There," Jeannie said ominously. "I am *not* responsible for what happens. When the guy gets smited—smote?—it's not my fault."

"Thanks," Connie managed, and scuttled down one of the cube aisles like a field mouse with a precious crumb.

"Haw!" the older woman said. Her "haw!" was followed by a spasm of coughing that lasted, subjectively speaking, about six hours. Steve checked the desk blotter for her left lung, but it was clear. "Should be interesting."

"All this?" he interrupted, thinking it was high time—*past* time—Jeannie noticed him, "for a card?"

"It's for Sucky McSuck," Jeannie explained.

"Uh . . . so?"

"So, he hates me."

"So?"

"So, he's in the hospital because of me."

"What'd you do? Shoot him?"

"I wish. Bob made me be nice to him."

"As if I could make you do anything," Bob remarked, reaching for the two-inch pile of phone slips his assistant was extending toward him.

"Shut up, Bob. Anyway, he made me be nice to Sucky. Oh—that reminds me, you got a new cover for your book. Anyway, the new cover was less awful than the last one, so I said, 'not too bad, Sucky,' and then he had a heart attack and Gloria here had to call an ambulance for him."

Steve frowned, so he wouldn't smile. It really wasn't very funny. Okay, it was. "Let me get this straight. You were nice to someone, and it shook him so much, he's in the ICU?"

"Yup. But that wasn't bad enough; now Connie wants me to sign the get-well card. They'll have to feed him through a tube!"

"They already are," Gloria husked, lighting a new cigarette with the stub of her old one. Steve noticed a halo of smoke hovering around the older woman's head and coughed pointedly. Jeannie caught his intent and hissed a warning, but it was too late.

"Say, isn't it against the law to smoke in buildings in this—"

Jeannie made a slashing gesture across her throat, and Bob palpably stiffened.

"—day and age?" Steve finished.

"I been doing it for forty-two years," Gloria grumped. "I'm not stopping now."

"Well, you don't look a day over one hundred," he said courteously.

"Knock it off, Hope. What are you doing here, anyway?" Jeannie bitched. "We're busy, and a prima donna author stopping by—"

"Is a delight," Bob interrupted.

"Liar!" Jeannie coughed into her fist.

"I brought those revisions for you."

"Oh, great." She accepted the disc with the same enthusiasm she would confer upon a wriggling bat. "I guess I'll just drop everything and get right to this."

"That's right," Bob said, deeply engrossed in his messages. "You will."

"Aw, son of a bitch!"

Steve smiled at her. He couldn't help it. She was just so . . . Jeannie. Today she was dressed like a miniature, younger Bob in a severe black suit with the jacket buttoned to her chin, black tights (only one run today) and black ballet slippers. Her wildly curly hair was tamed in a ponytail so tight, her eyebrows arched. She wasn't wearing any makeup. "Say, where's the son?"

"What are you babbling about, Hope? Did the pressure of having to do your best work fry your tiny little brain?"

Gloria hawed again, while Steve fixed his foul-mouthed harridan of an editor with a formidable frown. "I'm babbling, as you so crudely and annoyingly put it, about the sign out front. Anderson & Son. So, where's the son? If I'm getting the grand tour, I should meet everybody, right?"

"You're so not getting the grand anything—we all have work to do, if you didn't notice. And I'm the son," Jeannie added, unashamedly reading over Bob's shoulder.

"What? You?"

"Uh-huh."

"But—why?"

"Because Anderson-and-stepdaughter-who-resents-the-shit-out-of-him-for-taking-her-dead-father's-place didn't look too good on the letterhead."

"She's your stepdaughter?" he asked Bob, astonished.

"And worst enemy," Bob confirmed.

"Oh, shut up and go whine to my mother," Jeannie snapped. She jabbed an unmanicured finger at one of the message slips.

"And I did not call that newbie author a clinging vine; I said she was a needy idiot."

"Is it time for lunch yet?" Bob asked the air. "Because I'm getting unbearably thirsty."

"Thanksgiving must be fun at your place," Steve said, beginning to recover from the surprise.

"Haw!" Gloria said again.

Seven

Jeannie stomped off the plane and fumbled for her hotel confirmation. Ninety-six hours of pure unadulterated hell, that's what was in store for her. And she had *signed up* for it. Stars complaining about their book placement. Newbies complaining that nobody *told* them they'd need plot, or internal conflict, in their story. Mid-listers blaming poor sales on the house, never on a mediocre story. And wannabees too scared to talk to her, but not scared enough to stop stalking her.

And the food! If she had to eat one more limp salad, one more rubber chicken breast, one more molten chocolate cake oozing syrup . . . well, the chocolate wasn't so bad. . . .

"Going my way, sunshine?"

She nearly fell over her carry-on (a good trick, since she was pulling it behind her) at the voice, *his* voice: rich, deep, amused. In addition to being magically delicious, Steve was unnerving because nothing she said seemed to get to him. It wasn't natural for a guy not to get red-faced and throw things at her: shoes, watches, empty beer bottles. It was as if he found her . . . amusing and cute, or whatever. Which of course wasn't true. Couldn't be true. Maybe this was his way of sucking up.

"You're here already?"

"Yup. Figured, better come early, support my publishing house."

"Oh." *Weirdo.* "Okay."

He cast a concerned glance behind her. "Aren't those things supposed to have wheels? What'd you do, gnaw them off?"

"They broke," she said shortly. "Look, I have to get to the Marriott—"

"Me, too. We can share a cab."

"I didn't get a cab. I rented a car."

"How come?"

She clutched her shoulder bag, making sure the pack of cigarettes was still there. "Never you mind. Let's just say I need a car for a while. I guess I could give you a ride to the hotel."

"Such a gracious offer!" He staggered beside her. "I don't think I can stand it."

"Then fuck yourself and take the shuttle."

"Awwwwww . . . let's take it together."

"Pass."

"Are you *sure* you don't want to climb in a shuttle full of women ready to grill you on the smallest publishing trend? It's a twenty-five-minute drive," he added.

An eternity. "Bite your tongue. Where's the Enterprise desk?"

"Right next to Budget."

"Fine, you can hitch a ride with me," she said ungraciously. Which wasn't exactly fair, but really, it was her only defense. How come he was hanging around her so much? How come he didn't care when she tried to pretend he wasn't yummy by being mean?

His book wasn't *that* bad, and they'd fixed most of the problems. He was going to have the rest to her within two weeks, and they could slam it right to copy editing. Problem solved, and with a minimum of fuss. So why was he around all the time?

She wasn't so conceited to think he was interested in her—a rich classy guy like him. Although she was technically rich herself, since the day she decided to touch some of her trust funds. Which she had no desire to do—fer chrissake! Money dead people had earned, and inexplicably left to her. It wasn't *hers*. Besides, Bob paid her a decent salary, and she owned her apartment outright. She didn't need the dead people's money. One thing she had found out, the haves never had trouble getting more, and the have-nots had a helluva time just staying in place. It was stupid, but it was the truth.

Speaking of the truth, Steve was unnerving as hell. Maybe he was trying to get on her good side so the next editing job wouldn't be so arduous.

The thought made her laugh out loud. *Good* side?

"Onward, James," she commanded, thinking it really was too bad he'd worn a shirt to the airport.

"Budget! Don't make me barf!"

The Enterprise clerk raised his eyebrows. "Perhaps National, then?"

"Look, pal, I had a reservation *here*, at Enterprise. Do you know that word? Res-er-vay-shun?"

"We have your reservation right here, ma'am," he replied calmly, though sweat was nestling in his temples. "They're just cleaning the car right now and bringing it around. It'll only be another ten minutes. I only suggested an alternative because you seem so—um—rushed."

"Amazing! I *am* rushed, bud, you know why? Do you? Huh? Because it only took five minutes to get my bag, but it always takes at least forty minutes to do all the damn rental car paperwork. And now that it's done, you *still* won't give me the car! Y'know, if you guys are so paranoid about someone stealing, folding, or otherwise mutilating your cars, you shouldn't rent them out."

"Yes, ma'am."

"What's your beef with Budget?" Steve asked, interested.

He'd put his carry bag down and was leaning against the counter, hands in his pockets. She was afraid he'd slide off and hit his head on the shiny, yet filthy, airport floor.

"They don't take check cards."

"What, like you don't have a Visa?"

"I have five. That's not the point. I had two thousand bucks on my check card, but Budget was all, noooooo, we *can't* take check cards, ick, ptoo. Fascists. Then they made it out like it was *my* problem they had a sucky policy."

"Shocking," Steve commented.

"So; new rule: No renting from Budget, ever. Ever *ever!*"

"This is going to be a really fun weekend," Steve said sincerely, relaxing even more against the counter. "I can tell."

Eight

"Jesus Christ!" Steve screamed, grabbing frantically for his seat belt.

"I *told* you to buckle up," Jeannie said. "Now stop with the yelling. I can't concentrate on the road with the yelling."

"Look, it's easy enough to get to the hotel. This is Washington, D.C., not deepest Africa."

"D.C. in high summer," Jeannie muttered, peering through the windshield. "What were they thinking?"

"That it's cheaper to hold a convention in a hot place during a hot season, that's all. Truck! Truck! Truck!"

"I *see* the truck, calm down. Okay, here we go . . ." She fished in her purse for a long moment—she hated clichés, but it was true: she could never find anything in her purse when she needed it. At last she drew out a pack of cigarettes.

"Great," Steve grumped. "Something new to distract your attention from the road."

"Really new," she said.

"I didn't know you smoked."

"I don't. I mean, I do now. Remember that bet I lost? I bet Sammy that once I got him in a nice shelter he'd want to stay forever, and he bet me that if he wanted to leave, I'd take up smoking."

"Tell me you're kidding."

"I never kid." Man, the pack was wrapped tight. That wasn't cellophane; it was some sort of clear cement. "I don't have to smoke forever, just get through this pack. How hard can it be?"

"Jeannie, you're insane." He said this with grudging admiration.

"Look, eighty gazillion people smoke . . . they can't all be dumbasses. There must be some cool secret to all this."

"Yeah. Emphysema."

"Oh, what do you know about it?" At last, she had the cellophane off. She opened the pack and peered at the cigarettes nestled inside, lined up like white soldiers.

"Where'd you get that, anyway?"

"In this day and age, it wasn't easy. Because I couldn't do it where Bob would catch me—he'd rat me out to my mother."

"Your mom is . . ." He paused delicately.

"Steve, you have no idea. Seriously. She makes me look like Miss Congeniality."

"The horror," Steve whispered, hunching lower in his seat. "The horror."

"Okay, so, where's that lighter now?" She dug around in her purse some more. After all the trouble it'd been to get it, now she couldn't find it! It was kind of funny, actually, how difficult the whole stupid transaction had been . . . funny like a crutch.

"Pack of cigarettes," she'd told the clerk, a white-haired man in his sixties.

"What kind?" he'd replied, already reaching over her head for one.

"Surprise me."

He stared at her for a short beat, shrugged, then turned and groped for the packs she could see.

"No, not that one—the one next to it, the pretty one."

He'd pulled it down and slid it across the counter to her.

They were Ultra Lites, whatever the hell that meant to the cigarette-smoking community. "And I'm gonna need one of those, what d'you call 'ems? You know, to light them with."

"A lighter," he prompted.

"Right! Right. One of those. Um. A red one."

"Can I see some I.D.?" he'd asked with poorly disguised suspicion. And when she'd handed over her driver's license, he had taken a good minute to look it over.

"You're thirty-one," he finally said.

"Good math skills. Your talents are wasted here at Gulp N' Go."

"But you're just starting smoking now."

"I lost a bet," she explained.

"Not to mention," Steven said as she brought him up to date on her morning, "your mind. You really blanked on the word for lighter? You're supposed to be an editor? What'd you call it, the wand of fire?"

"Off my case. I don't welsh on bets, got it?" She stuck the cigarette in her mouth and nearly gagged on the faint scent. Then she started fumbling anew for her lighter.

"Watch the road! Look, isn't there just a cancer pill you can take? It'll be quicker, and less—look. *Look.* The car has one."

"Oh, excellent." She started to lean down, but he put his palm in the middle of her breasts and pushed her back. It was, sadly, the closest she'd come to sex in two years. "Watch the hands there, Grabby McGee."

"Watch the road. I'll get it."

"Okay, *okay.* Jeez, you're even grumpier than I am after flying."

"Yeah, it's the flight that has my teeth on edge." He leaned down, slapped the lighter, and it popped out a bare ten seconds later.

"That was fast," she said approvingly.

"We're living in a modern age."

She snatched the lighter out of its little holder and held the end to her cigarette. She held it and held it. Nothing appeared to happen. Her cigarette got a crimp in the middle. She narrowed her eyes, focusing on—

"Jeannie, will you *watch the road for the love of God?*"

She stood on her brakes in time to avoid rear-ending the semi (HOW'S MY DRIVING? was emblazoned on the back of the trailer), and now her cigarette was *really* crimped.

"Steve, just calm down, all right?" she mumbled around the cigarette. "I swear, shrill is *not* a good look for you. Look, I can see the whites all the way around your pupils . . . you're like a horse about to bolt."

"That's just what I am," he gasped.

"Everything's cool. You used to be a cop, right? And you're currently a New Yorker? Cripes. High strung much?"

"I'd go into a crack house without backup," he said through gritted teeth, "before taking a ride with you again." She noticed his knuckles were white where he was gripping the emergency brake. Although what he thought he was going to be doing with that, she had no idea.

"What? Were you, like, in a really bad accident or something, and that's why you got off the force?"

"No, and I'd like to avoid one. Now. Listen carefully. Smoke that fucking thing, put it out, and get us to the conference. *In one piece.*"

"You don't have to *scream.*" At last! Her cigarette was lit. She fumbled, and finally put the lighter back. Then she took a deep lungful. "Flavor country, here I c-ack!" She barked out a cloud of smoke. Everything was on fire! From her tongue down to her belly button! And her head was throbbing like day two of a hangover. And her mouth now tasted like the inside of an ashtray. A public ashtray next to a urinal. "Yuck! The magazine ads don't show any of *this.*"

Steve started to laugh, even as he was coughing and cursing and waving the smoke away from his face. It was amazing. The car was, like, *filled* with it. Already! "Those lying bastards," he said. "How dare they leave out the whole smoking-makes-you-vomit factor."

"Oooooh, don't talk about vomit." She sucked again, coughed again; then Steve grabbed the steering wheel and got them settled in the correct lane. "Thanks. This is intolerable!"

"You got that right."

"I'm supposed to smoke a whole pack of these? Without expiring? I don't think I can finish the cigarette!"

"I suppose welshing's not an option."

"Ha! I'll fix *him*. He didn't say how long I had to take to smoke the pack."

"Take a year," Steve suggested. "Take two."

She picked a piece of tobacco off her tongue. "Teenagers are idiots, that's all I have to say." She coughed again and felt her stomach heave. "No adult would put themselves through this."

Steve shrugged. "If your friends are doing it . . . you know how it is."

"Steve, do I strike you as someone who worried about peer pressure as a nubile teen?"

"Hardly. There's the hotel, up on the right."

"I see it; this thing didn't strike me blind. I'm pretty sure," she added, wiping her streaming eyes. "Cheer up, we're almost there, and then you can get out of my opium den on wheels."

"I'm counting the seconds."

She pulled into the parking lot, parked, and sighed. Then coughed again. "Well! That sucked."

"But it was an adventure."

"Yeah, so's a colonoscopy." She stared sadly at the pack. Only twenty-some to go. Well, she'd do one a month. A bet was a bet.

"Something we can tell our grandkids about."

"Sure, we—what?"

Then he leaned over and kissed her.

Nine

"No, really. Why'd you do that?"

"Forget it." He nodded at the hotel clerk and shouldered his bag and hers. "Come on, we're on the same floor."

She trotted after him. It was kind of funny how totally nonplussed she was. She had her palm slapped over her nametag so no one would recognize her. "No, come on. Tell me. What'd you do that for?"

"So I could experience the joys of secondhand smoke, tongue to tongue."

Panting to keep pace, she jumped into the elevator after him. "Come on, Steve, just tell me. I promise I won't get mad. Well, okay, I can't *promise* that, but I promise I won't punch you or anything. Probably. Well, I guess it depends on how piglike your reason is, but I'm willing to hear you out."

"Thanks tons. You won't get mad," he said, "but you'll get scared."

Her big eyes opened wide. He could practically see her lunge for the lifeline. A slur upon her courage! It would not be borne. "I can take it. You have no idea what I put up with at work. You're sick. You're dying. Worse—you're gonna miss deadline again. You're going with another publishing house. Did I ask if you were dying? You've undergone a religious conversion and won't write quote trashy books un-quote for us anymore."

"No, nothing like that. This is our floor."

"Screw our floor." He stepped out of the elevator, saw her come to the realization that a tantrum by herself in the elevator would likely only hurt her tights, then watched her leap out after him. "Okay, *now* screw our floor. Why'd you do that?"

"It was our floor." He tried not to grin.

"Not that! You know what I'm talking about."

"It really bugged you, huh?"

"I just like to know about things, is all," she said, sounding incredibly rattled.

"Okay, well, I did it because you're alternately cute and aggravating—"

"Which works nicely, because you're patronizing."

"—and I've decided we're going to get married."

"Look, if you don't *want* to tell me—"

"That's it, Jeannie. That's the reason."

She blinked, and thought that one over. "You were wrong," she said, voice quavering, "I'm *not* scared. But I am incredibly nauseated . . ."

She did look a little green. "That's the cigarette."

"Okay. Well, I'm flattered. I really am! I mean, you're cute and all, and halfway bright, and you're a good writer when you pay attention to theme, but I guess I should tell you, you're out of luck."

"Lone wolf, eh?"

"Kind of."

"That's okay," he said cheerfully, hefting their bags and starting down the hallway. "We can be lone wolves together."

She chased after him. "That's the stupidest thing I've ever heard—and I'm in American publishing!"

"You have another run in your tights," he said.

"That's okay. I packed twenty pairs. Listen, you were just

teasing, right?" She reached out and actually plucked at his sleeve. "Because it's okay if you were. I won't get mad or anything—really!"

"We're going to get married, Jeannie." He handed her her shoulder bag, then slid his key card through Room 3212. "Jeannie Desjardin Desiree McCord . . . got a nice ring to it, huh?"

"You're out of your fucking mind!"

"Stop it," he said, gently closing the door on her furious face. "You'll make me cry."

Ten

Jeannie rested her head on the toilet seat and wished she were dead.

Must be Thursday, she thought drearily.

Let's recap, shall we? She got stuck with a new author, practically rewrote his book for him, gave Sucky a heart attack, started smoking, got stuck at the R.A.C. with aforementioned author, who had now decided he was in love with her.

Well, no. He hadn't decided that; he'd decided to marry her. Big difference.

Oh, and to cap it off? She was in the hotel's public bathroom, first floor, deeply *deeply* regretting that cigarette.

She stared at the run in her tights and wondered exactly when Steve McCord had gone completely bonkers. Unless this whole day was a nicotine-induced hallucination.

No, the facts were firmly on her side. Steve was the crazy one; he was the writer. They were all, on one level or another, nuttier than a squirrel on crack-laced walnuts. She could think of a thousand examples. The geniuses never thought they were good enough; the mediocres thought they were too good. The geniuses were ignored most of their lives; the mediocres made millions. Neither a genius nor a mediocre could get read by an editor until they had an agent, and they couldn't get an agent until they had an editor. It was a fucked-up business, and that was for sure. Her capacity for the job did not speak well for her sanity.

She heard something slide and looked down as the something bumped her knee. A manuscript. Looked to be about 120,000 words. The title page was facing her. *Freight Train to Love.*

"That's me," she said hollowly, listening to rapidly retreating footsteps. "On the freight train to love."

Another sliding sound, another bump—this time from the other side. Another manuscript, easily twice as large as the first. "In the first place," she began, then rested her head on her forearms and tried to hold on to her gorge.

In the first place, the upper limit of an Anderson and Son manuscript is ninety thousand words. Do your homework.

In the first place, you don't give editors your book at a conference; you pitch them what your book's about, and they tell you to mail the damned thing. Otherwise . . .

sliiiiiiiiiiiiiide . . . bump . . .

. . . otherwise, you have to fly home with ten, fifteen, twenty reams of paper.

In the first place, you LEAVE EDITORS ALONE WHEN THEY'RE PUKING IN THE FIRST-FLOOR TOILET AT THE D.C. MARRIOTT.

sliiiiiiiiiiiiiiiide . . . bump

And people wondered why she was in a bad mood all the time! Here she was, being accosted—assaulted!—by manuscripts, by writers too chickenshit to actually meet with her, show their faces . . .

sliiiiiiiiiiiiiiiide . . . bump

. . . so instead they tried to bury her alive in the ladies' room!

Maybe one of them would hit her over the head with his or her *oeuvre*. That would be all right. One of those suckers would knock her right out. She could stay comatose through the conference . . . through 2005!

"Holy crap," someone said, her voice—so welcome and soothing in its no-nonsense cadence—bouncing off the tiles. "Are you okay in there? Should I get a Sherpa and dig you out?"

Jeannie actually laughed, and that's how she met Caro Swenson.

Eleven

"Come on," Caro said again. "Shouldn't I call a doctor? Or at least walk you back to your room? Your color is awful. Unless you're normally the color of bad cheese."

"Ugh, don't remind me." Jeannie averted her gaze from the row of bathroom mirrors, then straightened up from the sink in a hurry. "Are you being nice to me because I'm an editor?" she snapped, vibrating with suspicion.

"No," Caro said dryly. "I'm being nice to you because I can't resist your fashion sense; you look like a black Muppet. Especially when your eyes go all glarey like that. Relax, DUH-jar-din. I don't even have an appointment with you this weekend."

"Oh. It's duh-JAR-din, by the way."

Caro grinned. "I know."

"Well, um, maybe I'll take you up on that one."

"Which one? The doc, or the escort?"

"The latter. I was supposed to sit in on a panel this afternoon, but fuck that, I gotta lay down."

"What are you going to *lay* down?" Caro chortled. "Sorry. Grammar joke. What should we do with these?" She indicated the half dozen manuscripts scattered all over the bathroom floor.

"Um . . ." Dump them. Shred them. Burn them. Flush them. Leave them where they were.

Except . . . Jeannie knew full well that a book, even a bad one—sometimes especially a bad one—represented months of work. Sometimes years. It seemed so cold, even to her, to just turn her back on them. They had gone to the trouble to write the damned things, sacrificing free time, family time, sometimes work time. The least she could do was take a look at the first few pages.

It was her job, after all. Her commitment.

"Um . . . I don't want to just, you know, leave them . . ."

"Oooh, the rumors are true, you've got a heart buried in there somewhere!" Caro teased. "Wait'll I tip off the press!"

"You know, most writers are afraid of me," she said, slightly nettled. "Would it kill you to kiss my ass just a little bit?"

"I wouldn't go near your ass on a bet," Caro replied, "and that's a fact. How about this: I'll take 'em."

"You will?"

"Sure. There's a post office right across the street. I'll ship them to my house—all expenses tax-deductible, mind you—and take a look at them when I get home. If there's anything good, I'll forward it to you."

Jeannie was sooorely tempted. But it wouldn't be right. She didn't even *know* this woman, who looked like a forties' starlet with her wasp waist, generous bosom, and long, long legs. Except for the glasses—large purple frames—the woman would be breathtaking. With the glasses, she looked good, and interesting as hell. Her hair was plaited in a long blond braid that fell almost to her butt. She could have been a cover model. Maybe she *was* a cover model.

"Well . . . that's tempting . . . but they submitted them to me . . ."

"Incorrectly," Caro pointed out. "By rights you could leave them where they lie."

"Lay."

"No, it's lie. Anyway, you don't owe these guys anything, especially when they couldn't be bothered to look up Anderson and Son's writers' guidelines."

"Well . . . what about you? Why would you take on . . ." This incredibly thankless task, she didn't say, but Caro picked up on it.

"Oh, I love to read," she said cheerfully. "Love love *love* it."

"Me, too," Jeannie confessed, smiling a little.

"Yup, figures, you being an editor and all. I mean, how sucky would your job be if you didn't like to read? Anyway, I love it, almost as much as I love to write. And who knows? One of these could be the next Nora Roberts."

"Yeah, who the hell knows." Privately, she doubted it. There was way more crap than gold in the slush pile. Law of writing averages. But she admired Caro's enthusiasm. "What's your day job?"

"Pediatric nurse. Which means I get paid to poke small children with needles. It also means, thanks to the national nursing shortage, that I get to set my own schedule and have plenty of time for this little project. Plus, I've been writing for ten years and have a file full of rejection slips. If nothing else," she added with a grin, "I can recognize a rejectable manuscript, having written so many of them myself."

"Why *aren't* you pitching to me this weekend?" Jeannie asked, disappointed in spite of herself.

"Because I write time travel, and Anderson and Son doesn't do time travels."

Great. Clever, funny, gorgeous, nice, and does her homework. She wondered if Caro was a robot.

Use it. Who knows? Maybe Caro is editor material. We could sure use another one.

"Okay," she said. "I'll take you up on that. Who are you meeting with this weekend? Maybe I could put in a good word for you."

Caro actually shuddered. "Don't do me any favors, Desjardin. Seriously. Your reputation precedes you. I need a recommendation from you like I need another asshole."

Jeannie cracked up. She couldn't help it. And my, didn't laughing feel *fine*.

Twelve

"So," Bob Anderson said, tipping his Bruschetta upside down so the pieces of tomato fell off, "you've taken up smoking."

Jeannie narrowed her eyes at Steve, who smirked back. "Loose lips," she warned.

"Ah, your lips," Steve replied.

Jeannie hurriedly changed the subject. "Are you on the panel tomorrow morning?"

"Which one?"

"Whining Booksellers."

"It might be called something else," Steve said helpfully, "so don't bother looking it up in your schedule under that title."

"Yes," Bob replied. "It'll tie up most of my morning. So you'll be outing Steve, so to speak."

"Great." She wasn't exactly looking forward to telling several hundred romance readers that Hope Desiree was Mr. Hardbody. Well, at least it wouldn't be dull. "Remind me to bring my flamethrower."

They were eating dinner at The Palm: Anderson's Editorial Director, Anderson's CEO, and Anderson's top-selling author. Normally she despised such dinners: ninety minutes of stroking! She'd rather put up with ninety minutes of bikini waxing. This time it was unnerving to be sitting so close to Steve . . . she was acutely aware of his long, lean body beside hers. She wondered what she'd do if he grabbed her and kissed her again. She wondered what she'd do if he didn't.

"—sequel to the next book?"

"What? I wasn't listening."

"At least she's honest about it," Steve said to Bob.

"Her finest—possibly only—quality," Bob sighed.

"Excuse me for speaking my mind."

"I like it," Steve said so warmly that she accidentally knocked over her wineglass, which was full of ginger ale.

"I can remember when she was a teenager, lecturing me on the truth," Bob reminisced. He had a sappy—almost fond!—look on his face that she'd never seen before. "She'd say, 'Ninety-eight percent of everything is a lie, so I'll be two percent.' "

"So, you're like milk?"

"Shut up, Hope."

"At least," Bob said agreeably, "there's never a doubt where you stand on any given subject at any given time."

"You didn't think so when I told you to ditch the toupee," she retorted.

"You used to wear a rug?" Steve asked delightedly. Bob was as bald as an eight ball, except for a gray monk's fringe around his head.

"The phrase Jeannie used, if memory serves, was 'rotting muskrat carcass.' "

"I was doing you a favor! Tell me you didn't make tons more headway with my mom after you ditched Musky the Rug."

Bob smiled and shrugged.

Jeannie cleared her throat and continued. "Actually, you, um, weren't such a bad guy. I mean, I wasn't going to like any hound sniffing after my mother—"

"I'm getting misty," Bob commented.

"—and it's tough to enjoy a guy's company when you know the only reason he's there is so he can slip your mom the old beef trombone, but you were pretty okay. I mean, she could have done a lot worse."

"That's so touching," Steve said.

Bob, in midbite, inhaled as he laughed, and then all sounds from his throat stopped abruptly. His eyes widened, and he dropped his hors d'oeuvre.

Steve jumped to his feet . . . only to go sprawling as Jeannie threw an elbow into his ribs and knocked him aside. She jerked the older man out of his chair—a good trick, since Bob had fifty pounds on her—whirled him around, grabbed him around the belly, and yanked her fists in, hard.

Nothing. Other diners were slowly waking up to the fact that something was wrong, and several cell phones were flipped out.

"Come on, you stubborn putz," she panted, and jerked again.

Nothing.

Fuck! Jeannie held back panic by force of will. Was she doing it wrong? She was sure her thumb and fists were in the right spot. She could see Bob's ears, which were dark red and edging toward purple. She yanked again.

A clot of bread sailed through the air at the same instant she heard breath explode from Bob's lungs . . . and again, a scary silence.

She nearly dropped him in her effort to get him prone. "Somebody call an ambulance!" she shrilled, and bent to her stepfather.

Steve had his fingers on Bob's neck, and shook his head. "No pulse. He's not breathing. Lean back." She did, and Steve made a fist and slammed it down on Bob's chest. The pre-cardial thump, she remembered from her First Aid class.

If it didn't work, they would have to start CPR. *Oh, please, please let it work . . .*

"Bob, cut the shit!" she yelled into his face. "If you die, Mom'll never believe it was an accident!"

Before they could do anything else, Bob gasped in air and started coughing. His plummy color darkened for a moment, then started to lighten as he got the coughing under control.

Jeannie collapsed beside him. "Never do that again, you old bastard," she groaned. "I'm not breaking in another one of Mom's man-whores."

"Agreed," Bob gasped, and raised a hand, which she slapped.

"It's my fault," she fretted in the elevator.

"You jammed that piece of bread down his throat while I wasn't looking?" Steve's arm was around her shoulder—thank God, because she was afraid she'd fall down if he let go. Bob had been whisked away in an ambulance at the insistence of the restaurant manager, and she and Steve had lost their appetites, so they were on their way back to their floor. "How'd I miss that?"

"I was nice to him! Didn't you hear me being nice to him? And he choked! And almost died! This, *this* is what I get. You'd think I would have learned after almost killing Sucky."

"Jeannie, for crying out loud." She could see his lips twitching as he tried not to laugh at her. "You don't kill people by being nice to them. The idea is absurd. And slightly egotistical."

"It's not funny, Hope. This is it. The end. I can never be nice again."

"So you're strictly bad from now on. Well, more than usual. Which, frankly, boggles my mind. The universe," he added, "is in big trouble."

"Wicked will be my watchword," she declared.

"Well. How about being wicked right now?"

"That's a good idea," she said, nodding seriously. "I should resume badness ASAP. Innocent lives are at stake!"

"That's an excellent way to look at it," he agreed, and then he kissed her again.

Thirteen

They burst through the door and fell on the carpet, kissing and groping. Somehow Steve managed to kick the door closed, and then they were rolling around on the floor, wrestling their clothes off. Her thigh slammed into something and went numb, but she didn't care. His stubble was rasping across her nipples, and she *really* didn't care. His mouth was everywhere, he was kissing her with wild, fast kisses, and she was kissing him back as best she could. She could hear them panting and gasping in the dark, not speaking but letting their urgency speak for them, and then he was settling over her and nudging her knees apart. She reached down to help him, clasped him eagerly, and oooooooh, this might be a bad idea, he wasn't exactly small and she wasn't exactly drenched, but that was all right. Then he was nudging inside her, and then she'd locked her ankles behind his back, and then they flew.

"Did you say flew?" he panted in her ear. Her head was resting on his forearm and his other hand was bracing himself so he wouldn't fall on her.

"No, I said, don't stop, Hope."

He laughed, then groaned when she tightened her grip around his waist and thrust back at him. It had been uncomfortable for about three seconds, and now it was divine.

"I want you to give it to me, Hope."

"Jeannie . . ."

"Make me a woman, Hope."

"For Christ's sake!"

And now they were both laughing, and that was no good because he slipped out of her, picked her up, and tossed her on the bed. "Oh, Hope," she giggled. "You're so strong."

"No more talking," he growled, and pounced on her.

"Agreed," she said, and felt herself open before him like a flower. Her orgasm sang through her veins; there was that delirious feeling of being outside her body for a few seconds, then the languid fall back to earth.

"Oh, Jeannie," he groaned in her ear, and she felt him tense above her, then shudder all over.

"Steven," she said softly, and stroked his hair.

"Where are my cigarettes?"

He groaned again and threw a forearm over his eyes. "Is that why you insisted we go to your room?"

"A bet's a bet, as I believe I've mentioned before, and I can't think of a more perfect time."

"A more stereotypical time, you mean."

"Yeah, yeah. Whatever." He watched her root around, then straighten, holding the pack aloft. "Success!" she cried triumphantly. "Now what did I do with the lighter . . . ?"

He shook his head, but couldn't quite drag his gaze from her. Her breasts were medium-sized and firm, like Golden Delicious apples, and they bobbed as she leapt energetically around the room. She was too thin—and taking up smoking wasn't going to fix that—but had managed to hide a lovely body beneath those boring black suits and tights.

And she had some serious lower body strength going on, he thought, remembering the way her thighs had gripped him, the way her eyes had rolled back and she'd tightened around him; it had been like being in a heavenly sheath, one he'd never wanted to escape.

She had found her lighter, God help them, had lit up—it took only two minutes to get it going—and now coughed out a spectacular bloom of smoke. "Ahhhhh," she gasped. "Nothing like a cigarette after sex."

"You're starting to look green again," he observed.

"It's the shitty lighting in here." She bounded across the room and plonked down beside him. "You hungry? I'm hungry."

He smiled. "I don't think I've ever seen you so energetic."

"Oh. Well." She sucked on the butt again, this time trying not to cough, and her eyeballs bulged in an amusing, yet alarming, fashion. "I love to fuck."

"Oh, that's nice," he teased. "Is that what we did?"

"Sorry, Steve-o, I'm fresh out of hearts and flowers. I dunno, something about it, it totally energizes me. Especially when it's really really great." She looked at him hopefully. "Ready to go again?"

"Really really great, huh?"

"Oh, for sure. Top ten. Top five!" She counted on her fingers. "Possibly top one," she added in a mutter.

"I'm flattered. And I'd love to," he replied with perfect truth, "but I'm going to need another ten minutes."

"Oh." She giggled. It was a charming sound, and it delighted him. It was like finding a secret box with a bright red bow, one with your name on it. "That's okay. We can wait as long as you want. And since we're, y'know, passing time, can I ask you something?"

"My pecs are real, if that's what you're wondering. I'm implant-free."

"Very funny," she said, smacking him on the bicep. "Ow! Listen, is there a spare gram of fat on you anywhere?"

"Look who's talking, Skinny McGee! Is that your question?"

"No. Listen, I gotta admit, it's been on my mind—how come you quit the NYPD?"

"Because of my crippling amphetamine addiction."

Jeannie choked, then brushed pieces of tobacco off her lips. "No! Seriously? Come on, tell the truth."

"The truth is boring."

"Sure," Jeannie replied, "but it's the truth."

"Well, I was getting paid about thirty grand a year to have people shoot at me, and puke in my car, and insult me, and try to stab me. And then one of my books sold and took off—that was *True Heart*—"

"Great book."

"Thanks. Anyway, my first royalty check was twice what I made in a year. And my editor didn't throw up on me once. So I decided to write full time."

"Yeah, but how come romance?"

"Because there's a definitive ending," he said after a long pause. "And the fans kick your ass if you don't give them a happy one. I liked that, since I saw it so rarely as a cop. You can make a black-and-white world, and evil is always punished, and the good guys live happily ever after. I loved that."

Jeannie nodded. She looked around for a place to stub out her cigarette, gave up, walked into the bathroom, reappeared a moment later, then sat on the bed again and patted his leg. "I'm glad some fuckstick didn't shoot you in the face."

"You say the nicest things."

"Want to have a sleepover?"

"For the rest of my life," he said, and she blushed and looked away.

Fourteen

"Okay, we're gonna go up there, and I'll say how you're our best seller, and how much we all love your dazzling writing and intricate plots, blah-blah, and you'll say—"

"That my editor is a demon both in the office and in the sack."

"*Nooooo.*" She looked horrified for a moment, then grinned, then looked stern. "Don't even think about it, Hope, or I'll use your Jockeys as an ashtray. Anyway, you'll say you're honored to be here, happy to be writing for a distinguished house like Anderson and Son, yak-yak, and then we'll duck for cover."

"It'll be fine."

"Mmmmm." Jeannie was chewing her thumbnail, a loathsome habit she was unable to break. "It'll go either way. They'll either be thrilled you're a great-looking stud, or pissed off that you've got a penis but you've been passing yourself off as Hope Desiree. I foresee no middle ground."

"My real name is on the copyright page," he pointed out. "It's not exactly a deep, dark secret."

"Dude, I *work* there, and I didn't know."

"I think that's more a commentary on your single-mindedness, than on the intelligence of the average reader."

"I just don't want them to get mad. I've been worrying about this whole damn conference for the last two months, and that was *before* I had to boot you out of the closet."

"Jeannie, seriously. It's not going to be a big deal. There *are* male romance authors out there. Readers just want a good story. They don't care if I wear panties or jockies. Or both," he added, teasing her.

"Okay, jeez, whatever. Thanks for a truly vile mental image, by the way. Ready?" She took a deep breath.

"In a minute." He leaned over and kissed her on the mouth, softly, sweetly. "Okay. I'm ready now."

"What?"

"I said, I'm ready now."

"Oh. Okay." Her cheeks were red, but he didn't think it was from rage this time. "Let's do it."

"—Editorial Director from Anderson and Son, and Hope Desiree!"

They walked up to the podium, a wave of enthusiastic clapping washing over them, and then Jeannie stepped to the microphone and said, as the clapping faded to puzzled murmurs, "Hi. I'm Jeannie Desjardin. We've got a surprise for you guys—this is Hope Desiree."

"Hi," Hope said in a booming baritone.

The murmuring increased, and there was scattered clapping and even a couple of, "I knew it!" from the audience. Jeannie glanced down and saw Caro staring up at Steve.

"Hi," she said, waving down at her. "How are your appointments going?"

"Who cares? Damn!"

"I, uh, guess you're surprised that our number one romance writer is a man."

"And *what* a man!" Caro said, dazzled.

"Cut that out. Anyway," she said back to the microphone, "Hope here is available for autographs for the rest of the morning, and he'll be at the book signing tomorrow. Are there, um, any questions?"

A writer raised her hand—Jeannie recognized her as Catherine Spangler, a mid-lister currently toiling for Dorchester. "Yes?"

"Have you found that as a man it's more difficult to be taken seriously in the genre?"

"This genre," Steve said, "isn't exactly known for being taken seriously by anyone. Talked to any mystery writers lately?"

The crowd broke up.

"But to answer your question, I don't think it's any harder for a man to break in than a woman. You just need a good story. That's what we all want, right? A book that consumes us while we're reading it. A book you want to start reading all over again, that very minute. I don't think it matters who comes up with the actual story."

Nods all around, and scattered applause. Then, from the crowd, a slightly spiteful voice: "I suppose it doesn't hurt that you bear a passing resemblance to Fabio?"

"That's like implying only pretty female writers get contracts. It's kind of insulting," Steve said mildly. "Your looks don't have anything to do with it. Again: story. Good story."

"What happened when your publishing house found out you were a man?"

"Nothing. They didn't care, as long as I turned my work in on time." He winked at Jeannie, who barely noticed.

She was having kind of an epiphany here. Sure, she wanted their readers to accept Steve as Hope. But what if they didn't?

Well, what if they didn't? So he wasn't what they expected. Was she ever what anyone expected? Did she give a ripe fuck? Maybe Steve was right. Maybe . . . they were meant for each other.

Or maybe they were both heavily medicated.

"How did you get the idea for your first book?"

Jeannie nearly sagged against the podium. If they were on to "Where do you get your ideas," that was a very good sign. They weren't going to be skinned alive! Sure, an epiphany was nice, but it was even nicer not to have to dodge paper clips the rest of the weekend.

"Okay, well, Hope here will answer more questions at the signing. That's it." She stepped away—and bumped into Caro.

"Like you're going to leave without introducing me," she said. Today her hair was in another Valkyrie braid, her big brown eyes huge behind her purple glasses. "Fuhgeddabouddit!"

"Caro, Hope. Hope, Caro. Caro writes time travel."

"I love time travel," Steve said, shaking her hand and gifting her with a sexy smile. "Anything I've read?"

"God, I hope so," Caro said.

Jeannie jabbed her in the side. "Will you close your mouth? You're going to short out the mike with your drool."

"You know, Jeannie," Caro said, eyeing Steve like a diabetic checks out a hot fudge sundae, "I liked you just fine yesterday, and hoped we'd be pals, but now I definitely have to wedge myself into your life. So, Hope, looking for a critique partner?"

"Sorry, miss," Steve said politely. "I'm a one-woman—uh—woman." And he reached across and took Jeannie's hand and squeezed it.

"You *dog!*" Caro cried. "Not a word in the public restroom about any of *this.*"

"Shut up," Jeannie snapped, yanking her hand free.

"Don't mind her," Steve told Caro, who looked ready to follow him through the pits of hell. "She gets nervous around genuine sentiment. It'll take her a while to get used to the idea."

"Start signing," Jeannie said by way of reply. There was quite a line of fans forming, and she was heartened—it looked as though their little announcement was going to go over okay. "Woo later."

"I guess you're not bothered by her raging alcoholism,"

Caro said, grinning at Jeannie. "I, however, am as clean as the day is long, and I'd love to—"

"Never mind what you'd love to," she said, seizing Caro by the elbow. "Let's go, blondie."

"Hey, I've got a great idea for a book," she said as Jeannie dragged her away. Not that she was jealous, because she totally wasn't. Even though Caro was ridiculously gorgeous. And she and Steve would make a beautiful couple. And she'd probably be a lot nicer to Steve than Jeannie would be. That was all irrelevant. She just didn't want her author bothered unnecessarily.

Yeah. That was her story, and she was sticking to it.

"I said, I'VE GOT A GREAT IDEA FOR A BOOK."

"I heard you the first time. Here, let's get some coffee."

"Not a chance; can't stand the stuff. Say, you keeping any other yummy little secrets up your sleeve?"

"None of your business, Caro."

"Oooooh, she remembered my name! Flattering."

They sat down at a small table at a corner where Jeannie could keep an eye on Steve. "You're a hard one to forget. Now tell me your idea."

Caro leaned forward and planted her elbows on the table. "Okay, so, it just occurred to me. It was like a blaze of light!"

"Or the fizzle of a nightlight burning out."

"Check this: There's this woman, see, and everybody thinks she's a jerk, but she's really okay. It's just that she's driven toward jerkiness by prima donna authors and bean counters and corporate politics. She's a jerk to, you know, protect herself."

"Mmmmm." Jeannie sipped her coffee, which was alarmingly mudlike. "I'm listening. I'm going to kick your ass when you're done, but I'm listening."

"And say this woman works in publishing, and tries to keep to herself, and one day she gets a great slush-pile manuscript, and works with the author via, I dunno, e-mail or whatever. And then she finds out the author is this great-looking guy, and they fall in love. After the required amount of obstacles, of course. Which they overcome in a blaze of passion and a whirl of panties. The End."

"Lame," Jeannie commented.

"My ass! Everybody likes stories about surprises."

"So your heroine, she's—what? Redeemed by love?"

"Oh, hell no. She stays a jerk. But the author fella likes her just the way she is." Caro took a sip of her tea. "I mean, maybe it'd be okay if this editor figured out there's more to life than dashing hopes and dreams, but that's not as interesting, I don't think. And like I said, the hero thinks she's fine the way she is. So *that's* okay."

"I'd like to read a story where the heroine isn't redeemed by anything," Jeannie admitted.

"I'll bet." Caro leered.

"So, give me a partial. I'll take a look."

"Of course you will," Caro said comfortably. "You have to admit, it's a great story."

Fifteen

"That went over well," Steve began, walking into his room. Then: "Whoa!" as Jeannie jumped on his back.

"Time for sex," she said gaily, riding him to the bed.

"This isn't your jealous, territorial side showing its face, is it? Not that I mind, but I need some warning so I can keep it straight with your many other faces. Okay, your one other face."

"I hope you can talk and fuck at the same time," Jeannie commented.

"I'm a man of many talents," Steve said cheerfully, shrugging out of his suit jacket and tossing it in a corner.

They wrestled playfully for a couple of minutes, and then he helped her out of her jacket and blouse and—

"Oooh, braless."

"Like you didn't notice."

"That's true."

—panties, and then he was kissing her mouth and her chin and her neck, long, slow delicious kisses that made her shiver, and then his lips were brushing across her nipples, teasing them to stiffness, and then he was kissing her stomach, and then she forgot to keep track of everything he was kissing.

His tongue and fingers, darting and licking and stroking and teasing, quickly brought her to orgasm—faster than she would have believed, faster, in fact, than she could do it herself . . . and that was quite a trick!

He came up to her, but quick as a fish, she wriggled. Then he was on his back, and she was swinging a leg over him.

He grinned and said, "You've got this thing about riding, don't you?"

"Oh, keep quiet. Now let's see, what's the most romantic way to grab you and stuff you inside me?"

He burst out laughing, shaking the bed. "Cut it out! Laughter's a killer." She settled herself over him, and he abruptly quit laughing. "Oh, Christ, that's nice. Don't go away anytime soon."

"I'm done with all my appointments, anyway," she assured him. She started rocking back and forth, enjoying the slippery friction—on the down stroke it felt as though he was in her throat—and rode to another orgasm. "Oh, that's excellent," she sighed to the ceiling. Then he was gripping her hips, and she wasn't setting the pace anymore. He was using her as she had just used him, and she didn't mind a bit; in fact, she gloried in it. As he surged up toward her, she wrapped her arms around his middle and hugged him to her, and then he was stiffening in her embrace, and then relaxing, and hugging her back.

After five minutes of staring glumly at the pile of paper at the foot of her hotel door, Jeannie sighed.

"How did we miss *that?*" Steve said. "Especially since they couldn't fit the entire manuscript under the door, so they put it under in chunks."

"Hope they got an earful," Jeannie muttered.

"Ah, the misunderstood life of a New York editor."

"Pal, you have no idea. And while I'm thinking about it, let me set the record straight."

"As long as it doesn't involve you inhaling smoke, I'm all

ears." He laughed, then raised her hand to his mouth and kissed her knuckles.

"Because you seem kind of serious about this whole let's-stay-together-forever thing."

"Deadly serious," he said deadly seriously.

"Right. And I'm fine with that. I mean, it's weird. You know it's weird. We just met."

"My folks were engaged for sixty-two hours before they got married in Vegas," he said, yawning. "Forty-two years ago next month."

"Swell, I'll send them a card. But I'm getting used to the idea. And it's you—it's because of you. Just so you know. Because most guys take off when they find out there's not a scared little girl inside, or whatever. You know, when they find out—"

"That what they see is what they get."

"Exactly. And that—weirdly—doesn't seem to bother you. Which I like. A ton. But I wanted to tell you about truth. We sort of touched on it at dinner, but then I acciden-tally almost killed Bob and we got off the subject."

"Jeannie . . ."

"It's not like I get off on, you know, making waiters cry. I just love the truth. Fact is," she added, "I worship the truth. I think it's the most important thing there is. And I'd rather tell the truth and be thought a bitch than keep my mouth shut and have tons of friends but also an ulcer the size of the Lincoln Tunnel."

"That seems sensible."

"Right. Thanks. But anyway, I love the truth. And I think maybe I love you—I gotta think about that some more. But as long as you get that, I think we'll be okay."

"You're talking to a former cop," Steve said. "You think I've got any room in my life for someone who *doesn't* love the truth?"

Vastly relieved, she said, "Just so we're square."

"Oh, we're square."

"I wouldn't want you to say you were tricked or anything. You know, on *our* forty-second anniversary."

"Jeannie, you couldn't trick someone if they stuck a gun in your ear. You always speak your mind. Your crazy, sadistic, crass mind."

"You mean that?" she cried. "Jeez, that's the nicest thing anybody's ever said to me!"

"There's plenty more where that came from," he said, and kissed her again, and again, and one thing led to another, and it was okay, because it was the truth.

Instruction in Seduction

Jamie Denton

One

"Why do they call it a blow job when there isn't any blowing involved?"

Jackson Hunt choked and sputtered, spraying scalding coffee over the steering wheel and dash board of the police cruiser. "Son of a . . ."

"It's supposed to be more of a sucking action, isn't it? At least I think that's what I've always done."

He turned in the driver's seat to shoot his partner, Officer Eden Matthews, a heated glare. More hot, black coffee sloshed over the rim of the Styrofoam cup onto his hand. "Jesus, Eden," he complained, liquid dripping from his fingers. "Give a guy a little warning, would ya?"

The blame didn't rest entirely with her. She couldn't possibly have known his imagination would shift into overdrive with visions of her lush, full mouth poised over the head of his dick. He didn't normally engage in sexual fantasies involving his partner—at least not when she sat less than two feet away from him.

She glanced up from the magazine in her hands; a light frown creased her forehead as she reached into the glove compartment to hand him a stack of napkins to mop up the mess. "Sorry," she said, without an ounce of contrition evident in her amber gaze. "Now, answer the question."

He couldn't believe she'd initiated this conversation. In all the time he'd known her, sex was not a topic she'd ever openly discussed. Eden was a strict, by-the-book cop, who carefully dotted her *I*'s and crossed her *T*'s. That she would venture into one of the top taboo-in-the-workplace subjects had him curious.

"Why do you want to know?" he asked, against his better judgment.

"Don't be a prude, Jackson." Under the dim haze of lights from the dash, her amber eyes glowed a soft burnished gold. Her expectant gaze filled with a curiosity that elevated his libido several degrees. "Just answer the question."

Prude? No woman had ever called him a prude, not when it came to sex. There wasn't much he hadn't tried and didn't enjoy. The more frequent, the better.

She let out an exasperated huff. "Fine," she said when he didn't answer. Picking up the women's magazine again, she muttered something he didn't catch, but was fairly certain hadn't been complimentary.

They were twenty minutes into a Code Seven. With another ten minutes of their break left before they went back in service, he debated the wisdom of continuing the discussion, then decided to be thankful she'd let the subject drop. Opening the door to the cruiser, he poured the remnants of his coffee onto the asphalt.

"Do you get off when a woman masturbates in front of you?"

He nearly bit his tongue. "What?"

"It says, and I quote, 'Almost every man alive fantasizes about a woman bringing herself to orgasm in front of him.'" The look she cast his way was perfectly innocent, and highly erotic. "That's mind-blowing method number three, by the way."

He didn't think he could survive her telling him the number one technique. "I thought you were studying for the sergeant's exam?" he asked crankily, hoping to steer her into territory more conducive to his sanity.

"Later." She closed the magazine and set it in her lap. "This is important."

"I have a feeling I'm going to regret this," he said, slamming the car door. "Why?"

"I got dumped." She exhaled, her breath slow and uneven. "Again."

You didn't spend eight hours a day or more with a person and not learn a thing or two about each other's personal life, relationship pitfalls included. Five years ago she'd joined the Riverside County Sheriff's Department fresh from the academy. A year and a half ago, his rookie partner had been shot during a routine traffic stop, and he'd been assigned a new partner, Eden Matthews. Initially, he hadn't been thrilled being saddled with a female officer, but it hadn't taken him long to realize she wasn't like most of the women in the sheriff's department. She never took unnecessary risks to prove herself to her male counterparts, and she was probably more levelheaded than half of the guys he'd worked with over the past eight years.

It hadn't taken him long to realize she wasn't like most women, either.

"Would it help if I told you he was a jerk?"

A sweet smile curved her mouth. "You think they're all jerks."

She had a point. "Because they usually are," he said dryly.

When it came to men, Eden possessed a unique talent for picking the wrong guy. Not that they were all losers. The bank exec she'd dated a few months ago had potential, which had bothered him more than he would've liked. Yet, for such a strong, intelligent woman, Eden had no sense when it came to men. Rather than finding a guy who appreciated her qualities, she was perpetually drawn to men who were either too full of themselves or total wimps she easily intimidated and eventually pushed away. Within a matter of weeks the guy eventually figured out she wasn't the type of woman to worship the ground he walked on, and that would be the end of it—until the next bum came along that snagged her attention.

Fools, every last one of them, Jackson thought. If Eden wasn't his partner, she'd be the perfect lover. She wasn't a clingy woman, valuing her freedom and independence as much as he. With Eden, a guy smart enough to appreciate and willing to take the time to understand what made her tick would have it made. She wasn't one of those overly emotional females, either. In fact, he'd seen her reduced to tears only once in all the time he'd known her.

Two days before Christmas they'd been called in to assist on a particularly bad traffic collision. A drunk driver had run a stop sign, broadsiding a vehicle with a young family who'd been coming home late from a holiday celebration. The wife and two of the three children in the car had died at the scene, leaving behind a young father with an infant daughter to raise on his own. Jackson had been equally affected by the scene, but Eden's tears had unnerved him. After their shift he'd convinced her they needed to blow off steam. She'd agreed and had gone with him to his place where they'd proceeded to get hammered on tequila shots.

Eventually the salt and lime were forgotten. Sprawled on the leather sofa in his living room, they'd downed Jose Gold straight from the bottle. And that's when the real trouble started.

He'd kissed her . . . or at least he was fairly certain he'd kissed her. In all honesty, they'd both been so blitzed, he couldn't be sure whether the experience had been real or marked the launch of the wild fantasies he'd been having about Eden since. He'd considered asking her about it, but when there'd been absolutely no difference in her behavior toward him, he'd kept his mouth shut and for the past eight months had been relegated to sexual fantasies starring his partner.

"I know I'll regret this," he said, "but what does a return to singular status have to do with blowing minds?"

She leveled him with a direct stare. "He said I was a zero between the sheets."

Good thing he'd poured out the rest of his coffee; otherwise he'd be wearing the stuff. "You can't be serious?"

Her nod was solemn. "Dead in the sack. His words, not mine."

"Did you stop to think maybe he's the one with the problem?"

She glanced away, her focus on the patrons seated in front of the window of the all-night coffee shop. "It's not the first time I've heard that particular complaint," she said quietly.

No way in hell could a woman who kissed as passionately as Eden be considered a zero between the sheets. Granted, she had a tendency to be a little uptight, but if that kiss was anywhere near as real as his body constantly reminded him whenever he thought about her and not the product of a drunken fantasy, the problem was definitely not hers.

"Give me a break," he muttered, shaking his head.

"Just once I'd like to have a relationship that outlasts the expiration date on a carton of milk." She slipped a folded sheet of paper from the breast pocket of her uniform and handed it to him. "I've given this a lot of thought, and the one conclusion I keep coming back to is that I need to learn how to be a better lover."

He angled the paper toward the light for a better look. The *Kama Sutra* topped her neatly handwritten list of books. His eyebrows shot upward at the sensual possibilities jockeying for position in his mind as he zeroed in on a pair of particularly interesting titles. "*Awesome Afternoon Delight, All the Time,*" he read, holding back a grin. "*Every Man's Fantasy Revealed.*"

"I'm hitting the bookstore when it opens," she said with a nod. "So, what do you think? Are there any other books you'd recommend?"

She looked so serious, he didn't dare crack a smile. "I hate to burst your bubble, kid," he said, handing back the list, "but some things aren't meant to be learned from a book." He glanced pointedly at the women's magazine in her lap. "Or from a how-to article."

"So what you're saying is, hands-on experience, so to speak, would be better."

Suddenly, he felt uncomfortable as hell. "So to speak," he said carefully.

"Hmm," she murmured. She reached for the cup of soda at her feet and sucked hard on the straw. "Maybe you have a point. An actual instructor would be beneficial."

"Well, hell, let's boogie on over to the adult learning center and sign you right up," he said, his tone dripping with sarcasm. "This isn't like when you had a bug up your ass to learn about indoor gardens or how to line dance."

She drummed her fingernails on the arm rest. "True," she said in a contemplative tone. "It's not exactly the kind of class I'll find in the course catalogue at the UC extension center, either."

"Buckle up," he told her, then advised dispatch they were back in service. He didn't like the direction the conversation was heading, or the fantasies swimming in his head. He wasn't exactly in the market for a relationship, but he did care about Eden, in a way that cops weren't supposed to care about their partners.

He pulled out of the parking lot of the all-night coffee shop, then cruised five miles under the speed limit down Van Buren toward the 91 Freeway.

"You know, Jackson," she said as they approached the Galleria. "Why don't you help me?"

He turned into the mall parking lot to patrol the area and shot a wary glance in her direction. "Sure thing," he said sarcastically. "I'll post a notice on the bulletin board in the men's locker room for you at the end of our shift."

"Don't be ridiculous." She kept her attention on the shadows. "I'm not looking just to get laid."

The *just* in her statement was what had him worried. "Thank God for small favors," he muttered, negotiating a speed bump near the mall's main entrance. "The woman does have some sense left."

"You'd be the perfect instructor."

He hit the brakes and looked at her, hoping to see a teasing smile. Instead, she steadily held his gaze. He retracted his previous comment since she'd clearly lost her mind. "Forget it."

"And why not? Women talk in locker rooms, too. You have quite the reputation."

He stepped on the accelerator. "Yeah, well, don't believe everything you hear."

"Fine," she said in a huff. "If you won't do it, then I'll just find someone who will."

"This isn't like helping you study for the sergeant's exam," he complained. Or like the time he'd helped her move into her new apartment, or even when he'd accompanied her to her mother's funeral four months ago.

"What do you think of Cliff Batten? Rumor has it he's not too bad in the romance department."

He made a sound of disgust. "Batten wouldn't know how to please a woman if he had a gun held to his head."

"That could be an asset, if you think about it. He'd definitely be in it for himself. Besides, I'm interested in learning how to give, not take, pleasure."

"The two go hand in hand." He shook his head. She was twenty-seven years old. Surely she knew the hotter, more responsive the woman, the bigger the turn-on for the one getting her that way. She couldn't possibly be that naïve. Could she?

"I wonder if Cliff's on duty tonight?" She reached for the radio. "Slow down, Jackson."

"What do think you're doing?"

She shot him a tolerant look. "Giving the gals in dispatch something to perk up their shift. Officer requests an immediate Code Six Nine," she said, then laughed. Pointing toward the dark entrance to one of the mall stores, she indicated a dark figure hunched in the corner. "Hit the spot light."

He did, only to reveal a planter.

Eden returned the mike to the holder on the dash. "Glad I didn't call that one in," she said with a throaty chuckle. "On the other hand, maybe you are right. A man with experience, someone who really knows how to please a woman, might be the smarter choice."

"I never said that."

"Come to think of it," she continued as if she hadn't heard him. "The girls from dispatch were discussing Ross Findley from Vice tonight. He's hit on me a couple of times. I bet he'd be willing to tutor me."

God, he hoped she wasn't serious. With Eden's dry wit, sometimes he had difficulty determining when she was joking. "Stay away from Findley," he warned. "I've known him a lot longer than you have. The guy's a head case."

"It's a prereq for Vice. They're all a little edgy."

An understatement, in his opinion.

The radio crackled before he could answer. "Units in the vicinity of Van Buren and Magnolia. Code Four. Four-fifteen in progress, north end of the Travel Lodge parking lot."

Officer needs assistance. Damn. So much for a quiet end to their shift. He snagged the mike. "Four-four Edward responding," he said. "ETA two minutes."

"Affirmative, four-four Edward. Code Two," the dispatcher replied.

Jackson swore, hit the lights, and sped out of the mall parking lot.

"Probably just a couple of drunks pounding each other into the ground," Eden said. He caught the hopeful note in her voice and silently agreed.

He pulled into the parking lot, and Eden radioed in their location. One of the uniformed officers from the unit already on scene gave a warning shout as all hell broke loose. Eden called for more backup. The suspect bolted, heading straight for them at a dead run. Jackson waited, then at the precise moment flung open the door to the cruiser.

"Stupid son of a bitch," he muttered when the guy plowed into the door. The suspect sailed backward, his body landing with a hard thud on the asphalt and gravel.

Eden winced and leaned over to peer out the driver's side of the cruiser. "Suspect appears unconscious," she said into the mike. "Request EMT unit to location."

She looked at him and shook her head. "Do you realize how much paperwork you've just created for us?" She let out a sigh. "Again?"

He ignored her complaint and left the vehicle. The way he figured it, the extra time filling out reports would keep her busy and hopefully derail her current quest for higher education. Unfortunately, he couldn't say the same for himself. He had a bad feeling he'd be thinking of nothing else for a long time.

Two

Eden sucked in a deep breath and held it, tugging hard on the zipper of her jeans. If she didn't lay off the French fries, she'd have to add a pilates class to her gym time. As much as it pained her to say no to her favorite food group, the proof was in the snug fit of her Levi's.

The problem with working graves was all the dead time. Once the drunks and druggies were tucked in their beds sleeping it off, not much happened. Unfortunately, that left a girl with too much time on her hands to pack in the carbs and to think about everything wrong in her life.

She let the breath out slowly before easing onto the wooden bench in front of her locker to pull on a pair of socks. Just because she'd become a cop didn't mean she didn't want the same things most women her age were after: a home, a couple of adorable kids, and a golden retriever. A husband would be nice, too, but how did she find an eligible candidate when she couldn't hang on to a guy once they tangled the sheets?

Plenty of men were initially attracted to her. She usually had dates for all the big events like Valentine's Day and New Year's Eve, nor did she spend time waiting for the phone to ring on a Friday night. The problem came two to three weeks into what appeared on the surface to be a promising relationship, when the potential prospect usually disappeared faster than a suspect down a dark alley.

An exit line didn't exist that she hadn't heard, from the common *it's-not-you-it's-me* kiss-off, to the more inventive, *I only have four months to live*. She'd actually fallen for that one, until she'd run into the perfectly healthy jerk and his new bride a year later. Two weeks ago, Mr. Not-So-Wonderful-After-All threw her a curve ball she hadn't seen coming when he'd rudely announced she was as exciting in bed as a poetry reading. Normally his comment wouldn't have phased her. She would've written it off as just another inventive exit line, except she'd already heard that particular complaint—*twice*.

Before the sheets had cooled, she'd come to the conclusion she had a serious handicap working against her. Genetics. She might not have *doormat* flashing like a beer sign on her forehead, but when it came to men, failed relationships were a family specialty. As much as she'd fought against being anything like her mother, she realized she was dangerously close to carrying on the Varilee Matthews tradition. Like losing men was some secret family recipe handed down to each generation.

She'd had plenty of short-term relationships, but once she slept with a guy, he was history. It made no difference whether she waited three hours or three months before diving beneath the sheets. Her love life was the pathetic equivalent of a cry-in-your-beer country-western ballad. She'd gladly stand by her man, if she found one willing to stick around long enough for her to put on her shoes.

Must be something in the family DNA, she thought, because once a Matthews spread her legs, production of pheromones ground to a screeching halt. Whatever the case, without a doubt she knew she had to do something about her sorry state or she'd end up just like her mother—used up, bitter, and dead before her time because she'd brought home the wrong loser.

She let out a sigh, pulled the pins from her hair, and scrubbed her fingers over her tingling scalp. Jackson claimed she wouldn't develop a better sexual technique by reading a few books or magazine articles. She agreed. Having already devoured nearly every relationship how-to tome on the market certainly hadn't produced the desired results.

There'd been the book about "rules" which had driven her crazy. Subservience simply wasn't in her vocabulary. Venus and Mars might as well have been Pluto and Jupiter for all she cared because she didn't buy into prostituting herself to get what she wanted. She'd always thought of herself as more of a WYSIWYG kind of gal. Unfortunately, as her last lover had pointed out, she was more a case of false advertising. They saw a woman with a body made for sin, but who in actuality—wasn't. She was nothing more than a Volvo pretending to be a Porsche.

What she was asking of Jackson wasn't unreasonable, she thought as she dragged a brush through her hair. She really didn't see why he'd kicked up such a fuss. According to the female rumor mill, the man was a virtual legend between the sheets, and that qualified him as the perfect solution to her problem. Now all she had to do was make certain he drew the same conclusion.

Despite the heat, she decided to leave her thick hair loose, then slipped her feet into her sneakers and tied up the laces. With a squad full of eligible bachelors at her disposal, any one of them would be more than willing to accommodate her—if she had the nerve to ask them. In her opinion, though, only one would suffice—the one paid to watch her back on a nightly basis. Although Jackson did possess traffic-stopping good looks, she wasn't attracted to him in *that* way, so he posed no risk to her heart. He was one of her closest friends, *and* her partner. She trusted him, literally, with her life.

She snagged her purse from the top shelf and slung the strap over her shoulder, then grabbed her duffle before closing the metal door to her locker. Of all people, Jackson knew once she made up her mind to do something, she did it. He was usually such a smart guy. He should simply agree to help her and save himself the aggravation.

She left the women's dressing room and found him lounging against the wall waiting for her. He'd changed out of his uniform and wore a pair of dark jeans and a faded Hard Rock Café T-shirt which clung quite nicely to his thick biceps.

The women around the station often commented on Jackson's dark, classic good looks and the intensity of his sea green eyes. A couple of inches over six feet with a lean athletic frame and a cocky smile just a tad shy of arrogant, was it any wonder he turned heads? In uniform or out, any woman with a pulse could see he characterized the epitome of masculine perfection. Considering the sudden increase in her own pulse rate, apparently she was no exception.

She flashed him a smile her case of nerves belied. "Change your mind yet?"

His dark sable eyebrows drew downward. "Don't hold your breath," he said, and pushed off the wall.

She shrugged as if his opinion made little difference. "Suit yourself," she said airily. Instead of heading toward the parking lot, she went in the opposite direction and walked up to the watch commander's desk, prepared to initiate Phase II of The Plan—making Jackson believe she meant business.

He fell into step beside her.

"Did you want something?" she asked, glancing in his direction.

"You were supposed to drop me off, remember?"

"Oh, that's right." She snapped her fingers as if it'd slipped her mind she'd been playing chauffeur for the past two days since his pickup was in for repairs. "Don't worry. This shouldn't take long."

She approached the desk and kept up the confident woman pretext. "Hey, Commander. Seen Detective Findley around?"

The fifty-something watch commander glanced up impatiently from the paperwork in front of him. "What do I look like? A private secretary?" he groused. "Check the board, Matthews."

"Right, sorry to bother you," she said cheerily and took off toward the detectives' board near the rear exit of the station.

A red peg inserted next to Ross Findley's name under the "in" column indicated the vice cop was on the premises. She prayed Jackson took the bait, because she hadn't a clue what line of bull she'd actually feed Findley if Jackson called her bluff. Something about the guy gave her the creeps, but Jackson's severe dislike for the vice cop made him the perfect patsy.

She turned toward the staircase that would take her up to the detectives' area known as the bullpen and nearly collided with Jackson. He blocked her path, standing with his feet braced apart and his arms crossed over his wide, firm chest. Her pulse revved again.

Nerves. Most definitely nerves. Not sexual attraction.

"Just what do you think you're doing?" he demanded, thankfully in a hushed tone. She didn't relish drawing a crowd.

If the deep scowl on his face was any indication, apparently she had a better knack for manipulation than she believed. He looked as if he wanted to strangle her.

She let out an impatient breath. "What does it look like?"

"Like you're about to make an ass of yourself."

"My ass, my business. Now, if you'll excuse me . . ." She moved to step around him.

He moved with her. "Findley's got a big mouth, Eden. Word will get around. You don't want that kind of attention."

Another reason she'd chosen Findley as the unwitting ace in her bra to blackmail Jackson into aiding her in locating her MIA inner vixen. "Think of it as good press," she sassed, then darted around him. A third of the way up the stairs, his big, warm hand clamped down on her forearm, halting her.

Thank you, God.

She manufactured a warning look, then made a huge deal out of glancing pointedly at his hand on her arm before sliding her gaze to his. "Unless you've changed your mind, I suggest you let go." She'd managed to inflect enough hardness in her voice to sound convincing. "Now."

Heaven bless his chivalrous soul, his grip tightened. "You're not doing this."

"Wanna bet?" She attempted freedom, but his viselike grip kept her from bolting up the stairs.

"That's it," he said in a heated tone that made her tummy do a funny little flip. With a none-too-gentle tug, he hauled her back down the stairs. "We're out of here."

Trailing behind him, she gave in to the urge to grin as he dragged her toward the exit, debating whether to put up more of a fight. At least make it look good. All those books she'd read preached the benefits of playing hard to get. Except she wasn't trying to "get" Jackson. Well, other than in bed. She stifled a snicker. Strictly for instructional purposes, she silently added.

As an afterthought?

She pushed the thought away as he shoved open the heavy metal door and dragged her into the bright morning sunshine. She groped in her purse for her sunglasses and car keys. At a few minutes past nine, already the August temperatures were pushing hard toward record-setting triple digits. The air was still, moist with humidity that clung to her skin, promising another Southern California scorcher, typical for the inland valley this time of year. Waves of heat rose from the black asphalt, driving the heat index even higher. After tonight, she wouldn't be back on duty again until Monday. Maybe she should head up the coast to Pismo tomorrow after her shift and hang out with her oldest and dearest friend, Libby Morgan, for the weekend. The crowds would be horrendous, though, and cops hated crowds.

She'd never been much of a fan of summer, either, and now that she wore the uniform, her dread of the season had doubled. The higher the temperature, the shorter the fuse. Throw in a full moon, and the domestic disturbance calls alone tripled, especially on weekends.

Speaking of short fuses . . .

"What's up with this proclivity you've developed toward violence lately?" she asked him, still following behind him as he stalked across the parking lot to her GT. "You rendered another suspect unconscious."

He didn't bother with an answer. She hated to think he could be on the edge of burnout, but she'd been on the job long enough to know it happened. In a profession where gang violence, drug trafficking, and domestic disputes that all too often turned deadly were the norm, a cop had no choice but to develop a certain level of numbness or burnout occurred faster than a bargain-basement Fourth of July sparkler.

They were paid to protect and serve a society that viewed them with varying degrees of contempt as if they were the enemy, making the thin line they walked between compassion and detachment even more precarious. Eventually, even the best cops made mistakes. When her own partner made them twice in as many weeks, she had a right to question him.

He finally stopped when they reached the back end of her car. "I'm driving." He released her, only to hold out his hand for her keys.

"Think again, buddy." It'd taken her months to save up enough for the down. "I haven't even made the first payment yet."

His left eyebrow hiked upward, and he gave her a challenging stare. "Hand them over."

She glared right back. "If you're on some macho guy trip, cancel it. Since when can't you be seen in the passenger seat with a woman behind the wheel?" They split the driving during their shift, even during the rainy season when most of the male cops insisted otherwise.

He leaned toward her, and she couldn't make up her mind whether the heat from the asphalt or his body was responsible for making her so uncomfortably hot all of a sudden. "Right now, I have a strong urge to put my hands around something and squeeze. Your scrawny neck or the steering wheel," he said with a shrug. "Ladies' choice."

There were two things she knew with absolute certainty—that life didn't come with guarantees or a handy instruction booklet, and that Jackson Hunt would *never* hurt her. She made a definite *un*vixenlike snort which told him exactly what she thought of his empty threat, but slapped the keys in his hand anyway. "One scratch and it's your ass, Hunt."

"Don't sweat it."

Once they were settled inside the sleek leather interior of the vehicle, he turned the key, and her precious Ford GT roared to life. He gunned the engine, testing the power. Her baby purred in response to his touch. Would she purr in response to his touch, too? God, she hoped so.

"Buckle up, kid," he said, snapping his own seat belt in place. "And get ready for the ride of your life."

Oooh, now he's talking. Except she had a feeling he wasn't referring to the kind of ride that started with hot, wet kisses and ended with deep, slow strokes of his body inside hers. Yet.

She pulled the safety harness across and slid the buckle into the catch. "I wish you'd stop calling me that," she told him. Occasionally he'd say the word, and it almost resembled an endearment, or least held a modicum of affection. Today it sounded more like an insult.

"Oh, and thirty is *so* old." She was only three years his junior. "And I'm hardly a kid," she added, sounding suspiciously like a petulant child.

He turned to look at her, and her breath caught. Something indefinable and intense smoldered in his eyes, turning them a vibrant shade of turquoise and reminding her of the ocean. Vast, deep, and dangerously unpredictable.

"I know."

The low, rough quality of his voice sent a wild and delicious tremor rumbling down her spine. He deliberately swept his gaze down the length of her. Beneath the fabric of her serviceable cotton bra, her nipples tightened. Her panties were damp before he reached the waistband of her jeans.

Lifting his gaze back to hers, he let out a long, unsteady breath. "That's my problem."

Three

Jackson needed his head examined for seriously considering such an outrageous proposal. Regardless of the opportunity for no-strings-attached sex, something no guy in his right mind would dream of turning down, Eden was his partner. A smart cop didn't fuck his partner—figuratively or literally.

Rather than pushing the speed limit through the winding, hilly roadways of Canyon Crest to her apartment, he should've hopped on Interstate 15, taken Highway 30, and floored it north to the psych hospital. He didn't even need a room with a view of the country club-like grounds. One with soft, heavily padded walls would do. A matching straight jacket couldn't hurt, either.

Eden gripped the arm rest when he took a curve a little too fast. "You're going to miss"—her head whipped around as he zipped past her apartment complex—"the turn."

She let out a gusty sigh. "Okay, so we're not going to my place. Mind telling me where we are going?"

"Crazy." He dropped into third and gunned the engine. "Don't worry," he said, and shot her a quick glance. "You've made sure it'll be a short trip."

He crested the hill and flew down the other side. At the top of the next rise, he slowed and pulled to the side of the road. She remained silent when he turned off the ignition and left her sitting in the car. Walking across the wide patch of gravel to the barricade at the edge of the turnout, he steadied his breathing and concentrated on the view of the canyon below.

A few low trees dotted the immediate landscape amid the dried grass covering the sloping hills where he and his siblings had played as kids, long before the housing developers had arrived and changed everything. What had once been a quiet, rural neighborhood had been devoured by housing tracts and an overcrowded, dispassionate bedroom community of strangers.

He'd grown up on these hills, had explored every ravine, every crest, had climbed every tree. Where a cul-de-sac of Spanish-style homes with tile roofs now stood, he'd played cowboys and Indians, cops and robbers, knights of the realm or wherever the imagination of his four brothers and two sisters had taken them. He'd been the fourth born out of seven. Just another face in the crowd, he thought, lost in the shuffle.

The cluster of mulberry trees at the base of the hill below him was long gone, but the memory of the time he and two of his brothers had filched a few cigarettes when they thought their old man wasn't looking remained fresh in his mind. The three of them had sat beneath the shade of those now missing trees on a scorching summer day, attempting to perfect the art of inhaling. Not only had he turned an unappealing shade of green, but the old man had busted the three of them cold. The middle Hunt boys had had their asses fried, but the spare-the-rod-spoil-the-child philosophy of child rearing hadn't paid off, either, since he, Beck, and Clayton had still managed to pick up the habit.

With the tip of his boot, he toed a weed poking through the gravel and sand. Most of his life-altering decisions were made in these hills, so it made sense to come here now. Despite the hornets' nest of trouble agreeing to her sensuous request would stir, the temptation to finally have her tested the limits of his self-discipline. Maybe she'd even manage to take his mind off the restlessness that had been hounding him for the last couple of months, too.

Jackson had grown up wanting to be a cop, just like his dad, someone respected by his peers and the community he served. With the exception of the oldest sister, Kylie, who'd moved to New York to become a fashion designer, each of the Hunt kids had followed in Damon Hunt's law enforcement footsteps in one form or another. Aidan, the oldest brother, had spent five years as a street cop while earning his law degree and had become a prosecutor for the county. Clayton, his older brother by two years, had gone into criminal justice as a parole officer for conditionally released parolees, a shit job if one ever existed, in Jackson's opinion. The FBI had claimed his younger brother Beck and sister Jewel. Beck was a profiler, and his kid sister had recently transferred into deep-cover ops. Tucker, the youngest Hunt brother, whom Jackson hadn't seen in over two years, was involved in the federal witness protection program for the U.S. Marshal's office. Jackson and Aidan had been the only two to wear the uniform, but Jackson had made the old man proud by remaining a street cop.

He realized now his idealistic notions of making a difference were impossible to achieve when the system worked against him. After less than a year on the job he'd learned when he locked up the gang bangers the chances of them being be back on the street with their "homeys" before he started his next shift were greater than the Oakland Raiders coming back to L.A. The creeps who beat the crap out of their wives, girlfriends, or kids would be cut loose to return to their homes for dinner, until a well-meaning neighbor called in another domestic disturbance dispute. He could throw drunks in the tank because they were too stupid not to climb behind the wheel until the end of time, and he'd still be sent to deliver the bad news to a family that their husband, wife, or God forbid, son or daughter, wouldn't be coming home because of another schmuck with a drinking problem.

A brisk wind kicked up suddenly. He shrugged off his morose musings before they threatened to darken his mood further. Behind him, the car door slammed, followed by the crunch of gravel from Eden's footsteps as she approached. He glanced down at her when she came up beside him. Here, on top of the hill of the canyon, the hot, Santa Ana wind tossed the wavy ends of her long onyx hair across her face. She pushed the strands away, then slid her sunglasses to the top of her head in an effort to keep her hair in place. Questions filled her amber gaze as she looked up at him. Questions he didn't know if he could answer, or if he even wanted to know the answers.

The distraction her offer could provide from his own disillusionment was tough to ignore. If he lost himself in her, maybe he'd forget about the restlessness and cynicism plaguing him—at least for as long as her instruction in seduction lasted.

"This probably isn't a good idea," he said. "We are partners, Eden. I kinda like knowing you're there to watch my back every night. I wouldn't want that to change."

She tucked her hands into the back pockets of her jeans, drawing his gaze to her gentle curves. His groin tightened as he imagined his hands skimming over the surface of her skin, pressing her thighs open and driving into her slick feminine heat.

"There's no reason it has to," she countered calmly. "It's not like we'd be having an actual affair. If we're not romantically involved, we won't be reassigned, so we have absolutely nothing to worry about."

"What about friendship?" he asked. "Sex enters the equation and things could be different between us. Are you willing to take that risk?"

A gentle smile curved her lush mouth. "This is about sex.

Friends often become fuck-buddies. It doesn't mean the dynamics of the relationship will change. It's not like we're attracted to each other in that way. Oh." A sudden frown tugged her dark eyebrows together. "Unless you don't think you could"—she held her hand parallel to the ground, palm down, slowly lifting her index finger upward—"you know."

He cleared his throat. *"That* won't be a problem," he promised arrogantly. If she had an inkling how often she starred in his fantasies, she wouldn't be asking. Hell, he was already sporting a hard-on, and all he'd done was look at her.

"We're consenting adults, here, Jackson. Neither one of us is in a relationship at the moment." She shot his arguments down one by one, using her fingers to tick them off her list. "No one will get hurt. Our jobs aren't even at risk. The worst that might happen if word *did* get out that we'd slept together is reassignment. If I pass the sergeant's exam next month, that's a fact we'll probably have to face, anyway."

"You honestly don't see a problem, do you?"

"No, I don't." She let out a long, slow breath and gave him a hard stare filled with determination. "If you aren't willing, fine. I'll find someone who is."

"Someone like Findley?" he said sharply. He wasn't jealous, but the thought of Eden with the vice cop gave him an ulcer.

"Maybe," she said, and shrugged. "Why do you have such a problem with him?"

"He's not a nice guy."

"If you're trying to tell me Findley's a player, I'm well aware of that fact." Impatience laced her voice. "But he has the kind of experience I need right now."

"Oh, he'll screw anything that moves, all right. But he's not a nice guy," he repeated with meaning that was lost on her. The curiosity in her eyes told him loud and clear she didn't get it.

He let out a sigh of his own. "His ex had the bruises and broken ribs to prove it."

Her skin paled beneath her summer tan, as he'd expected. Eden possessed a helluva lot of inner strength he thought admirable considering her background. She had zero tolerance for abusers of any kind. He'd watched her single-handedly take down more than a few mean SOBs when they'd responded to domestic disturbance calls, and she hadn't been nice about it, either.

"Jesus," she whispered, and sat on the edge of the heavy gauged steel barricade as if her legs were no longer capable of supporting her. "I had no idea. You'd think word would get around the station."

"The rumor mill isn't always reliable," he told her. Even when one of their own was involved in domestic violence. Occasionally, the brotherhood got it wrong. "The charges were dismissed because Findley's ex was too afraid to testify."

He'd accomplished what he needed to, spooked her away from Findley for good. Since he no longer had to worry about her making that particular error in judgment, why didn't he just tell her there was no way in hell he'd be a party to her harebrained scheme?

But he knew the answer. There wasn't anything complex about his reasoning. Despite the risk to their friendship, he wanted the chance to turn all those fantasies into reality.

No way could he refuse her, he decided. He simply didn't possess that much willpower.

He held out his hand to her. "Let's go," he said, caving like the hood of a cheap car.

She lifted her eyes to his. Hope, caution, and a trace of triumph mingled in her golden amber gaze.

He'd been had, he realized with sudden amusement. Set up. Duped. And he'd played right into her hands.

Things could be worse, he supposed as she trustingly took his hand. She might actually figure out exactly how he felt about her.

Four

In Eden's trembling hands, an innocuous mascara brush had become a lethal weapon. She'd nearly poked herself in the eye twice already, and she hadn't managed to add an ounce of color to her lashes.

She let go of an impatient huff, then made another vain attempt to lengthen her eyelashes. "Oh, for God's sake," she muttered to her reflection in the bathroom mirror. "Get a grip, dammit."

Not for the first time since hatching her plan, doubt overcame her. These were no little niggles of the stuff, either, but tsunamiesque waves of it, rapidly making a mockery of her bravado.

She took aim. Without blinding herself, she applied a thin coat of mascara. What if having sex—no, instructional sex— with Jackson *did* alter their friendship? Was learning how to pleasure a man so he'd stick around long after the sheets cooled worth the price of a friendship? Her address book wasn't exactly overflowing with entries of people close to her. Acquaintances, she had plenty, but the number she considered as intimates were few and far between.

Growing up in a powder keg set to explode without warning had taught her the wisdom of keeping others at a distance. Early on she'd learned the hazards of inviting classmates over for slumber parties or afternoons of play. Of the few friends she did make, her time was spent at their homes for as much to escape the chaos as to avoid the embarrassment of anyone witnessing the circumstances of her home life. The one exception had arrived her first day of junior high school when she'd met Libby Morgan. Sadly, they were kindred spirits. They understood each other and carried similar baggage from living in domestically violent environments. They'd been as close as sisters since.

Unlike Libby, Eden did recall two separate brief periods when her life hadn't consisted of screaming matches, drunken brawls, or tiptoeing around the house the morning after because her mother and the boyfriend of the hour were sleeping off a hangover. There were memories of happier times, and to this day she clung to them. Although her parents had only lived together, at least she'd had a loving father, something poor Libby had never known.

But, at the age of six, Eden's life had changed. A uniformed officer had come to their door one night with the news that her father had died at the scene of an accident. On his way home from work, he'd fallen asleep behind the wheel, crossed the median into the oncoming traffic of a busy highway and died in a head-on collision. Life as she knew it had been irrevocably altered at that moment and had spiraled more and more out of control with every passing year.

She'd been eight the first time one of her mother's boyfriends had put Varilee Matthews in the hospital. At nine, she and her mom had lived in the car for a week because the next boyfriend had thrown them out on the street.

Libby had shown her how to safely sleep with a kitchen knife under her pillow shortly after they'd met. A good thing she'd taken her friend's advice, because one of Varilee's losers-of-the-month had dared to enter her bedroom one night while her mother had been working graveyards re-stocking shelves for a grocery store.

The end of her thirteenth year had spawned a fresh set of unfortunate circumstances when Varilee took up with a particularly mean SOB. Eden spent a week in the hospital after attempting to stop him from beating up on her mom, and had been rewarded for her efforts with broken ribs and a collapsed lung.

The summer before her freshman year in high school, by some miracle her mother had dried out, hooked up with a nice guy, and married him. Kenny Fuller had been a widowed auto mechanic with two daughters close to her own age. He was a huge bear of a man with a deep, booming voice and hands bigger than anything Eden had ever seen, and she'd been absolutely terrified of him. He'd been twice as gentle as a kitten and never mistreated her mother or her. His kindness and patience had reminded her that not all men hit women, and for the first time in nine years, Eden had lived in a safe, loving environment. Gradually, she learned to trust again, even if she still tended to proceed with an abundance of caution.

Even though Kenny had eventually divorced her mother the year after Eden graduated high school, in her heart, he would always be her dad. She called him at least once a month to check in and catch up, made sure she remembered his birthday, and when she wasn't on duty, spent holiday celebrations with him, her stepsisters, and their growing families. Kenny and his daughters were the only real family she'd ever known, and even though Varilee had eventually remained true to her DNA and had driven him away with her excessive drinking, Kenny made certain Eden understood he was divorcing her mother, not her.

Eden had sworn long before the arrival of Kenny in their lives that she would never follow in her mother's footsteps. No way in hell would she ever allow some guy to use her as a punching bag, and she'd been successful. Unfortunately, Varilee's failed-relationship gene ran as strong as ever in Eden's bloodstream. Hopefully that would change now that she'd convinced Jackson to assist her in improving her bedroom basics and beyond.

Despite his misgivings and protests, once she'd changed his mind, he'd proven his willingness to see the job done. After the drive through the canyon yesterday morning, he'd suggested neutral turf to lay down a few terms and conditions. During a breakfast of bagels and cappuccino at a local coffee house, he'd insisted that for him to successfully put her in touch with her inner vixen, the best way to start would be to observe her in full-blown serious, next-stop-sex, relationship mode.

Where did it end? she wondered suddenly. With full-blown serious heartbreak? She quickly abandoned that train of thought and gave her lashes another swipe with the mascara brush.

Initially, she'd quibbled. All she'd been after was a few games of one-on-one under the covers to improve her technique. But he'd stood firm. His honest opinion and advice required an accurate assessment of her natural actions and reactions.

Whether she'd had too much caffeine and not enough sleep, or pure desperation drove her, by her third cappuccino she'd agreed. What she still hadn't figured out was how on earth she was supposed to act naturally when he'd not only be watching her every move, but teaching her how to drive a man wild in bed.

"Talk about performance anxiety," she muttered to her reflection.

With her lashes suitably coated and her eyes still intact, she tossed the new tube of mascara into her makeup drawer before reaching into the black-and-white striped bag sitting on the blush-toned marbled vanity. The new makeup she'd bought that morning after work had been department-store expensive, as had the glittery copper halter top and the impossibly short, black silk skirt a few inches shy of illegal. She hadn't been able to resist the sales clerk's promise that men would fall begging to their knees, so she'd whipped out her credit card and had only mildly cringed when she signed the receipt.

Concentrating on her task, she carefully applied the lip liner, then followed up with the matching berry-breeze lipstick before adding a few strategically placed smudges of coppery gloss for added shimmer. After a few moments of intent study, she declared she looked a helluva lot more confident than her rioting insides indicated.

Regardless of her apprehension, she still believed she'd made the right decision. Guilt had given her a few hard shoves for manipulating Jackson, but the worst of the conscience-induced body slams had occurred last night during the lulls on their shift when she'd had way too much dead time to think. Today as she'd prepared for her first lesson, she'd done so with the belief that any vixen worthy of her vibrator wouldn't dream of wallowing in recriminations or waste time making excuses for a desire to educate herself in the arts of pleasure. Why should developing her skills as lover be different from any other educational experience?

Knowledge was power, regardless of the subject matter, she reminded herself. When she'd had a desire to improve her culinary skills, she'd signed up for cooking classes in Italian and French cuisine. The colorful ceramic pots filled with lush herbs in her kitchen garden window were a direct result of a workshop she'd taken at the local community center. Southern California, an area rich in cultural diversity, had prompted her decision that a second language would be an asset for a cop. She'd enrolled in courses at the community college and now spoke fluent Spanish and even knew a smattering of Vietnamese. In each of those specific instances, the results of her quest for self-improvement had proven beneficial. She could think of no reason why her latest quest for higher learning should fail.

She finished slipping the pair of glittering chandelier earrings into her lobes just as the oven timer dinged, signaling the seafood lasagna she'd prepared for dinner had finished baking. After one final check in the mirror to ensure the complicated up-do she'd attempted would hold, she declared herself ready for her first night of study in Wicked Woman 101.

She left the bathroom with less than five minutes to spare before Jackson arrived. After a quick stop to slip into a pair of black strappy heels, she hurried into the kitchen to retrieve the lasagna from the oven.

He'd better give her an *A* for creating such a picture perfect romantic setting. Music from a soft rock station on the stereo played subtly in the background. The table in the cozy dining area was set with the china and crystal patterns she'd been slowly collecting since she first moved out on her own after high school, complete with a creamy lace tablecloth, linen napkins, and a large crystal bowl filled with vanilla-scented floater candles in the center. She'd even splurged on a bottle of '84 chardonnay from one of the local wineries.

"Screw that," she said, lowering the oven door. "He'd better give me an A plus."

She turned off the oven, then set the seafood lasagna in its baking dish on a pair of trivets to cool as another wave of doubt crashed into her. Maybe she hadn't been perfectly honest with herself in insisting their friendship wouldn't change. They were going to become lovers—albeit temporarily. No, she thought as she scored the crusty loaf of Italian bread. Not lovers, she amended. The word implied a deeper emotional connection than their relationship dictated.

So what was Jackson to her now? She couldn't exactly call him her fuck-buddy because once her vixen-in-training sessions ended, so would their bedroom liaisons. How did one define the parameters of their association? If they weren't lovers in the romantic sense or even casual sex *compadres*, then the only definition that remained was instructor and student.

She frowned as she poured melted butter over the bread, certain she liked the sound of "friend" best. After sprinkling freshly grated parmesan cheese on top of the crust, she wrapped the loaf loosely in foil and set it in the cooling oven to slowly warm.

The doorbell rang, and she nearly jumped out of her skin. The oven door slipped from her hand and flew shut with a loud clang. Or had that been the sound of her heart careening into the pit of her stomach? Impossible, she thought, because it was currently lodged in her throat.

What the hell was wrong with her? She couldn't remember ever being this nervous when faced with the inevitability of the real thing. Refusing to remotely consider she was about to make a gargantuan mistake, she left the kitchen and headed purposely toward the front door.

Her heart dislodged from her throat to frantically ricochet around in her chest like a psychotic air-hockey puck at the first sight of Jackson on her stoop. Her ability to form a coherent sentence, let alone find an appropriate word to describe how incredibly virile and all-out sexy he looked garbed in something besides his uniform or the jeans he usually wore when off duty, fled. Not that the man wasn't a credit to any wardrobe choice, but she hadn't been mentally prepared for Jackson looking so impossibly handsome dressed in a pair of tan khakis and a crisp white linen shirt. He still had that cop aura about him, as any who wore the uniform did, but he certainly didn't resemble the friend she knew so well. The man standing on her doorstep with a heart-stopping smile and appreciation shining in his bedroom eyes as he swept her with his gaze quite simply stole her breath.

Bedroom eyes? Since when?

Friends didn't have bedroom eyes. A friend wouldn't look at her as if she were the most mouthwatering item on the menu. And her breasts sure as hell weren't supposed to tighten and pucker, either. That sort of nonsense wasn't for friends or partners, but was reserved strictly for soon-to-be lovers.

We are *soon-to-be lovers.*

Because she didn't trust herself not to start babbling like an idiot, or to commence drooling as if she were one of Pavlov's dogs, she stepped back and silently motioned him inside her apartment. She drew in the scent of his citrus after-shave as he passed. Her hold on the door became a death grip. Heavens, the man smelled positively scrumptious.

He handed her a mixed bouquet of fresh-cut summer flowers she hadn't even noticed until now. "For you," he said.

She took the flowers, her fingers brushing against his. A warm jolt zinged powerfully along nerve endings she'd forgotten existed. "Uh . . . thank you. They're lovely." Despite the noticeable tremor in her voice, she came off appearing relatively capable of mastering basic language skills. She cleared her throat. "Excuse me for a moment while I put these in water."

She closed the front door, took two steps, then stopped suddenly to look up at him. If they were truly involved, she wouldn't hesitate to show her appreciation of his thoughtfulness with a kiss. He was judging her, dissecting her actions and reactions. Once they moved into a horizontal position, he'd have plenty to critique. No way could her tendency toward perfection tolerate him finding her inadequate outside the bedroom, too.

Her fingers flexed, causing the clear plastic wrap covering the long stems to crackle loudly. She covered the short distance separating them to wreath her arms around his neck. Even with the heels adding a couple of inches to her five-foot, four-inch height, he nevertheless towered over her by a good seven or eight. Funny, she'd never noticed he was so tall. Or the exact width of his chest and shoulders.

Because she hadn't been looking, she wondered, or because she hadn't *wanted* to look?

The color of his sea green eyes deepened to the richest, most brilliant shade of turquoise she'd ever seen. Heat flared in his gaze when his hands feathered down her bare back to settle just above the curve of her bottom. He pulled her so close her tightened nipples brushed provocatively against his chest.

She forgot to breathe.

"Thank you." Her voice barely rose above a whisper thanks to such severe oxygen deprivation. "For the flowers."

"You're welcome."

The sexy rumble of his voice vibrated through her. She stared into his eyes, held by a sensual, hypnotic spell she couldn't possibly resist. She lifted her lips toward his. Each nanosecond crept by with aching slowness as he lowered his head. Anticipation stirred her blood.

Every nuance of the moment became suspended in time, magnified as her awareness of him came vibrantly alive. The way his warm, masculine scent clung to his skin, the rapid cadence of her heart, the heat of his fingers through the thin fabric of her skirt, the knowledge that after tonight, nothing between them would ever be the same.

She refused to dwell on anything but the sensual possibilities that lay immediately ahead. Her lashes fluttered closed when his mouth settled over hers, his lips simultaneously soft and firm, the kiss coaxing yet demanding. The velvety glide of his tongue as he deepened the kiss sent heat spiraling through her, and she moved against him.

He groaned, tightening his hold. The length of his very impressive erection pulsed against her belly, and her thighs tingled in response. Moisture pooled between her legs when his hand slid down to fully cup her bottom in his hands.

Plastered against him as if she belonged there, a strange sense of familiarity overcame her. She attempted to write the odd sensation off as a freaky case of déjà vu, but she couldn't, not when she knew the heat of his mouth, his taste, the way he teased and taunted her with his tongue. This wasn't some cosmic predestination that fate intended to have happen all along, but the whisper of something real and concrete flirting on the fringes of her memory.

She'd swear she'd kissed Jackson before. And she'd liked it. A lot.

Five

Jackson skimmed his hand along the swell of Eden's hip, his fingers brushing past the hem of the filmy scrap of black material passing for a skirt. A man could handle only so much temptation before he caved, and she'd effortlessly maxed his limit the second she'd greeted him at the door. Her sweet moan as she clung to him, along with the inviting way she widened her stance for him now, and he was toast.

Gliding his palms over her sleek skin, he softly caressed her. The bouquet of flowers slipped from her hand, landing on the carpet with a crackling thud. She raked her fingers through his hair, slanted her mouth beneath his, and left him with no question exactly where they were headed. Straight into a minefield.

On the drive to her apartment, he'd considered a variety of scenarios taking place tonight. Fantasies, actually, and every one he'd dreamed up ended with him buried inside Eden's slick heat and her slender thighs wrapped tightly around his waist. But not a single image started with him fucking her within two minutes of arriving.

His dick swelled and throbbed. She'd wanted to learn how to be a better lover, but gauging from the way she kissed him and how sensuously she moved against him, she knew precisely what she was doing—making him crazy. Tonight, he realized, had zilch to do with teaching her anything, and everything to do with the promise of giving and receiving pleasure.

Since agreeing to her quest he'd been incapable of concentrating on little else but Eden, sex, and more sex. Only he'd imagined moving slowly until she was completely at ease with him in the role of lover before turning up the heat. The hotter the better, too, but she'd killed his noble plans the minute she'd pressed all those curves against him.

God help him, he wanted her so badly he ached. He wanted her with a fierceness that should have left him shocked and shaken, not rock hard and more than ready.

Dragging his mouth from hers, he kissed his way along her jaw to nuzzle the side of her neck, gently nipping and laving the tender flesh below her ear. He drew in her light floral perfume and caught the unmistakable musky scent of her arousal as it rose around him, intoxicating him and obliterating the final remnant of what little common sense he had left.

Her hands slid from around his neck and landed on his chest. Regret slammed into him, thinking *she'd* come to *her* senses, but rather than pushing him away, she grabbed hold of his shirt. Hauling him with her, she backed up until she came in abrupt contact with the short space of wall between the entry and the kitchen.

"It wasn't supposed to happen like this." His voice was strung so tight with need, he hardly recognized it as his own.

"I know." Desire burned hot in her eyes. Her fingers trembled as she worked the buttons of his shirt, pushing the fabric aside to run her hands over his chest. "I didn't even know it *could* happen like this."

"Eden, maybe we shouldn't—"

A determined light fired her gaze. "Shut up, Jackson." She rubbed her open palms across his flat nipples. "For God's sake, shut the hell up and just go with it."

She pressed her open mouth over his nipple and suckled

him. Whatever stupid thing he'd been about to say died a silent death when his brain short-circuited.

"Sweet Jesus," he rasped as heat hotter than a brand seared his groin. Only an idiot would dare call Eden an unskilled lover. The woman had him harder and thicker than he imagined possible. He was so hungry for her, if he didn't have her soon, he'd go insane.

She fumbled with his belt, but he took hold of her wrists and placed them directly above her head. If she so much as brushed the tip of her finger over his cock, he'd explode.

She looked at him with a heavy-lidded gaze. Curiosity and desire blended together within the amber depths until the color of her irises practically glowed in a rich, shimmering golden hue.

"Let me touch you." Her voice went low and husky. She sounded like sex, and his dick pulsed and throbbed in response.

"Later," he promised her. Provided he survived that long.

With his left hand, he kept her wrists locked in a relaxed pose above her head, then traced the slender column of her throat down to the slope of her breast with his right. He held her gaze and palmed the weight of her breast through the rough, scratchy texture of her top. The sharp intake of breath she sucked in between her teeth when he circled her nipple with his thumb excited him beyond belief.

"I'm so wet for you, Jackson." She dragged her tongue across her plump bottom lip in an erotic display that nearly killed him.

With his knee, he gently nudged her thigh, urging her to part for him. "How wet?"

"Hmm," she moaned softly, and rolled her hips against his leg. "Dripping."

An invitation didn't come any more engraved.

He slid his hand down to her slender waist, over the curve of her hip, and along her leg to slip beneath the hem of her skirt.

"Touch me," she whispered.

He couldn't deny her if he tried.

Trailing his fingers upward along the inside of her thigh, his knuckles brushed against her damp, dewy curls. Sharp need clawed his gut.

"Christ, Eden," he rasped. "You aren't wearing . . ."

"Panties?" Her easy, sinful smile exceeded anything even his fantasies had conjured the past eight months, and he'd conjured some damned erotic images. "Are you shocked?"

He drew his fingers along the slick, moist folds of her labia. She rolled her hips, moving against his hand, anxious for more of his touch.

"More like turned on," he admitted. "So much it hurts."

"Then let me touch you," she whispered huskily. She attempted to tug her hands free, but he tightened his grip. He wouldn't last thirty seconds if she touched him.

Her eyes glowed with the intensity of her need. "I want you hard and hot in my hands." Her breath caught. "In my mouth."

His heart thudded heavily in his chest. Hell, he could barely stand after that carnal demand. "Later," he somehow managed to say. "I promise."

Slowly, he circled the outline of her velvety smooth opening, delving slightly deeper inside her hot wet core with each revolution. She was so wet, so slick, so hot and ready for him, he summoned every last ounce of self-control he could muster to keep from making love to her.

Her breathing deepened as her arousal heightened. Her lips parted, evoking more fantasies. He imagined her naked, on her knees going down on him, her rich, dark pink lips sliding over the head of his cock as she made love to him with her mouth. Some women climaxed while giving head. In his fantasies, Eden always came.

With the barest amount of pressure, he pressed the pad of his thumb over her swollen, throbbing clit. Her lashes fluttered closed, and she emitted a sexy series of low, throaty,

"Oooh," sounds with each breath she expelled. He lengthened the slow, steady strokes around the pulsing bud. Her response to his touch tested the limits of his threadbare control.

Pushing down with her hips, her hot, slick center contracted, pulling him deeper inside her. "Don't stop," she whimpered, bending her knees slightly to take more of him.

He wouldn't dream of putting an end to her pleasure. She grew hotter, wetter, and her clit thickened and pulsed. She was so close, it wouldn't take but a few more measured strokes to send her soaring.

"Open your eyes, Eden," he rasped. "Watch me make you come."

Know it's me *making you lose control.*

She obeyed his demand without an ounce of hesitation. Short, hard pants of breath coalesced with her enticing little whimpers as he carried her closer to release. He thrust two more fingers inside her, pushing her, filling her until her whimpers segued into a low keening moan signaling how very close to the edge she teetered.

Once her body stretched to accommodate his invasion, he stroked her again. Slow. Easy. Her cries became more desperate, more demanding, so he kicked it up a notch, driving her harder, taking her faster toward the brink.

Her legs trembled, and he supported her with the weight of his body. The sharp edge of her fingernails sliced into his wrist. Her eyes widened in wonder as his name poured from her lips when she flew apart from the force of the orgasm that rocked her.

He released her hands, and she gripped his shoulders, digging her fingers into him as he kept the intensity of the orgasm going for her, pushed her to take all she could handle, then encouraged her to reach for even more. His erection throbbed, heavy, hot, and painful as he watched the beauty of her so wholly consumed by the sweet bliss of fulfillment.

Slowly, he brought her down. Breathing ragged and her

body limp with exhaustion, she collapsed against him. They'd exceeded the boundaries of friendship, and God only knew what damage their professional relationship would suffer. He'd known they were making a mistake, yet instead of talking sense into her, he'd given in because he hadn't the strength to resist her.

Telling himself the only reason he'd agreed to her wild scheme stemmed from friendship was a load of bull. He'd known it, and he still ignored the alarms that had gone off warning him he would regret his decision.

He let out a slow, uneasy breath. Frankly, he simply hadn't had the balls to face the reality of the situation. As much as he'd tried to deny it, the truth was he'd been blindsided by white-hot jealousy at the thought of some other guy touching Eden the way he'd just done. To him, that said loud and clear he cared about her a helluva lot more than he'd initially believed.

He smoothed his hands over her sweat-moistened back as the last of her tremors subsided. Supporting her weight, he held her close, next to his heart, because he didn't know what else he was supposed to do. There wasn't a chance in hell they could ever return to the status quo.

Fuck.

Effective immediately, he was tendering his resignation as her instructor in how to pleasure a man. Oh, he'd gladly guide her through the many ways she could please him. He'd been fantasizing about them for months. But the rules were definitely changing. Unless she agreed to his only condition, that they become lovers in every sense of the word, then he was out of there—no matter how much it killed him.

"Eden?"

"Hmm," Eden murmured, unwilling to leave the comforting warmth of Jackson's chest. She hadn't thought a person could actually doze off while on their feet, but as close as she was to doing just that, she figured she'd better alter her opinion.

"We need to talk."

Uh-oh. She didn't like the sound of that one bit. With supreme effort, she eased out of his embrace and straightened, teetering slightly in her heels.

"No. We don't," she said, then turned and walked unsteadily into the kitchen.

"Eden, wait."

As she washed her hands at the sink, she sensed his presence behind her. Dammit, she did not want to hear his recriminations or regrets. Remorse had no place whatsoever in the satisfied afterglow of one of the most gratifying orgasms of the decade.

"We can't do this," he said. "I can't. Not like this."

Unexpected anger slammed into her so hard she nearly stumbled. "It's a bit late for that, don't you think?" she snapped at him. She turned off the faucet and yanked a paper towel from the holder to dry her hands.

What the hell had made her think he'd be different from the others? He was, after all, a man. Apparently the entire gender had been infected with the same testosterone poisoning. Screw her and skip out the door, that was their motto. Christ, she must have detailed instructions tattooed on her ass—*remove dick and proceed to the nearest exit.*

Okay, so maybe she and Jackson *hadn't* physically gone all the way, but if he was ready to cut and run before they even made it into the bedroom, then something was definitely wrong with her. A sad little fact of her life, but she'd find a way to deal with it. What she absolutely could not handle was her friend and partner lying to her.

She tossed the paper towel on the counter and removed the loaf of bread from the oven before facing him. Folding her arms, she propped her backside against the edge of the sink, then dipped her gaze pointedly to his crotch. The outline of his erection remained impressively evident beneath his trousers. "Looks to me like you wouldn't have any problems finishing what you started."

He scrubbed his hand over his face. "Don't blow this out of proportion, Eden. I nev—"

"That's not all I won't be blowing," she said sarcastically. She clung to her anger. If she didn't, the abject disappointment that even Jackson could do this to her would take over, and she might actually cry.

Like hell.

No man was worth her tears.

He stalked across the kitchen to loom over her before her heart took its next beat. "This isn't about not wanting you, dammit," he fired at her, the frustration in his voice equaled the heated emotion lining his sea green eyes. "It's about me—"

"Oh, please, Jackson. Can't you be more inventive than that?" She forced a caustic laugh around the lump the size of a bullet-proof vest lodged in her throat. "If you're going to lie to spare my feelings, at least have the decency not to feed me a line that predates the Ice Age."

"Would you stop interrupting and let me finish?"

"I'm listening, but make it good. Just remember, I've heard them all. Go ahead," she said, gesturing with her arm. "Give it your best shot. Dazzle me with your creativity."

He drew in a long breath and let it out slowly. No doubt a stall tactic to borrow time as he searched for the words to blow her off in a way he hoped wouldn't hurt her.

Too late, pal.

"There's nothing I want more than to make love to you, Eden," he said in a calmer tone.

"But?" In her experience, there was always a *but* somewhere.

"I'm resigning as your sexuality instructor. If you're willing to learn how to give me pleasure, then I have no problem showing you everything you want to know. But only as your lover."

Her eyebrows winged upward. "As my what?"

His lips tugged into a frown. "I think you heard me."

Oh, she definitely heard him. She just couldn't believe

what she was hearing. So much for offering a no-strings, casual, anything goes, sexual liaison. No guy in his right mind would prefer to complicate obligation-free sex with . . . what? A commitment?

She had a feeling she was looking at just that guy.

"You sure about that? Do you even know what the term implies?" She certainly did, and no matter how she viewed the situation, the results made her queasy. In the end, the kind of involvement he was proposing would translate into the demise of their friendship and her having to break in a new partner, or worse, completely transfer to another squad.

"Mutual exclusivity, for one."

She stared at him, utterly stunned. Jackson Hunt, in a mutually exclusive, committed relationship? They'd laugh her off the force if she carried such a wild, unbelieveable tale into the ladies' locker room. She'd known him to have two, sometimes even three, women dangling from the proverbial string at a time. Hell, the man practically made a career out of avoiding commitment-minded females.

Understanding dawned in one big *Ah-ha!* moment. The old caveman, stand on mountain, pound manly chest, double-standard bullshit.

"Look," she said, "if you're worried about me sleeping around while we're doing our thing, then don't. I'm not exactly planning on rolling out of bed with you in the morning to go try out some new technique on the first potential stud that bleeps on my radar screen."

"I didn't think you would. You're not the type."

He really did know her too well. There wasn't a chance in hell she'd ever sleep with another guy while she and Jackson were involved. Not that she'd ever dreamed he'd screw up a good thing by demanding mutual exclusivity, but promiscuity in general simply wasn't her style. Relationships were complicated enough without trying to simultaneously juggle two or three at the same time, as he well knew.

So if he wasn't concerned with her bed hopping, then

what was he trying to say? Offer her reassurance that for as long as they were involved he'd only put his boots under her bed? She wanted more of what he'd given her earlier, not reassurances she hadn't asked for and didn't need.

She rubbed at her throbbing temples with the tips of her fingers. "You're confusing the hell out of me. Why are you doing this now?"

He dragged his fingers through his hair. "I don't like the thought of you using me to prep for some other guy."

She blew out a frustrated stream of breath. Why did she suddenly feel as if she were the equivalent of a fire hydrant and he a big, furry German shepherd attempting to mark his territory? "For some *unknown* guy," she corrected him. "I haven't exactly zeroed in on my next intended victim."

"I don't see a difference," he said stubbornly.

No, he probably didn't. He was, after all, a mere chest-thumping man. "Well, I don't see a difference, either. People do move on when relationships end, Jackson. Or did you forget that part of it?"

He folded his arms over his chest and gave her an impatient look. "You don't know that."

"Yes I do," she argued, "because that's the way it works. And when the relationship is over, it's rarely pretty. Besides, we'd practically be flushing a great friendship and a solid partnership down the toilet, too."

"It doesn't have to be that way," he said, and started buttoning his shirt.

"I'm offering you sex, a lot of sex. Adventurous sex. No strings, no complications, and you seriously want a commitment? Have you lost your mind?"

"Maybe I have," he said, looking perfectly sane. His careless shrug belied the hardness of his stare. "The decision is yours, Eden. Take it, and we'll finish what we started. Leave it, and I'll see you when our shift starts Monday night."

"You're issuing an ultimatum?" she asked incredulously. "Your way or a cold shower?"

A positively arrogant smile curved his mouth. "You bet your sweet little ass I am." He glanced pointedly at his wrist watch. "Clock's ticking, babe. What's it gonna be?"

Six

Eden seriously contemplated the benefits of a cold shower. As she suspected, not a single advantage came to mind.

"Just so I'm clear," she said, sitting primly on the edge of the chintz covered chair in the living room, "all this macho territorial bullshit is because you want a commitment. From me. Do I have it right?"

Facing her, he sat on the ancient travel trunk she'd found at a yard sale and used as a coffee table. With his arms braced on his knees, the look he gave her she could only describe as marginally tolerant.

"It's not difficult to understand, Eden."

"We haven't even had sex yet. Don't . . ." She glanced toward the closed draperies as if the word she needed were embroidered there on the creamy-colored fabric for her easy reference. "Don't people"—she refused to use the term *couple* to describe their association—"usually wait until after they know for certain they're sexually compatible before committing to a relationship?"

He smiled in a way that jump-started her heart and made it skip a few beats. "I doubt that's going to be an issue for us," he said with an arrogant chuckle.

Oh, you foolish, foolish man. How quickly you forget.

Sexual incompatibility had been the very reason she'd propositioned him in the first place. He'd most definitely pleased her. He'd graciously proven his ability in that regard. In earth-shattering spades. Unfortunately, she had yet to return the favor, so he had no clue how one-sided their relationship would be on a sexual level.

"I wouldn't be so hasty if I were you," she warned. "I'm a lousy lay, remember? I'm practically famous for it. This could end up being the shortest committed relationship in recorded history. Even yours."

He let out a long, impatient sigh and stood, crossing the narrow distance separating them. Planting his hands on either side of her, he leaned in and trapped her between that heavenly body she was dying to explore and the chair, threatening her comfort zone. How had she managed to work beside him all these months, spend so much time with him on and off duty, and not once realize he possessed such a powerful presence? He was her partner, her friend, and now he was insisting on a commitment from her before they became lovers. When exactly had he transformed into such a forceful personality without her notice? For a cop, her observation skills were indeed questionable.

"You really have no idea how sensual you are, do you?" he asked.

Wisely, she kept her mouth shut. She wasn't touching that one with a ten-inch dildo.

The heat of him surrounded her, taking up all the oxygen in her cozy living room. Breathing became next to impossible. He dipped his head to nuzzle the side of her throat. Any trace of her usual rationale vanished.

"All I have to do is think of how you respond to me"—he caught her earlobe between his teeth and lightly bit down—"and I imagine all the ways I want to fuck you."

What little air she'd been hoarding for survival whooshed out of her lungs. God, but what a way to go, she thought. Her breasts swelled, tightened. Her nipples formed into tight peaks and ached for his hot, wet mouth. Dampness collected between her legs. "Jackson," she murmured, amazed by her body's response to the sexy words he whispered in her ear. She wasn't a corpse. She knew perfectly well how sexually magnetic he was, but having him turn all that power in her direction was more than she was prepared to handle. He was too much . . . everything.

He straightened and pulled her with him. She wrapped her arms around his neck as his hand slipped beneath the hem of her skirt, his palm skimming her bare hip. Lowering his head, he whispered in her ear, "You're wet for me again, aren't you?"

His mouth burned a path from her ear to her throat where he teased the hollow with the tip of his tongue before dipping lower to lave the curve of her breast. His fingers feathered down her back to the tie securing her top in place. With a quick tug, the fabric fluttered, coming together to drape in the front. With her top held in place only by the thin tie around her neck, her breasts were partially exposed. He smiled and pushed the fabric aside, then took her nipple inside the velvety smooth warmth of his mouth.

Sensation ripped through her, and she felt a sharp tug low in her belly. She raked her fingers through his thick sable hair, holding him to her. His hands cupped her bottom, gently massaging as his fingers drew closer to her damp wet center.

He lifted his head and looked up at her. "Aren't you, Eden?" he asked again, easing closer, closer, until she felt the tips of his fingers brush lightly against her.

"Yes," she uttered on a strained whisper, widening her stance, inviting him to touch her again. She wanted him to push inside her, fill her. She craved the wildness his touch promised so all she'd be capable of comprehending was raw pleasure.

He inched closer and separated her folds from behind. Cool air brushed against her heated center, and she trembled from the conflicting sensations. The warmth of his skin, the chill of the air, the heat of her arousal gathering.

He settled to his knees in front of her. The tenderness in his oceanic gaze caused her throat to catch. Oh God, what was she doing? Her previous worries were minor compared to her concerns now that he insisted on changing the rules of the game. By upping the stakes, the ramifications were gargantuan. Didn't he realize what could happen? Their friendship and partnership aside, what if she started to care about him—in a forever kind of way? A guy like Jackson would shatter her heart in a nanosecond when he walked away, as he inevitably would do. *If* she was stupid enough to fall in love with him. Which she wasn't.

"Don't ever think you won't please me," he said, "because it isn't possible." He rose up and kissed her then, slow, deep, and with so much emotion she couldn't help but feel a twinge of doubt over her IQ score.

She had to touch him, to feel the length of him pulsing in her hand. The trembling of her fingers caused her to fumble with the buckle of his belt. Before she could slip the leather from the clasp, he ended the kiss and released her. He stepped out of her reach, and she felt the loss clear down to the bottom of her soul.

Desire burned hot in his gaze. "Yes or no, Eden?" he asked, his voice tight.

She shook her head. "Don't ask me now." Snagging a fistful of his shirt, she hauled him close, then eased her hand down his torso, cupping the head of his penis through his trousers. Gently, she squeezed him. "Give me *this* instead. We'll talk later."

He grit his teeth and hissed out a rush of breath, followed by a rough groan. Slowly, she rubbed her palm along the thick, impressive ridge.

He grabbed hold of her wrist. "No," he said. "Not until you give me your answer." He urged her back down into the chair.

"Jackson, I really don't see what dif—"

Her protest died when he dropped down on one knee in front of her. A scandalous grin curved his mouth as he tugged her bottom forward to the edge of the cushion, then hooked her knees over the arms of the chair. He flipped up her skirt, exposing her. She had no idea what erotic delights were zipping through his mind, but she was more than game if it meant delaying the response he sought. He simply didn't know what he was asking of her. If she agreed, then they were doomed. Why couldn't he see that?

Probably because he was currently transfixed on the evidence of exactly how aroused he'd effortlessly made her— again. Her feminine moisture pooled thickly between her legs, her need for him blatantly obvious. He drew his hand slowly up her thigh, then cupped his palm over her mound. She lifted her hips toward the warmth, pressing her clitoris against the heel of his hand. Heat fired along the surface of her skin. Nerve endings sizzled as if overloaded by an electrical current.

She gripped the arms of the chair so hard her fingers ached. Closing her eyes, she let her head fall back and pushed everything but the glorious pressure of his hand against her from her mind.

"You like that, don't you?" he asked her.

"Hmm," she murmured. So far, the guy was batting a million.

"And this?"

With the heel of his hand still applying pressure to her sensitive bud, he separated her folds to fully open her, then employed the use of his other hand by dipping his fingers deep inside her. Her answer was a cry so primitive and needy she didn't recognize it as her own.

She opened her eyes and stared down at his hands, watching in awe as he withdrew and thrust into her again and again, slow, methodical, reaching deeper inside her to massage her inner core. She was dying, she was certain of it. No human being could possibly withstand the acute building of such incredible pressure and survive.

"There's more, Eden," he said, looking at her. "So much more. Hotter, better, and I'll take you places you'll never read about in a magazine." His voice sounded as tight and strained as the tension coiling inside her. "Say yes, and it's yours."

How dare he force her to think of things better left alone when he had her in such a vulnerable position. Didn't he realize that in a matter of moments he'd already managed to send her careening closer to the brink of another orgasm that threatened to be twice as powerful as the last?

He kept his gaze locked with hers as he expertly zeroed in on her G-spot and lightly massaged. A fuse ignited, guaranteeing she'd detonate from sheer bliss within seconds. Her entire body grew even tighter with anticipation. She arched her spine, searching, reaching, needing that perfect slice of heaven his touch promised.

His skillful hands stilled. The exquisite explosion of ecstasy floated out of her reach.

"Say no, and it stops here and now."

She whimpered a protest. Extortion? At a time like this? The nerve! The man made her manipulation tactics look puny and amateurish in comparison.

The sexy tilt of his lips went beyond arrogant. He had her right where he wanted her, and they both knew it. "Was that a yes?"

"Yes," she relented. He'd forced her into an emotional quagmire she had no desire to navigate, yet left her with no choice but agree to his terms.

His grin turned devilish. The look suited him to perfection.

"Are you sure?" he asked, and rubbed the tip of his finger against her inner wall. She shuddered. The pressure stopped again, and she glared at him. "Yes. Whatever you want. Just do me, dammit."

He leaned close. "Smart choice," he whispered, then caught her mouth in a rough, tongue-tangling kiss. So possessive, she thought fleetingly before the last shred of her common sense fled as he expertly rocked her world and sent her coasting along the waves of the purest pleasure she'd ever ridden.

Guilt was an overrated emotion in Jackson's opinion. He refused to harbor so much as an ounce of it, either, for playing down and dirty to get what he wanted from Eden. As far as he was concerned, the end justified the means—getting Eden in his bed.

And *only* in his bed.

With his arms braced on the retaining wall of the semiprivate balcony off Eden's bedroom, he leaned forward and stared up at the full moon riding in the midnight sky while she dozed. He'd led her into the bedroom after their tryst in the living room with every intention of finally making love to her, but she'd looked so exhausted, he'd decided to give her a chance to rest first. She'd fallen asleep in his arms almost immediately, and that had been over two hours ago.

The Santa Ana winds continued to blow fierce and hot through the canyon, stirring up enough dust to make the lights from the homes and street lamps below appear distant and inconsequential. Contemplating Eden's prediction they were destined for the shortest relationship in recorded history, he absently patted his front shirt pocket for the habit he'd given up almost a year ago. He'd never considered quitting until Eden had complained one night while they'd been on patrol that he smelled like a dirty ashtray. He'd gone cold turkey the next day.

He blew out a steady stream of breath. Christ, had he had a thing for her for that long?

He hadn't appreciated her crack about his inability to commit, but knew her well enough to know she was projecting more than objecting. Granted, his track record in that department proved no better than hers, but at least he could lay claim to two relationships that qualified as long-term. That was more than she could say.

He frowned. Now that he thought about it, his relationships really weren't all that lengthy. The longest had lasted a little over two years. But when he made a commitment, he made it all the way. What he lacked in longevity, he made up for in loyalty.

Eden had spoken out of fear more than any real shortage of faith in him. He understood that, and with her history, he couldn't really blame her. What she didn't see, however, was the jackasses she usually picked took a hike because she pushed them away before they could catch a glimpse of the baggage she carried, not because she wasn't any good in bed. He had no intention of running and hoped to show her he was nothing like the rest of them.

Standing on the sidelines as he'd done these past months gave him an advantage over the competition he hadn't realized until now. Eden came with issues, and he understood that about her. Hell, he understood *her*. On his watch, that counted for something.

Although she'd never admit it, for as much as she claimed to be looking for forever possibilities, the idea of anyone being that close scared the shit out of her. He didn't doubt his edict tonight had pushed a few of her panic buttons in that regard, too. But, the way he figured it, their friendship, combined with the fact they depended on each other to stay alive out there on the streets, gave him an "in" the competition would never have. She knew she could count on him because he already had her trust.

All he had to do now was make her realize that trust extended beyond the job.

He pushed off the retaining wall, quietly opened the sliding glass door, and walked inside her bedroom. Cool air from the quietly humming central air-conditioning brushed over the heat of his skin. As his eyes slowly adjusted to the darkness of the room, he realized the bed was empty.

"For a minute there, I was afraid you'd left."

He turned toward the sound of her sultry voice. She stood in the doorway between the bedroom and master bath bathed in moonlight wearing nothing but those sexy strappy sandals and a smile filled with sin.

A ball of fire settled in his groin and burned. "Not a chance," he said, and held his hand out to her. "Come here."

She shook her head. "Oh, I don't think so." Casually, she strolled toward the bed with a confidence that belied her misguided belief of inadequacy. "You've been calling the shots all night. Now it's my turn."

His cock swelled and throbbed in lustful anticipation. "What did you have in mind?"

She bent over the bed to straighten the covers. A perfectly innocent move, except he wasn't buying it. From the way she kept her legs straight and her ass high in the air granting him an awe-inspiring glimpse of paradise, she knew exactly what she was doing—tempting him beyond belief.

She snagged a pillow from the bed and walked toward him. "Well, let's see," she said, and let out an airy little sigh. She kept her gaze locked with his and dropped the pillow at his feet. "There is a question that's been on my mind recently."

He swallowed. Hard. "Such as?"

She settled to her knees in front of him.

His stomach bottomed out.

Her eyes gleamed as she reached for his fly. "I would like to know why it's called a blow job when only sucking"—she moistened her lips with her tongue—"and licking are involved."

Seven

Eden had gained more knowledge and experience in the past three weeks courtesy of Jackson's expert instruction than she'd garnered in the nine years she'd been sexually active. Her first experience had left a lot to be desired, namely desire itself. Like many of the eighteen-year-old girls she'd known, she'd been equally anxious to rid herself of virginal stigma and had gone all the way for the sole purpose of having her cherry popped. The event had been so unremarkable, all she really remembered was that it had been over quickly. Thankfully, her sex life had improved in the coming years, but she knew with absolute certainty, not a single brief encounter compared to the all-consuming passion she'd discovered with Jackson.

He left her breathless, satisfied, and always eager for more. As a lover, he could be demanding and ruthless in their pleasure. He relentlessly forced her out of her comfort zone to explore new sensual delights she'd once viewed as forbidden, then made sweet and tender love to her as if he were treasuring every moment as their last.

Sexually, she never knew what to expect from him or what path their journey toward mutual satisfaction would take. Yet, of all the erotic delights he'd shown her, nothing had prepared her for the emotional impact she'd felt when she discovered he not only stuck around long after the sheets had cooled, but he kept coming back for more.

She folded her bath towel, then used it as a cushion as she sat on the edge of the tub to smooth tangy, tropical-scented lotion over her legs. For as much as she was enjoying every single minute she spent with him, she wasn't a total idiot. Without question, Jackson was a dangerous man, at least insofar as her heart was concerned. Luckily for her, she'd wisely kept him in her bed and nowhere near the vicinity of her heartbeat.

On the job, she'd been downright militant in making certain no one knew they'd crossed the line of friendship by becoming lovers. Since partners often hung out together after their shifts, she didn't concern herself with gossip. Of course, she thought with a smile, no one knew she and Jackson went to her apartment or his small house in the older section of town to fuck like rabbits at the end of their shift, either.

She hadn't seen him in two days, since he and one of his brothers were relocating Jackson's dad to a retirement community in Palm Springs. Although she did miss having Jackson around, she hadn't minded all that much, since she'd spent the down time cramming for the sergeant's exam she'd taken yesterday morning. With four days off after pulling twelve straight nights of patrol, she planned to make up for lost time by putting all the intimate knowledge she'd learned to very good use.

Finished with the lotion, she applied some makeup, then dried her hair, leaving it loose to cascade down her back. Jackson may have insisted hands-on experience beat whatever she might learn from the written word, but she bet he wouldn't have a single objection to the few helpful hints she'd picked up on her own. While he'd been in Palm Springs with his dad and brother, she'd spent last night alone with a bottle of blackberry merlot and the latest best-seller. After spending the morning shopping for a few essentials guaranteed to bring Jackson to his knees, she felt confident he'd develop a deep appreciation for her study habits.

She left the bathroom and dressed with care in the new filmy lingerie she'd purchased on her shopping expedition. The plastic tarp crinkled when she sat on the edge of the bed, the sound echoing through her head until her bravado nearly crashed and burned.

"Be brave," she quoted from the book for which she'd gone to three different bookstores before she found a copy. "You are a vamp, a vixen, a wicked woman. You *are* a walking, talking, fucking fantasy in the flesh."

She let out a rush of breath, not quite convinced the pep talk she was supposed to repeat whenever she felt her nerve slipping had the desired effect. To play it safe, she repeated the mantra again, more firmly this time.

Putting on the new pair of spiked red leather pumps, she stared down at the angle of her feet and suffered massive doubt over her navigational capabilities. The chapter titled "Sex Kittens are Pussies" had insisted the five-inch skyscraper heels were an essential ingredient of a man's *vampasy*. Furry bedroom mules and white lace, virginal lingerie, were for sweet and coy sex kittens content to spread their legs and not take responsibility for their own orgasms. Not vamps. Vamps kicked sex kitten ass. They wore red or black, the colors of hot, raunchy sex. Preferably leather, but satin was an acceptable alternative for the newly vampish. And vamps liked their sex hot, and they demanded it often.

Eden giggled. The latter alone qualified her as definite vamp material.

The saleswoman at the adult specialty store had promised her the strapless, black satin corset with no bra cups had become one of their most requested items since the acclaimed best-seller *Every Man's Fantasy Revealed* had topped the charts. Eden hadn't argued and made the spendy purchase along with a matching thong with red satin rosebuds designed to massage her clitoris when she moved, and a pair of black seamed stockings. Now that her inner vixen had been coaxed out of hiding, she'd even purchased a few other items that had caught her attention and sparked her imagination.

With studious care, she circled the bed to check her seams in one of the three, full-length mirrors she'd purchased at a discount warehouse. She'd arranged the mirrors at the foot of the bed, leaning them against the chairs she'd brought in from the dining room. A fourth chair sat in the center for a more immediate surprise destined to drive Jackson wild.

A couple of minor adjustments to her stockings later, she then surveyed the room one last time. For uninterrupted passion, the "Erection Stoppers" chapter suggested removing all time keeping devices and telephones from the room. She'd disconnected her alarm clock and tucked it on the shelf in her closet. If they indulged in watching adult movies together, which she didn't think her new vampishness was ready for quite yet, she was even supposed to place a strip of black tape over the lighted panels of the DVD player.

The phone rang, and her pulse quickened. She'd left a message for Jackson to call from his cell when he pulled into the parking lot of her apartment complex. As the book had instructed, she waited until after the third ring to answer. Of course, she fully realized she'd only pulled off the suggestion because it took her that long to negotiate the distance to the phone in the god-awful stilts pretending to be shoes. "Hello?"

"Hey," Jackson said. "I'm here. Parking as we speak."

"The door's unlocked. Come straight to the bedroom. Oh, and Jackson," she purred in a way she knew would turn him on, "it's gonna get hot tonight. Very, very hot."

His growl of pleasure made her smile. She snagged the extra large bottle of water-based lubricant she'd put on the nightstand earlier and held it close enough to the phone for him to hear the sound of her snapping open the cap.

"What was that?" he asked, a hint of caution in his voice.

She laughed, low and throaty, the sound as sinful as she

knew how to make it as she drizzled the lubricant liberally over the tarp spread over the stripped down bed. "Jackson?"

"Yeah?" he asked carefully.

"Just get your dick up here and fuck me."

"Jesus, Eden," she heard him mutter seconds before she disconnected the call.

Jackson had created a monster. A wildly sensual, insatiable monster. God help him, he was loving every sexually adventurous minute of it, too.

Once his heartbeat slowed and he'd been capable of movement, he'd locked up his truck and made a beeline for Eden's apartment. He let himself in and locked the door behind him. The drapes were drawn to keep out the late evening sun, and she had the a/c running on high, making the cozy apartment chillier than usual. He had no idea what she had in store for him, but anticipation stirred his blood with each step that brought him closer to her bedroom.

He headed down the short hallway, coming to an abrupt halt when he reached the open door. His heart pounded heavily in his chest. Blood filled his cock until it swelled and pulsed. The beautiful, erotic vision awaiting him filled him with awe.

"Wow," he said, because that was the only word willing to materialize.

Dozens upon dozens of candles were scattered throughout the room, from tapers to pillars to votives, filling the room with a tangy, citrus scent. The flickering light bathed the room in a soft, warm glow, but that wasn't the sight that stole his breath. That honor had been reserved for Eden by her sensual self.

She sat at an angle in one of the dining chairs gently caressing her exposed breasts outlined by a black corset with miniscule bloodred satin roses. Three tall, full-length mirrors were arranged behind her, like an erotic triptych where her sexy image went on indefinitely.

With her hips tilted upward and her legs unashamedly open, she straddled the chair, gifting him with a damned provocative picture. A scrap of black material shielded her dark curls, but his attention was focused on the single row of bright red roses pressing enticingly against her glistening feminine flesh. The line of red disappeared, he imagined, to caress the seam of her sweet, rounded ass.

With the most wicked smile he'd ever seen on her face, she put her middle finger between her red-tinted lips and sucked on the tip. She held him transfixed with her glowing amber gaze, then pulled her finger from her mouth, drawing the digit down her body with agonizing slowness until she caressed the line of roses.

He couldn't move. Hell, he couldn't breathe. He stood in the doorway, mesmerized as she plucked at her nipples with one hand while she rotated her hips, thrusting them lightly when she began to masturbate in front of him.

"Do you know how much I've missed you?" Her voice was a throaty purr of sound. She gave a sexy little pout and peered down at her hand between her legs. "I can show you."

The tip of a bloodred fingernail slipped inside. He nearly came out of his skin.

"Hmm," she murmured, stroking herself. "So hot."

He couldn't take another minute without touching her. "Is this a private party?"

She dragged her tongue across her plump bottom lip. "There's always room for you," she said huskily. "Inside me."

She couldn't have any idea what she was doing to him, taunting him this way. Couldn't possibly understand the dark, primal, and a little bit dangerous need to have her that consumed him. The unrelenting desire to completely possess her drove him so hard it made him edgy and as close to irrational as he'd ever come in his life.

He was across the room in two long strides. Still fully

dressed, he took hold of her hand and brought it to his lips, drawing her finger into his mouth to taste her essence.

She looked up at him with desire blazing in her eyes and reached for him, ripping open the button fly of his jeans with her free hand. Tugging her other hand from his grasp, she freed him and settled her lush mouth over the head of his cock.

Searing heat fired his blood. She worked him into a frenzy of animal lust with her lips and tongue. Need pounded through him, and he pulled away before she took him too far. Roughly, he hauled her to her feet and spun her around to face the triad of mirrors. "Bend over," he ground out harshly.

She did, and placed her hands on the pad of the chair. Leaning over her, he aligned his body with hers and rubbed his cock against the soft flesh of her ass. He caught her breasts in his hands, kneading the weighty globes, teasing the nipples she'd readied for him into tight, beaded peaks until she finally uttered a whisper-soft moan.

She ground against his crotch, and fire sped through his veins. A harsh breath hissed out between his teeth from the pain of his erection straining against her tight ass. God, he had to have her.

He shoved her long, black tresses aside and kissed the nape of her neck. He laved and nipped at the tender flesh of her back, gliding his tongue over her spine to the satin edge of the corset. Dropping to his knees behind her, he picked up where the corset left off, kissing the indentation at the base of her spine and over her bottom.

"Open your legs." His voice was rougher now as sharp-edged desire continued to push him beyond the limits of his control.

Without protest, she did as he asked, but it wasn't enough to suit him. "Wider, Eden," he said in a demanding tone. "Now."

She widened her stand more, and he breathed in the rich,

musky scent of her arousal. The added height of her heels, bent over the chair with her legs parted for him, lifted her ass high in the air and put her in a vulnerable position. He had a fleeting thought of the level of trust she bestowed on him, but the desire to overwhelm her took control. He pressed her open, exposing her, making her even more vulnerable to him.

Greedy bastard that he was, he would have all of her, every last inch and all she had to give; then he'd demand more from her. Until she understood he'd settle for nothing less, he wouldn't stop. He couldn't. He simply wasn't that strong where his feelings for her were concerned.

She loved him. He knew it, even if she didn't. Before the night was over, she would because he planned to make certain of it. The realization would scare the hell out of her, but all that mattered to him was that she acknowledge what he knew was in her heart.

A long, sultry moan erupted from her when he lapped at her, slowly licking her from behind. He forced himself to take his time with her, drinking her essence as it pooled on his tongue. So hot, so sweet. With lazy swirls, he tongued her throbbing pearl, making her shudder with the sensation. Her legs trembled, but he wasn't about to let her off easy and with a quick release. Tonight he'd make her work for it, make her beg him for it.

He circled the outer edges of her dewy center, teasing her with little half thrusts, pushing the little satin rosebuds inside until the keen sounds of her frustration grew loud enough to drown out the heavy pounding of his heart.

Before she reached her climax, he rose to his feet. He ignored her protests, and pushed into her. Watching their unending reflection in the mirrors, he buried himself inside her slick, wet core. Taking her from behind this way, he penetrated her more deeply than he'd done before. It was sheer heaven.

Her outcry was a sensuous blend of pleasure and surprise. When she didn't attempt to move away, he dug his fingers into the soft flesh of her round bottom and pumped into her hard, over and over again. He buried himself as far as she would take him, then slowed the pace, penetrating her with long, deep, measured strokes while she milked him with her sweet, moist heat.

Her moans grew even louder, and her fingers gripped the edge of the chair, her knuckles whitening from the force. She dropped her head forward, but he wanted her to watch, to see what she did to him. Grabbing a fistful of her thick, dark hair, he tugged, forcing her head up until she looked into his eyes through the reflection of the mirrors.

"Watch," he said gruffly. "Watch me fuck you."

Fire burned in her eyes, and her lips parted hungrily. She moved her hands from the pad of the chair to one of the rungs, the shift in her position tipping her pelvis, deepening the penetration. He ground into her, and she held his gaze, taking all of him.

Something inside him snapped. He released her hair and took her hips firmly in his hands. Furious, intense pleasure slammed into him, and he lost it. His release came hard and swift, and was as wild and abandoned as their lovemaking.

In the back of his mind he heard her call out to him, but he'd leapt beyond comprehension, unable to rein in the animalistic impulses driving him. She'd pushed him too far, and he was incapable of recognizing whether her cries were from her own release or from fear because he'd lost total and absolute control.

The world took its sweet time righting again. His breathing slowed, and the ringing in his ears quieted. His senses slowly returned, bringing regret crashing down on him. The words she called out to him finally penetrated his thick skull.

Jackson, stop.

Jesus, if he'd hurt her . . .

He withdrew and helped her to straighten. Afraid of what he might see in her eyes, he kept his gaze averted as he turned her toward him and pulled her to him. Wrapping his arms around her, he held her close. "I'm sorry, Eden," he said, his voice rough with emotion. "God, I'm so sorry."

She let out a shuddering breath. "You should be," she said, sounding . . . miffed?

He loosened his hold to look down at her. She tipped her head back and gave him one of her single, arched eyebrow expressions. "That was pretty damned selfish of you," she complained.

He cupped her cheek in his palm. "I didn't hurt you?"

A sweet and tender smile curved her lips, chasing away his doubt. "No, you didn't hurt me." She pressed her mouth to his hand. "But you could have waited for me," she chided him.

He let out a sigh. "I'll just have to make it up to you."

"Damned straight you will," she sassed him.

He took her face in his hands and kissed her, long and slow. "You do know I'd never hurt you, don't you, Eden?" he asked when he lifted his head.

She stiffened, then pulled away from him. She turned and moved to the bed without comment.

"Eden?"

"Of course you wouldn't." Her voice held a hint of brittleness that worried him. She looked over her shoulder at him, but the saucy grin fell short, courtesy of the caution banked in her eyes. "Because you know, I'm a helluva better shot than you."

Because he knew she expected him to, he laughed. He didn't doubt for a second she'd blow the balls off the first guy stupid enough to physically threaten her.

But what about emotionally, he couldn't help worrying. He supposed he'd find out soon, because once he told her he loved her, he expected her to let him have it—with both barrels.

Eight

An unmistakable sexy glimmer lit Jackson's sea green eyes as his gaze shifted to the bed she'd covered with the paint tarp and lightly coated in the sensual lubricant she'd bought. An appreciative smile curved his lips. "I'm not even going to ask," he said, shucking out of his jeans. He drew his navy blue T-shirt over his head and tossed it on the floor near her feet.

The sassy reply she'd been about to taunt him with never materialized. The beauty of his erection stole her breath. After the way he'd just made love to her, she couldn't help but feel moderately surprised, not to mention damned impressed, to see him rising to the occasion again so soon.

Throughout the day she'd worried she might have been the tiniest bit hasty in skipping ahead to the "Amorous, Adventurous, and Absolutely Audacious" chapter of the sex manual she'd been reading. But the intensity in Jackson's gaze as he moved purposely toward her put her doubts to rest and had her pulse revving in no time flat.

With that traffic-stopping smile still in place, he reached for her to gently pull her into his arms. Resting her cheek against the wide expanse of his chest, she wound her arms around his waist. His hands swept lightly down her back in a loving, reassuring caress. The steady beat of his heart thrummed beneath her ear, strong, sure. Just like him, she thought. Rock solid.

He was so big, so strong and powerful, but she'd never feared him. With Jackson, she would always be completely and utterly safe. She hadn't needed to hear the promise he'd made because she knew he'd die before he'd ever physically harm her.

Emotionally, her convictions were nowhere near as concrete. So long as they'd kept their relationship free of all the usual, messy romantic entanglements, she'd had no qualms about continuing to see him on a mutually exclusive basis. Except lately, she couldn't shake the impression that the state of their involvement had somehow undergone a dramatic shift she hadn't seen coming. If she hadn't been so busy concentrating on all the phenomenal sex they'd been enjoying, she might have noticed the difference in his touch, the tenderness in his eyes, or the heartfelt emotion behind every kiss sooner.

On the surface, their friendship appeared unchanged, but she admitted they now shared a deeper understanding of each other. She easily sensed his moods. He'd become a whiz at pushing her hot buttons to get her riled, just as she knew exactly what to say to fire him up. Although she could hardly stomach the stuff, she kept chunky peanut butter on hand because he liked it with his toast. A devout chocolate chip ice cream connoisseur, he made room in his freezer for her all-time favorite butter nut crunch. She supported his convictions, and he understood her passions. His yin to her yang?

Not a chance, she thought. Sure, the bond between them had definitely grown stronger; that she couldn't deny. But, she refused to believe for a second that she'd gone and fallen in love with him. That she would never do.

Oh, yeah? Then why do you suddenly feel so . . .
Entangled?
She didn't. She absolutely would not, could not, *had not*

fallen for Jackson. After the way she'd just driven him wild enough to finally lose complete and total control with her, what woman wouldn't be feeling a little . . . entangled?

Oh, shit.

No. Not happening. Her emotions were maxed, that's all. She was on a power trip, not some warped I'm-in-love-with-him emotional high. She wasn't *that* stupid.

She hoped.

His hands drifted up and down her back, his fingers dancing over the black satin enclosing her rib cage. "Okay, what gives? Is there some key to getting you out of this thing?"

She laughed, grateful for the distraction he unwittingly offered from the dangerous path her thoughts had taken. Pulling back, she conjured up a saucy grin. "Yes, but it's a hidden key. You'll have to follow a very special map to locate it."

"A buried treasure?" He scrubbed his hand over his jaw as if contemplating the possibilities. "I wonder where you could've hidden a key?"

She rolled her eyes and snagged his hand. "If I have to tell you"—she turned to lead him closer to the bed—"then what fun will that be?"

His laughter warmed her. "If I have to tell *you*," he said with meaning, "then you haven't been paying attention."

"Guess I'm going to need a refresher course," she teased him.

His hands landed on her waist, and he hauled her up against him. The heat of his chest seared her from her shoulder blades all the way down to where the length of his penis pressed against the seam of her behind.

"Is that all you want, Eden?" he asked, his tone suddenly serious.

His arms went around her waist, his hands traveling upward to cup her breasts. Dragging his thumbs rhythmically across her nipples had her trembling. "That's all," she said. That's all there could ever be.

"When does it become more than just fun?"

She closed her eyes and tried to concentrate on the delicious shockwaves rippling over her skin and not the underlying meaning or the hint of urgency in his voice. "Tonight is about pleasure," she whispered.

"And what about tomorrow?"

She rocked her hips, and the strip of satin rubbed enticingly against her clitoris. Reaching between their bodies, she wrapped her hand around the thick, velvety length of his shaft, then pumped him gently in a desperate attempt to change the subject.

"When I have a hard dick in my hands," she said boldly, "I can't think that far ahead."

She refused to consider anything beyond the here and now, and focused her attention on Jackson growing thicker, heavier, hotter in her hand. The sound of his breathing as it deepened with each stroke, the soft glow of flickering candles, and the subtle aroma of citrus candle wax blending seductively with the warm musky scent of their arousal became her salvation.

"Make love to me, Jackson," she said. "Tonight is only about pleasuring each other."

His hands stilled on her breasts, and she held her breath, waiting for him to issue another one of his my-way-or-a-cold-shower ultimatums. But then his hands thankfully coasted from her breasts to skim over her waist to tease the tops of her thighs above the band of her stockings, and she could breathe again. A minor victory, she knew, but she'd gladly take what she could get if it meant not having to think about tomorrow.

He dipped his head to nuzzle the side of her neck, slowly nipping and laving a steamy path to her earlobe. "You want pleasure, babe?" he whispered.

His hot breath fanned the shell of her ear.

She lightly squeezed his shaft. "Oh, yes."

He tenderly kissed her shoulder and quickly undid the front hooks of the corset before urging her to release him. "If a woman experiences prolonged orgasm, did you know she can ejaculate?"

She'd read that some women ejaculated, but as far as she knew, the tale was more urban legend than reality. Although if any man existed with the skill to bring his lover such incredible pleasure, his name was more than likely Jackson Hunt.

"She has to journey through the seven peaks of ecstasy." He spoke in a low, hypnotic tone, granting her a reprieve.

He urged her to sit on the edge of the bed, then crouched in front of her to remove her shoes. She stared, mesmerized by him, by the soothing sound of his rich voice, by the sight of his big body kneeling before her, by the reverence of his touch. Something inside her shifted, but she lacked the courage to define the change.

"Each peak you climb will be stronger and more powerful than the last," he promised. Leisurely, he smoothed his hands upward to the band of her stockings, then rolled them down one by one, tenderly nipping at the sensitive skin he exposed. "Only then will you have an orgasm so intense you'll ejaculate."

Her body quickened in decadent anticipation.

He lifted his head and leveled her with a direct stare. "But before I slip my cock inside you and we journey together to what the ancients call the wave of bliss, there's a rare gift you must give to me first, and it has a price," he said in that same hypnotic tone. "The legend is that once a man is bestowed the divine nectar of his lover, he can never be fully satisfied by another."

Her breath hitched in her throat at the raw emotion filling his gaze. This wasn't what she'd signed on for, dammit. Sex. Yes, she'd agreed to mutually exclusive sex. Simultaneous orgasms and mind-blowing passion were more than welcome. But no emotions, no entanglements, and no ridiculous ancient fairy tales or orgasmic myths were allowed.

"That's a tall order." She shot for flippant but had skidded too close to scared shitless to pull it off effectively. She added a shrug that felt too mechanical to be truly careless. "I'll take the orgasms, hold the legend."

His tolerant look left her with the distinct impression she was more transparent than saran wrap.

He rose, seriously invading her space, his smile perfectly predatory. Her tummy did a flip.

"The menu doesn't allow for substitutions," he said. "What you see, is what you get."

Out of options, she lay back against the mattress and gave a tiny yelp when the chilled lubricant she'd doused over the tarp initially made contact with her bare skin. "Oh, God," she said, moving sinuously beneath him as he literally crept over her, preventing escape. "This stuff is awesomely slick."

Dragging her fingers through a pool of the velvety thick liquid, she summoned up a determined smile all her own and took Jackson in her hand, stroking the length of his shaft. She deliberately evaded his question, but she figured he'd probably had that one nailed before she started the next downward stroke.

"What is that stuff?" he asked her, his voice strained.

"A sensual lubricant. Second only to mother nature," she said, quoting the advertising slogan on the bottle. She collected more, then applied her other hand to him and stroked him hard. She loved the feel of him so thick and heavy in her hands, and the way he grit his teeth and closed his eyes. As a distraction, her ploy qualified as a significant success. "Feels incredible, doesn't it?"

"Good God, yes."

With him on his hands and knees above her, she rose up to swirl her tongue over his flat, brown nipples. Arousal spread languidly through her, dampening her with need. His breathing deepened and hips began to rock with easy, gentle thrusts. She continued working him into an even thicker erection using the technique he'd shown her brought him the most pleasure, stroking his thick shaft, while caressing and teasing the head of his penis with the pad of her thumb.

"Eden, you have to stop."

"Why?" she asked, stilling her hands. She pressed her open mouth on his warm skin and tasted him.

He rolled her to her side. "No substitutions," he said. "There's room for only one item on the menu tonight. Your pleasure."

Lying partially on his side, he slid her next to him, with her slippery back cradled against his chest. He held her to him, strumming his hand over her rib cage, along her belly, to her hip, then back again as if he were exploring her for the first time. She rested her head against his granite-hard bicep, and he tipped her face with his index finger. He kissed her thoroughly, with a reverence that caressed her heart. Effortlessly, he made a mockery of her resistance, crashing through the sturdy brick wall she'd erected to protect herself from loving him.

His slow, delicate touch, his fingers slick with lubricant gliding over her skin, brought her to a new level of heightened awareness. She wanted to believe the chaos he created within her was a result of physical need. The ache deep in her chest told another story. One that frightened her.

Damn him and the loving, tender way he kissed her. Screw him and the gentleness with which he touched her. She didn't need or want all the riotous emotions crowding her, but the pulsing of her body and the throbbing of her clitoris had her aching for relief she wasn't strong enough to deny.

Moving his hand down her belly, he teasingly swept by her curls to her thigh. He parted her legs, then guided her calf until it rested over his thigh. She made a sound of greedy anticipation, needing him inside her, needing only to feel the luxurious sensations he'd promised her so she wouldn't have to think.

Ending the kiss, he grazed his tongue over her jaw to her

ear. "I love the way you respond," he whispered to her. "How your clit swells and throbs when I caress you there." His hand skimmed over her rib cage. "How slick and hot you feel when I put my dick inside you."

His mouth clamped down on hers, the kiss rough, demanding. She whimpered and reached for his hand to guide him where she needed to feel him the most. He ignored her demand and ended the searing kiss.

"When you take me in your mouth, it makes me even thicker and harder," he whispered naughtily in her ear. He lazily massaged her inner thigh, and her hips came off the bed.

"God, and the way you taste when all your moisture pools on my tongue . . ."

A moan ripped from her chest. "Jackson, please."

". . . drives me fucking wild."

He didn't know the meaning of the word. "Dammit, Jackson. Touch me. Now. Please."

He rubbed velvety-textured lubricant over her sex. "Better?"

"Oh, God, yes."

He saturated her, his deft fingers lovingly coating her with the luxurious, creamy sex grease. The pleasure was too immediate and extreme. The steady buildup of pressure too hard and intense. She went wild, became decadent under his hand, and it still wasn't enough to cool the inferno he'd fanned inside her.

She wanted so much more. Needed the release he'd held out of her reach more than her next breath. "Make me come," she demanded in a strained whisper. "Do it, Jackson. Do it now."

"Once we start, I won't stop until you give me everything you have." He slid his middle finger inside her and massaged her deeply. "I'll take you there, but not unless you promise it all."

"Take me there," she cried.

The tip of his finger found her G-spot. The first wave of pleasure immediately slammed into her, taking her breath.

"I'll never give it back, Eden."

"I don't care," she said, then let go with a low, primal growl when he kept his promise and deepened the intensity of her pleasure. He made her so mindless, she'd have promised him anything if it meant continuing to feel the beauty of the climax rippling through her.

Without allowing her a moment to catch her breath, he pushed her farther along the wave, holding her steady in a minefield of sheer bliss as he'd promised he would, guiding her over the next peak, and the next, each more powerful than the last. She'd never felt more uninhibited, never more free or so in tune with another human being. God help her, she didn't think there'd ever be another to make her feel the way Jackson could.

He loved her alternately with his hands, his mouth, but not with his body. The teasing thrusts of the petal pink, rotating vibrator he stroked her with sent her soaring, and then he pushed her even harder by suckling her clit and cranking up the vibrations of the toy to an even higher level.

She came unhinged.

She clawed at him as her body strained for sweet release. She pushed him away when the intensity became too much to bear. She begged him to stop, then insisted he take her to the next level. She wanted it all. His hands, his mouth, every blissful second of the unrelenting passion he gave her.

Her need drove her beyond the boundaries of her safe world. Once she left, he wouldn't allow her to return, leaving her ruthlessly open and raw with her heart fully exposed and vulnerable.

Just when she thought she couldn't withstand another second of such intense lovemaking, of the constant humming pulsating through her, he upped the stakes on her and pushed her again until the force of another powerful orgasm rocked her. He took her world and turned it upside down, but still he withheld what she yearned for the most, to feel the weight of his body sliding over hers, to welcome him inside her as their hearts beat together and their breaths mingled, for their bodies to be linked in ultimate intimacy.

He moved between her legs and slid his hands beneath her bottom, lifting her to his mouth. He lapped her, pushed his tongue inside her, then sucked hard on her pearl, loving her with such lavish decadence she flew toward the next peak with rapacious, unfettered abandon.

The explosion of sensation that overcame her was so sharp and brilliant, she was blinded by its vibrant richness. She felt the vibration of his low, throaty groan against her as wave after wave tumbled through her. She gave him all she had to give, then wept from the magnificence of such profound, infinite pleasure.

Finally, the weight of his body passed over her, and she wrapped her legs tightly around his waist, lifting her hips to welcome him inside. He took her with a long, swift stroke, and she clung to him, awash in sensation.

Supporting his weight with his elbows, he gently smoothed the hair clinging to her face. The tenderness in which he made love to her combined with the deep affection in his eyes filled her with a poignancy she was ill-equipped to handle. She did the only thing she could to keep the words she read in his gaze from tumbling from his lips—she dug her fingers into his backside and urged him to take her hard and fast back to that place where thoughts ceased and only sensation existed.

He rose up, extending his arms, and she pulled him deeper inside her. She met him thrust for thrust, inciting a wildness in him that made her as equally ravenous. Beneath him, she crested the next peak, then flew apart. When he came with her, she knew she'd never experience anything as beautiful or pure as the man she loved consumed by the power of their mutual climax.

* * *

Eden had no idea how much time had passed when she awakened sometime later with Jackson's thick biceps wrapped around her. She lay on her side, her back cradled by the warmth of his big body tucked along the length of hers. "I love you," she whispered, so overcome with emotion the words slipped out before she could acknowledge they existed.

Panic gripped her. Oh, God. What the hell had she done?

"Take a breath, babe," he said, his tone gentle as she struggled fiercely to escape his embrace.

"Leave me alone." She needed space. Air. *Now.* "I don't want to do this anymore."

He held her tighter. "Eden, look at me."

No way. She wasn't that good of an actress. If he took one look in her eyes, he'd know she was lying.

"I know it frightens you," he said as she struggled against his firm hold on her. "I'm here, Eden. I'll always be here. That's a promise."

The affection in his voice tore at her, threatened to weaken her resolve, but she refused to fall victim to it. She couldn't. Her survival depended on her staying strong.

Thanks to the slippery tarp, he had no trouble turning her to her back where he could loom over her. She made the mistake of looking up into his eyes. The emotion reflected in his gaze caused the ache in her chest to triple. "Don't do this to me." She struggled for air. "Oh, God. I can't breathe. I can't breathe."

"I love you, Eden."

She shook her head. "No."

"Why not?" he insisted, frowning. "What are you afraid of? Me?"

She pushed hard at his chest, and he let her go. She scrambled away from him. Away from the truth of her feelings for him. "This conversation is over."

"The hell it is," he said roughly. He reached for her, but

she was off the bed before he could stop her. "Dammit, Eden."

"Leave, Jackson." Panic made her voice rise sharply. She backed up until she reached the foot of the bed. "Go before this turns ugly."

"Don't hold your breath." He followed her off the bed. "I'll be damned if I'm going to let you push me away, too."

She spun around, anxious to put as much distance between him and her vulnerability as possible. Her foot tangled in his jeans, and she momentarily lost her balance. Reaching out to keep herself from falling, she put her hand up and bumped into one of the chairs. The mirror wobbled precariously, then finally tipped forward and crashed loudly to the floor.

She barely spared a glance at the broken shards scattered over the carpet and made a mad dash for the safety and solitude of the bathroom. Locking the door behind her, she slumped against the hollow wood and waited for the sound of the front door slamming closed. Only then would she breathe a sigh of relief.

He jiggled the doorknob. "Don't think I'm leaving," he said loud enough to be heard from the other side of the door. He didn't sound angry, just determined. "We will finish this. Tonight."

He would, too. He'd lay siege if he had to, she knew, just to prove a point. When it came to determination, he made her look like an indecisive wuss.

"Just my luck," she muttered, and pushed off the door. She shook her head at her rotten timing. According to superstition, she'd just been handed seven years' worth of bad luck for breaking a mirror. Whatever entity reigned supreme in that department obviously didn't believe in wasting a second in doling out punishment.

Nine

Over an hour later, Eden still hadn't emerged from what Jackson suspected she envisioned as sanctuary. Since she'd been hiding out in the master bath, he'd showered in the guest bathroom, cleaned up the disaster she'd made of the bedroom, and had already downed his first cup of strong, black coffee.

She was scared to death. He got it. But there wasn't a chance in hell he was going to allow her to sabotage their relationship, especially not after she'd admitted she loved him. If she thought he'd let her work through her fear alone, then she was in for another shock, as well.

He wasn't giving up on her. Or them.

The water shut down in the master bath, so he left the bedroom and headed into the kitchen to pour himself another cup of coffee to give her privacy to dress. The shower ranked as progress. She hadn't even turned on the taps until after he'd started the coffee brewing.

What the future held for him, he couldn't state with any degree of certainty, except he knew in his heart he wanted a future with Eden. He wasn't prepared to reserve a church for next June, but the thought didn't give him a case of hives, either. With a shake of his head, a wry smile tugged his lips. He couldn't say the same for his sanctuary-seeking Esmerelda.

158 / *Jamie Denton*

After her reaction when she realized the depth of her feelings for him, the only way he'd get her into a church would be under armed escort.

He took his coffee into the living room to wait her out, wondering what type of reaction he'd receive when he informed her he was leaving the force. Nowhere near as dramatic as her realization she loved him, but he expected her to have an opinion or two on the subject. Once they made it over the current hurdle, she'd no doubt grill him hard, if only to assure herself he was making the right choice for himself.

Now that he'd actually made the decision and had taken the first step toward his goal, he didn't know why he'd even hesitated in the first place. He supposed much of his reasoning for staying on the force for as long as he had stemmed from the misguided belief that turning in his badge equaled failure. As his dad had firmly told him, his only failure would be in doing nothing.

During the two days he and his brother Aidan had spent moving his dad down to Palm Springs, several lengthy discussions had taken place once his dad had asked him out of the blue if he'd made up his mind about leaving the force. Jackson had been floored. He hadn't realized his discontent had been obvious to anyone other than Eden. But once he'd admitted that he'd been feeling restless for some time, the rest had been easy.

Upon returning from the desert community early yesterday afternoon, he'd immediately put in an application for U.C. Riverside's masters program in child psychology. He expected his chances of acceptance were good, but knew he'd have to wait until the spring semester since he'd applied too late to make the fall term. Making a difference still mattered to him, but he felt he could do more good working with disadvantaged and troubled kids before they turned into the lost causes he dealt with on the streets. With his blue collar roots, he had no trust fund to draw from for financial support. A cop's salary wasn't bad, and while he had a decent sum of money saved, it was no fortune by any stretch of the imagination. In the meantime, he'd remain on first watch working patrol until he found another job better suited to his long-term career goals.

He lifted the mug of coffee to take a drink when Eden walked into the living room. A pair of faded jeans hugged her curves. The skimpy red tank top showed off her slender arms, and the matching chips prominently displayed on both shoulders. She barely resembled the wickedly sensuous woman who drove him insane with lust. She looked young, vulnerable, and mad as hell.

"Why are you still here?" she rudely demanded.

He added "too defensive to listen to reason," and then threw in "too emotionally charged to engage in rational discussion" to his assessment of her. Setting his mug on the end table next to the blue corduroy sofa, he let out a sigh and settled back. He propped his foot over his knee and looked at her. "Because we need to talk."

She folded her arms and shot him a mean-assed glare that would've been more effective if she'd been able to mask the stark fear in her gaze. "I already told you the conversation was over. The words weren't too big for you to understand, were they? Or are you being deliberately obtuse?"

He ground his teeth in frustration. In her continued effort to drive him away, she was spoiling for a fight. He refused to give her the satisfaction.

Her eyebrows winged upward. "Well?" she said when he kept silent. "Which is it?"

"The tough chick act won't fly with me, kid," he said calmly. "I'm onto your game."

"Yeah? Well, the *games* are over, too," she said in a bitchy tone. "Your services are no longer required." She spun around and stalked into the kitchen.

For all of five seconds, he considered taking her advice

and leaving, at least until she cooled down. His patience only stretched so far. But if he walked out now, he'd play right into her hands.

Or would he?

The woman wanted a fight; then he should probably give her one. Then, just maybe, she'd finally believe there wasn't a chance in hell he'd ever hurt her no matter how much he might want to wring her sweet neck.

"We have unfinished business."

Eden closed her eyes and gripped the edge of the counter. What did she have to do for him to stop pushing her? She thought for sure the raving bitch trick would've driven him away. Most guys bolted at her first growl.

She didn't understand why it hadn't worked on Jackson. He should've been peeling out of the parking lot by now, not leaning with his shoulder propped against the fridge. She'd watched her mother hone the skill to perfection over the years, and one of two things inevitably occurred—the jerk either walked out when she turned into Varilee the Viper, or she'd get knocked on her ass and then the jerk would leave.

She slanted Jackson an intentionally smoldering glance, attempting a different tact. "I thought we'd finished up our business quite nicely." She dipped her gaze to his fly. "Unless you're interested in a repeat performance."

"Tempting offer." He moved away from the refrigerator and slowly closed in on her. He didn't appear the least bit furious, but the sheer determination in his eyes heightened her degree of nervousness to record levels. He backed her up against the counter, then planted his hands behind her. He had her trapped, which she suspected was his intent.

Damn, he smelled good.

"Tempting," he said again. "But not one I'm interested in at the moment." He spoke in the modulated tone she recognized as one he used when talking down a crack addict or a drunk worked up over some imagined slight. Calm. Reasonable. She hated it.

"Tell me again that you love me," he said. "There's a performance you can repeat. Often."

Once was more than enough for her, thank you. "Sorry. Show cancelled." She shrugged with a carelessness she was nowhere near feeling. "It was a limited engagement, anyway. Not meant for public viewing."

This close, she could see the dark, midnight blue rims surrounding his colorful irises. Heat radiated from him. And his determination was palpable.

And, damn, he smelled *really* good.

"I know what you're trying to do, Eden. It isn't going to work with me."

"Oh, really?"

His nod, and the sexy cant of his mouth, were way too confident. "Try all you want to piss me off. It's not going to change how we feel about each other. This callous I-don't-give-a-shit-about-you act you're trying to pull now won't get off the ground, either. I know better," he said. "If you weren't in love with me, you wouldn't be running scared."

She wondered if a Feng Shui cure existed for warding off six-foot-plus of determined male. "You're feeling all warm and fuzzy because you just had amazing sex. But *I* know better. Once the afterglow fades, so will the generosity."

"Not possible."

"Trust me, I know what I'm talking about. Wham!" she said, slapping her hands together. "Right when you least expect it."

A dark frown replaced his arrogant expression. Slowly, he straightened. "You don't believe—"

"You bet your ass, I do," she said sharply. "I lived it, Jackson. I'm still living it. Every time we go on a call where a woman is getting the crap beat out of her, it's *always* by some stupid jerk she fell in love with. Jesus, do you even pay attention out there? How many times do you have to hear those lowlifes say 'the bitch wouldn't shut up' before you'll get it?"

"So that *is* why you're spoiling for a fight," he said, shaking his head.

"Oh, forget it," she said in a snide tone. "You're incapable of understanding anyway."

Why waste her breath when it wouldn't make a difference in the end? Of course she knew he'd never hurt her in that way, but he'd tear her to shreds emotionally, and that would be no less painful. They had had a good time while it lasted, but the fun was obviously over. The time had come to cut and run, and that's exactly what she would do—once she figured out how to pull it off.

She walked away from him and strode into the living room. She turned down the a/c, then opened the drapes, surprised to see the grayish pink fingers of dawn breaking over the horizon. There was something to be said for locking away all those time keeping devices.

"Make me understand."

She flinched at the unexpected sound of his voice, but kept her back to him. If she ignored him, maybe he'd go away.

His hands settled gently on her shoulders, and he turned her to face him. "Aren't we worth fighting for? If you want a fight, then at least make it worthwhile."

"Is that what you think I want?" She let out a breath. "Jackson, I do not want to fight with you."

"Bullshit," he said, his tone rising. "You're itching for one because you want to see how far you have to push me before I blow. Give it your best shot, kid. God knows you're testing the limits of my patience now, but don't think for a minute I'd ever hurt you that way, no matter how pissed off I might get."

She rolled her eyes. "I know that."

"I might raise my voice, but never a hand to harm you. *Ever.*"

She let out a sigh. "I know, Jackson," she said again.

He raked his hand through his hair. Frustration lined his gaze. "Then what are you so afraid of?"

She briefly closed her eyes and shook her head. God, she couldn't believe what she was about to say. "It's not you, it's me."

He dropped his head forward and actually chuckled. "Try again," he said when he lifted his head. He moved to the sofa and sat. "And dazzle me with your creativity this time."

Her lips twitched at the reminder of the challenge she'd once issued him. After a moment's hesitation, she went to the chair and perched on the arm. Essentially, she was putting an end to their relationship. As much as she detested the vulnerability the realization evoked, he did deserve an explanation.

"My mom didn't always drag me from one shit hole to the next," she said. "What I remember about the time with my dad, and then the years she was married to Kenny, is actually pretty good. Those in between years, though . . ."

"I know it was rough," he said. "You don't have to go there if you don't want to."

If she'd been close enough to touch, she didn't doubt he'd do so, silently offering her his strength because he sensed hers waning. His unselfishness was one of the reasons she loved him, his willingness to share a burden that wasn't even his.

A wry grin touched her lips. "After my dad died, my mom became a bum magnet. If there was a bum within a ten-mile radius, Varilee was attracted to him. Before the booze took a toll on her, she was a pretty woman, so it wasn't like nice guys weren't drawn to her; she just didn't want them.

"Some of the creeps weren't too bad, but once she'd start in on them, it was let the games begin. The better ones walked out. The others would rough her up, some worse than others, then they'd split or toss us out. I never understood why she'd start up, but Kenny inadvertently explained it once not long after they divorced. He'd said that Varilee was afraid of happiness. I didn't figure it out until the night she died."

She drew in a deep breath and continued. "She was lucid for a change, and I guess I knew that would be it for her. It probably had something to do with all the painkillers they were pumping into her," Eden said. "I think she was trying to comfort me when she said she wasn't afraid to die, because she'd be with my dad again. She talked about how proud he would've been of me, he'd been her only love, and how hard he'd worked to make her happy. I remember sitting there thinking that her crazy life finally made sense."

His expression turned skeptical. "How so?"

"The truth is, she died long before she ever succumbed to AIDS. She died when my dad did. She loved him so much, when she lost him, it destroyed her. I've spent my entire adult life trying not to be anything like her, but I'm very much my mother's daughter."

He scrubbed his hand down his face. "Eden, don't—"

"No," she said forcefully. Despite the deep sadness weighing her down, she needed him to understand why she couldn't let herself love him. Moisture clouded her vision, and he became a watery blur. Her throat ached as she fought to hold the tears at bay and drew in an unsteady breath. "I won't do it, Jackson. I have to be stronger than she was or everything I survived will mean nothing."

She lost the battle, but he was next to her, hauling her into his arms before the first tear rolled midway down her cheek. She didn't want to cling to him, didn't want to need the strength of his arms around her. But she greedily took all he offered, further proving Varilee Matthews's blood ran strong in her veins, evidenced by the river's worth of tears she now spilled over some guy.

No, she amended. Not just *some* guy. Jackson.

He said nothing as she cried. He just held her to him and offered her his strength since hers had become nonexistent.

Just like he had . . . the last time?

A memory nudged her. Just like he had . . . the first time?

The familiarity that had been flirting on the fringes of her mind since the night they'd become lovers slowly crystallized. He held her, comforted her now, just as he had done the first time he'd ever kissed her.

She pulled back and swiped the moisture from her face with the back of her hand. "The night of that accident last December. We were trashed on Tequila and you . . . you kissed me, didn't you?"

He winced, but the truth was in his eyes.

"Why didn't you say anything?"

He shrugged. "You never mentioned it, so I wasn't even sure it happened." He skimmed his hands down her arms, catching her fingers and lacing them with his. "If you were pretending it never happened and I brought it up, that would've been uncomfortable for you. If it was just another fantasy and I said something, then you'd know that"—he shook his head—"it was a lose-lose situation."

Just *another* fantasy? "Wait a minute." She frowned. "Then I would've known what?"

"That I've had it bad for you for months." His tone turned defensive.

And she'd called him obtuse? She'd never once suspected his feelings for her were anything but platonic. His insistence they become lovers suddenly made perfect sense.

"I wish you'd have told me."

He laughed, but the sound held no humor. "Okay, just so you know the difference," he said, his tone as razor sharp as the glint in his eyes. "*Now* I'm pissed off."

She stared at him, not sure what, if anything, she should say. No confusion on her part whatsoever. A blind woman could see he was seriously ticked at her.

"What difference would it have made?" he fired the question at her and let go of her hands. "You thinking of all the time we've wasted? Or are you feeling slighted out of the cheap thrill you missed out on putting me through more hell?"

She planted her hands on her hips. "How is this my fault all of a sudden?"

"It wouldn't have made a difference. You still would've pushed me away, only sooner rather than later." He made a sound of disgust and turned away from her, only to spin back around and level her with a lethal glare. "If you don't want to be anything like Varilee, then stop acting like her."

"Now wait just a—"

"Christ, wake up," he thundered. "She didn't fall into the pattern she did because of a broken heart. Her self-destruction was intentional because it was easier than accepting the responsibility that comes from loving another person. She made the choices she did because she knew she'd never fall for the losers she brought home."

"No. You're wrong," she argued. "She was married to Kenny for more than five years."

"Oh, there's a shining example," he spat sarcastically. "You said she'd start her bullshit and the games would begin. She pulled her crap with him, too, Eden. He told you himself, your mother didn't know how to be happy. You are your mother's daughter, because you don't have the first clue any more than she did."

A wave of nausea hit her. Shock? No doubt considering he'd just annihilated twenty-one years' worth of a belief system in one fatal blow. In her determination not to repeat the same mistakes as her mother, she hadn't stopped long enough to see the truth. She might not have made the same poor choices, never subjected herself to the same physical abuse, but in every other respect, Jackson had nailed her. Hard.

She stumbled backward, but he caught her before she did something really stupid—like break a few more mirrors and double or triple her rotten luck.

"Fight or flight, Eden?" he said with unmistakable challenge.

She shook her head, not sure what he wanted from her, but positive it would cost her more than she could emotionally afford. She couldn't do this, not now. Not when she no longer knew her own identity.

For over two decades, she'd wrapped herself in a shroud of illusion, wrongly believing it would provide protection from pain and heartbreak. Jackson was only half right. She did push people away, but because it was easier than accepting her share of the responsibility for her own heartache.

"Come on, babe. Fight or flight?" He quieted his tone, but held her upper arms in his big, strong hands in a tight grip. "What's it going to be?"

She attempted to shrug out of his grasp, but he refused to release her.

"If you can't run, then you're going to have to fight," he continued relentlessly. "But you don't see a difference, do you?"

"I don't like this."

"Because you can't run," he taunted her. "You've always run because you've never had anyone with the balls to back you into a corner and make you face what you're afraid of. Until now."

"No."

"You're going to have to deal with it. With me."

She glared at him. "I said, *no.*"

"Too bad."

"Stop it, Jackson," she snapped at him. "I'm not going to play your stupid games."

A purely predatory light lit his gaze, making her nervous. "I'm here for the long haul. No matter what it takes."

No, not nervous, she decided. Furious. With him. Her entire body shook with it. How dare he push her, pressure her when she was so vulnerable—when she had nowhere to hide from the chaotic, confusing emotions overwhelming her.

She jerked out of his grasp, but she didn't run, she advanced a step and tried to give him a hard shove. He didn't move so much as an inch.

"What the *fuck* do you want from me?" she shouted. She

glared up at him, seething. He just stood there, watching her, absolutely unfazed by her angry outburst.

He'd pushed her, forced her to fight him, and he wasn't fighting her back? "What, Jackson? What more could you possibly want from me?"

"Everything."

"I don't know how to give you everything," she fired at him. "If I did, it'll be too much, and I don't know how to temper it. I keep people at a distance because if they get too close, they see too much. After one good look at the flaws, the fears, all the scars, they decide you don't fit into the box they wanted you to, so they throw you away. Do you have any idea how much it hurts to realize you weren't good enough? That you didn't matter enough?"

And then you were left alone to cover up the fresh scars, doing your best to mask the flaws and bottle up the fear just so you could survive the next round of disappointment.

"That you weren't worth fighting for . . ." She bit back a sob and looked at him, her comprehension dawning bright as she clearly saw what he'd forced her to face. Like the warmth of the sun evaporating the foggy morning mist, her understanding slowly dissolved the red haze of her anger, leaving her raw with her emotions exposed and vulnerable to the burning intensity of the sun.

She went to him and hung on tight. "I don't want to throw us away," she told him. Because they didn't fit into the box she'd wanted them to, one where she wouldn't have to feel too much, she'd hadn't thought twice about setting their relationship out on the curb. She wasn't hurting only herself, but more importantly, Jackson, because she'd been too afraid to fight for them. "But we're gonna need a bigger box."

He chuckled, and his arms came around her. "Then I guess we better find one."

She let out a sigh and hugged him to her. "I'm a wreck, aren't I?"

He tipped her head back to look down at her. A sexy, half grin curved his mouth. "No," he said, gently. "Just human."

He didn't say the words, but he didn't need to. She knew he loved her, just like she had no doubt she'd never tire of seeing the love she felt for him reflected in his stunning, sea green eyes whenever he looked at her.

Lifting her lips to his, she kissed him. She could offer him no guarantees that wherever their love took them would be easy, but with absolute certainty, she knew she'd fallen in love with the *right* man. One strong enough to break past her barriers, brave enough to make her see the truth, and just crazy enough to love her right back.

WICKED
WAYS

Susanna Carr

One

What am I doing here? Peyton wondered as the man's groin invaded her personal space. It took all her willpower not to flinch, even as the musky scent of masculine sweat assailed her flared nostrils. She tried to maintain a casual pose, but every muscle in her body hummed with tension. Her hands clenched underneath her chair. Her rigid fingertips brushed against something gooey.

It's gum. She assured herself. *Please let it be gum.*

"Hey, I know you," the blond god said as he placed his hands behind his head and displayed his magnificent chest. He rotated his hips to the relentless beat of the eighties' song "Holding Out for a Hero". "You're my boss at Lovejoy's Unmentionables."

Peyton flashed him a tight smile. "That's right," she admitted. Was there no end to this night? Why did she think she would have gone unnoticed? Nothing else was going her way.

But who was he? She hadn't really been looking at his face. She squinted as the disco ball spun crazily, swirling white dots of light over everyone. "Bubba Joe from Shipping?" she guessed. "I'm sorry, I didn't recognize you . . ."

"Yeah, that's because I'm incognito," he said, and punctuated each syllable of the last word with a short pelvis thrust.

Okay . . .

"You know, this is my alter ego." He gripped the back of her chair. She felt as though she was caged in testosterone. "But call me by my stage name, Hubba Bubba."

"Did you come up with that all by yourself?" Peyton willed her arms to stay at her sides, although her elbows started creeping in.

"Nah. I ain't that creative. The girls gave me that nickname in high school." He got off of her, and Peyton slowly let out a relieved sigh. It lodged in her throat as he turned around and straddled her again, this time clenching and unclenching his buttocks. His bare buttocks. To the beat of the music. In her face.

"So whatcha doing here, Miz Lovejoy?" he asked as he turned around again. "This ain't no place for someone like you."

Tell me about it. "Entertaining some business clients." Why wasn't this song over? She didn't remember it lasting this long. Wagner's operas were shorter than this.

"All these women wearing black?" He nodded his head to the women sitting at the table, flexing their fingers wildly as they hollered about what they wanted to do with his butt. "I thought you guys just came back from a funeral or something."

No, it just felt that way. "They're here to relax." And to see if Peyton was one of them. A team player. It wasn't clear she succeeded.

"They could save Lovejoy's?" He did a cat stretch before dipping his spine. Peyton, momentarily entranced by the play of muscles, suddenly realized he was rubbing his full erection against her black straight skirt.

Her knees knocked together. "We might reach an agreement that could bring us a lot of money," she replied hoarsely. Did everyone know about the company's financial troubles? "Nothing's definite yet."

Bubba Joe leaned in close until all she could see was his tight nipple. If she spoke, her lips would press against his slick skin. Peyton's cheeks turned a vivid red. "You want me to be real nice to them?" he whispered into her ear. His hot breath stirred the tendrils of her hair that escaped from her French twist. "Give them a private showing?"

Peyton winced. Oh, yeah. That's what she needed to do; make her employees studs for the night. "Thanks for the offer," she said graciously. "It's very generous, but I want you to come out alive."

He flicked a look at the group of women. His smile overflowed with confidence. "Don't worry, Miz Lovejoy, I can handle it."

It seemed as if everyone could handle the evening but her. "I think it would be best if you didn't treat them differently. Why don't you go over there now?" She hoped Bonnie Tyler's ah-ah-ahs from the speakers drowned out the desperation in her voice.

He glanced down. Pointedly. Peyton reluctantly followed his gaze. Were the strobe lights doing something to her eyes or did those leopard spots seem bigger?

"You need to tip me."

"Oh. Oh!" She forgot about the dollar bill scrunched in her fist and probably stuck to the gum. Peyton tore it from under her chair and offered it to him.

Bubba Joe dipped his head next to hers. "No, Miz Lovejoy, I can't take the money. It's against the rules. You have to put it on me."

On him? He was her employee! Peyton's polite smile wavered. She cleared her throat nervously. "Of course." The heat emanating from his snug G-string scorched her hovering hand. She changed her mind and crammed the mangled dollar over the miniscule string on his hip, the farthest place away from any private parts. "I don't want to injure you."

"You couldn't. This is designed for protection from

overeager hands." His splayed fingers framed the leopard skin.

Peyton was at a loss. "Love the fabric," she finally said.

Bubba Joe smiled proudly. "Thanks. My mom made it for me."

An image of his quiet mother hunched over an industrial sewing machine popped in her mind. "She always does excellent work."

"I'll tell her you think so," he said as he strutted away. "See ya, Miz Lovejoy."

Peyton closed her eyes. Oh, God. She didn't want his mother to know she was anywhere around Bubba Joe's G-string! Her stress headache threatened to erupt into a full-blown migraine. Peyton shot up from her seat. She needed a break. She almost wished she smoked so she could have the excuse to escape outside.

"Hey, Peyton," Macey yelled over the lusty music. She motioned for her to get closer. Peyton grudgingly obeyed. Macey Bonds was the hottest name in naughty lingerie these days. Her line was in every sex shop and adult catalog. If she used Lovejoy for her manufacturing needs, Peyton wouldn't have to worry about money for a very long time.

The strange thing was, Macey didn't look like someone who was taking the adult industry by storm. Peyton had expected someone who looked and dressed like a porn star, not a brunette pixie who preferred trendy pantsuits.

Macey's idea of entertainment, on the other hand, would make a frat boy blush.

"You like that guy?" Macey asked as she tossed back the rest of her martini. "You had him dance for a long time." The woman wagged her eyebrows suggestively.

Peyton shrugged. "Just seeing what he had to offer." No way was she fessing up about forgetting to tip him. Had she remembered, she would've thrown the money at Bubba Joe before he was an arm length away. "Excuse me, I'll be right back."

"Where are you going?" Macey asked.

She had no idea. "Bathroom." Peyton could have kicked herself for uttering the first thing that came to mind. She hoped Macey wouldn't make the trip a group outing.

Macey's blue eyes sparkled with knowing. "Hubba Bubba got you all excited, did he?" She winked. "I had no idea these good ol' boys were well hung."

"It's in the water." Peyton took a step back, but Macey grabbed her elbow.

"Come on, I'm dying to know. What was he whispering in your ear?"

"Uh . . . his phone number."

Macey frowned with disappointment. "Oh." She wrinkled her nose. "That's no fun." She dropped Peyton's arm and motioned for the spandex-clad waiter.

Peyton gave a small smile. "I'll be right back," she said as she walked away. Well, maybe it was a boring answer. She couldn't think of anything more exciting. She sure couldn't get excited about this place. What was wrong with her? Why couldn't she be as enthusiastic as the other women in the crowd? They acted as if they'd been trapped in a convent since puberty and were just recently released. She felt that if you've seen one half-naked man show off his package, you've seen them all.

As she waited in line for the bathroom, Peyton noticed the empty men's room. That would be the place to get a moment's peace. She decided to risk entering. Chances were she'd seen what was in there already displayed on the stage. When she stepped across the threshold, Peyton gagged from the stench. She clasped her hand over her mouth and nose and tiptoed her way through the debris to the row of sinks.

She pinched the edges of a coarse paper towel dangling from the chrome dispenser and blotted the sweat from her face. The humid June night managed to invade the strip joint despite the air conditioners chugging continuously.

Peyton looked at the row of sinks and tried to decide

which was the least infectious. Turning the faucet knob with her elbow, she ran tepid water over the paper towel and pressed the damp wad onto the back of her neck.

Closing her eyes and sighing with relief, she blew the wisps of hair that tickled her forehead. Peyton opened her eyes and looked at her reflection. Some strands plastered against her flushed face. Her brown eyes were dull with fatigue and the effect of her two wine spritzers.

Peyton cringed as she saw her outfit. Her camisole glared against the limp black suit. The magazine article insisted that wearing a white camisole would—presto!—turn her business suit into appropriate dress for a night on the town.

They lied. Peyton squeezed her eyes shut and rested her forehead against the cool, streaked mirror. She looked like a dork. A loser. A woman who forgot to put on her blouse. When she got home, she was canceling her subscription.

Boring. Peyton hissed as the word reverberated in her mind. Why did that hurt so much? The word "bitch" held no power over her. She laughed when someone once called her a slut. So why did the label "boring" cut like a knife?

Maybe because she knew there was a strong possibility they were right.

No, that wasn't true. She wouldn't let it be true. Peyton straightened away from the mirror. There was nothing boring about her. Her job wasn't boring. It was challenging. Her social life wasn't dull. She had a group of interesting friends.

No boyfriend right now, but not because she was boring! Peyton straightened her shoulders and tossed the wet towel in the stuffed trashcan. None of her ex-boyfriends ever had complaints in that area. She knew how to have fun.

Even in bed. Peyton snapped her jacket collar into its perfect position. She'd had plenty of amazing sex in her life. Fantastic. Unreal. Okay, she hadn't quite accomplished multiple orgasms, but she was beginning to think that was an urban legend.

And so what if she hadn't had any sex recently? She'd

been busy. Peyton briskly tugged the edge of her suit jacket. Everyone thought she was so lucky to have inherited the family business. They didn't see the struggle behind the scenes or understand the fear of being the Lovejoy who lost it all.

And, yeah, most days were spent at the office. She'd even go so far to admit that her idea of a great night these days meant being asleep before eleven. Which she wasn't getting, because these women thought life started after midnight.

Peyton's shoulders slumped as she realized she was sounding like her mother. Being like her mother would definitely turn off her clients. She couldn't risk offending these women, but she craved a good eight hours of sleep.

She had two options. She could (a) forget about the whole thing, button up her suit jacket, scale the bathroom stall, and escape through the window, or (b) stick with it, take off the jacket, and schmooze with those women until she got the deal she needed.

She stared at her reflection. Her gaze traveled to the window above the stalls. Peyton firmly drew her stare back. Her eyes focused on the wilted business suit. She glanced at the window that beckoned her to go home where it was safe. Comfortable.

Boring.

Peyton watched her left eyebrow arch. Her mouth set into a determined line as she hiked her chin up a notch. *I'll show them. I'll show them all. Peyton Lovejoy has what it takes to turn around the company.*

She ripped open her jacket like a first-time flasher. What she didn't have in content, her enthusiasm should have made up for with extra bonus points. She shrugged off her jacket and clenched it in one hand, her eyes intent on her reflection.

Peyton Lovejoy is not a dork or a loser. She is a wild, wicked woman who gets what she wants.

Her hair was next. The French twist had to go. She clawed out the pins with determined fingers and gave her straight brown hair a good toss. It didn't billow like the hair color commercials, but fell onto her bare shoulders.

Peyton Lovejoy . . .

She made a face.

. . . has got to stop referring to herself in the third person because it's really annoying.

Peyton studied her appearance with the same concentration as if she was presented with a spreadsheet. The camisole was demure, but it showed a lot of skin. It wasn't designed to be seen in public. Peyton twisted from side to side. She shouldn't make any sudden movements. Hunching shoulders and bending down were no-nos. So were taking deep breaths and— "It's fine," she muttered to herself.

The hair was too much, but the twist was too refined. Peyton held her jacket between her teeth and quickly braided her hair. More wisps fell around her face. They were going to drive her crazy, but too bad. A wild woman didn't let hair get in her way.

Peyton gave her appearance another once-over. With a sharp nod of approval, she swung her jacket over her shoulders with two fingers and strutted to the door, pausing only to kick a fragment of paper off her heel.

Watch out world, here I come.

She exhaled sharply and swung open the door. The exuberant screaming drowned out the pulsing song "Brick House." Peyton caught a glimpse of Macey lying on stage as a man wearing a glittered G-string straddled her. His dance was akin to an epileptic seizure as he shook his unusually long penis in Macey's face.

It was like waving a red cloak to a frenzied bull. Macey decided right then and there to do a public display of her fellatio skills. Peyton's mouth fell open as she stepped back into the men's room and let the door swing shut. She raised her hands up in surrender. *We are so going to get arrested.*

Forget it. Peyton tossed her shoulder bag strap across her chest. There was no way she could convince these women that she was fully capable of handling their manufacturing needs. That she appreciated the sexual confidence that oozed from Macey's designs. That she understood because she was just as sexy, wild, and wicked.

She could find other designers looking for a manufacturing company known for their quality goods, Peyton decided as she strode to the stall below the window.

She could turn around Lovejoy's Unmentionables without them. Just because the majority of lingerie designers wouldn't give her the time of day didn't mean the rest of the fashion industry would be the same. There was that one retail chain that adored her. So what if they catered to men who had a thing for women's cotton panties?

Peyton gingerly stepped on the toilet seat and reached for the window. Her fingers were nowhere near the paint-chipped sill. She pressed her lips together and reached harder. S-t-r-e-t-c-h! She grunted until her spine popped. Her balance weaved. Peyton froze, her feet wobbling in the black heels as she gave a quick prayer that she wouldn't fall into the rust-stained toilet bowl.

When her feet steadied, Peyton warily allowed her arms to drift to her sides. Her shoulders sagged in defeat. As a final insult, her camisole gaped, flaunting all she lacked.

Who was she kidding? Peyton dipped her chin. She needed those women execs more than they needed her. "If I have to walk across town stark naked, I will do whatever it takes to save my family's company."

Peyton blinked and looked around the scuzzy stall. Not exactly Scarlett O'Hara shaking her fist with the sun setting behind her in blazing red.

It didn't matter, Peyton decided as she delicately hopped off the toilet seat. She was going to be a sexy young thing if it killed her. She was going to walk the walk, talk the talk. But how was she going to convince those women out there? They were the real things and could spot a pretender.

Peyton paced the floor in front of the urinals, dodging

sodden paper towels. She mulled over the problem before she opened her purse and grabbed her cell phone. She needed information quickly. Peyton hit the speed dial. Accurate info because she didn't have the luxury to make any mistakes.

"Main Library Answer Hotline," the low masculine voice rumbled in her ear. "This is Mike. How can I help you?"

A shiver of awareness skipped across her bare shoulders. There was something about this librarian's voice that curled her toes. She hadn't met him, and she was sure she wouldn't want to. The image in her mind most likely didn't match reality. The guy probably wore high-waist pants and smelly wool cardigans.

"Hi, Mike. I was wondering about something. How long do I have to let a man shake his assets in my face before I can give him his money?"

Mike Ryder rubbed his hand over his face. How the hell did he get stuck with this job? It was his nightmare come to life. He was stuck behind a desk in a building that reeked of dust, mildew, and regulations. Worse, he was required to deal with women who spoke in euphemisms.

And this particular lady was the worst. He wanted to correct her. *Not assets. Ass. A-s-s. He's shaking his ass.*

He could tell she was in her late twenties or early thirties. Her cultured voice was half whisper, half drawl. It caressed his ears and made him think of a woman's soft hands dragging across his skin.

Mike's stomach clenched as he imagined the hands drifting past his hips. If he wasn't careful, his gentlemanly manners—which weren't strong to begin with—were going to crumble and expose his masquerade. He had to get the woman off the phone. Fast. "Why do you have to give him money?"

"So he'll get off of me." The unspoken "duh!" in her voice set his teeth on edge. She was lucky he wasn't in front of her, otherwise his glare would make her run for cover.

"Have you tried shoving him off?" he asked.

WICKED WAYS / 183

"I can't do that!" she said, scandalized. Her screeching matched the high-pitch guitar riff in the background. "It would cause too much of a scene."

Mike frowned. "And the man dry humping is going unnoticed?"

"In this place? Yes."

"What place?" He might regret asking.

She cupped her hand over the phone and mumbled, "Jack's."

Like that was supposed to explain it all. "Jack's?"

"The male strip club," she answered with great reluctance. "This is the answer hotline, right?"

"Yeah. Yeah." The chick was at a male strip club? Never in a million years would he have placed her there. Mike leaned back in his chair and propped his feet on the desk. He couldn't wait to hear her reasons.

"Well?" the woman asked impatiently. "What's the answer?"

"What was the question?"

She huffed with exasperation. "How long do I let him do a lap dance before I can give him the tip?"

Mike shrugged. "As long as you like." Why did this woman think there were rules for everything? Women went to Jack's because they were looking for a free-for-all.

"I don't like that answer."

Mike pinched the bridge of his nose as he gathered the last reserves of his manners. "Then give me a different question."

"Fine. A few . . . friends of mine wanted to be at this strip club. I want them to have a good time, and I don't want to be a spoilsport."

"Gotcha." Now it was making sense. Her friends probably dragged her to that joint so they could shake off the prissy attitude. "Do you have a lot of cash on you?"

"Yes."

"Large denominations?"

"A few." Her hesitation suggested she wasn't sure about

Mike's information. "I was told you could never have enough one dollar bills."

"True. Here's the plan. Don't sit down."

"Not a problem. You should see some of the chairs. I don't know what's on—"

Mike didn't want to know, either. "Take one of the large bills, or a handful of the one dollars, and wave it around your friend's head."

"Why would I do that?"

"It's a sign that you want the guy to give his attention to your friend."

"Oh. I didn't know that." The woman sighed. "Why don't they give you a list of rules when you go to these places?"

"Anything else?" He shouldn't ask, but he knew she would call back anyway.

"No—yes!" Urgency shot through her voice. "Does my friend do the dollar stuffing, or do I?"

"Whichever." He decided to give her a break. "Place the money on your friend."

"Place?" Suspicion entered her voice. "Like where?"

Mike tossed up his hand. Can't this chick use her imagination? "Sticking out of her shirt, between her legs . . ."

"Wait a second, wait a second." The woman was ready to argue. "They can't take the money from you. Hubba Bubba just told me that."

Mike rolled his eyes. Only in a small town could you get away with that name. "There are other methods of removal. Like with his teeth, or his thighs, or . . ."

The woman backed off immediately. "Okay, thank you! By the way, how do you know all of this?"

I've been known to leave the house. I'm a consultant for Chippendales. I'm making it all up just to mess with your mind because I have nothing better to do. The sarcastic replies were bombarding his gentlemanly façade. He had to get off the phone. "We librarians don't know everything," he parroted the canned response through clenched teeth. "We just know where to look for the information."

"And you're sure this information is accurate? You're not getting this off the Web, are you?"

Mike felt his nostrils flaring. *Just one zinger. Just one.* "Positive."

"Okay. Thanks a lot, Mike. Bye!"

"Good luck." Mike heard the disconnecting click. "You're gonna need it."

He slowly relaxed his jaw as he replaced the phone back in its cradle. Whoever she was, the woman was in way over her head.

She had been calling since the Answer Hotline was created a week ago. When she'd asked what a "yoni" was, he'd had to bite back the slang word and cull his memory for the clinical term "vulva." Her strangled "oh" response had made him wonder if he needed to explain vulva.

But she hadn't been offended. She kept calling asking more questions. Strange ones. Sometimes she took the answer with ease; other times she hung up abruptly. It was hard to predict how she would handle the answer.

He wasn't sure what to worry about most: that there was something going on in the middle of this cornfield to provoke these questions, or that he knew the answers without looking them up.

Mike returned his attention to the paperwork strewn on the desk only to have the phone ring again. He growled in the back of his throat and snatched up the phone. "Main Library's Answer Hotline. This is Mike. How may I help you?"

"Hey, Mike, you need to sound friendlier," his sister Skylar said, "or you'll scare the patrons."

"Some of them could use a little scaring," Mike said distractedly as he scanned another handwritten paper.

"Aw, is playing librarian wearing you down?" Skylar

asked as if she was talking to a grumpy toddler. "Finding it more difficult than toting around AK-47s and karate chopping bad guys."

"I don't use an AK-47. It's a Beretta."

"Whatever. So, were you able to find any information?"

"It's been difficult since I had to assume a geek identity, work at the library during the day, and answer this damn phone at night. The hotline is popular, but not for real research questions. There were a lot of hang-ups, a guy asked me what I was wearing, a few questions from drunks, and a teenager who tried to do a prank call. For the record, he won't do that again, and his bed wetting has reoccurred."

"Is this your way of saying you haven't found anything?" Skylar asked.

Mike rested his elbows on the desk. Either his sister was too stupid or too used to him. "I broke into the Friends of the Library file cabinet. The minutes of their meetings are a real bore."

"You're wasting your time with those," Skylar decided. "No one reads them, but Miss Schultz works very hard on them."

"Well, Miss Schultz is getting a big, fat kiss from me."

"Please, don't. She's the one with lavender hair and a pacemaker. Your kiss will send her over the edge."

Mike ignored her. "After I deciphered her handwriting, I found out that she has recorded everything, from Millie's bunion operation to what the Friends of the Library made at their last bake sale. And, guess what. Her notes about the money don't match the library's records."

Skylar gasped. "So, it's official. Someone *is* embezzling."

"It's probable." He had hoped it was yet another Nancy Drew wannabe moment for Skylar, but he guessed she grew out of that.

"So how are we going to catch the bad guys?" She practically crackled with energy. "Do we get to set a trap?"

Maybe not quite out of the phase. "Now is not the time to

act. You don't want the perp to know you're onto the crime just yet."

"Perp." She squealed with delight. "This is so exciting."

"Calm down," Mike insisted. Skylar's unbridled enthusiasm had caused trouble on more than one occasion. "The paper trail is very thin. If you don't have a plan on how to catch the guy, you'll wind up with nothing."

"Right, right. And I could lose my chance of becoming Head Librarian."

That concern was not on the top of his priority list. "Not to mention offending a lot of people in this town."

"How are you going to narrow down the suspects?" Skylar didn't seem to hear the subtle message. She had a real-life mystery that she could sink her teeth into.

"I've already done it." He rifled through the paperwork and found the list of names. "It's between the treasurer, Owen Lovejoy, IV, or the president, Peyton Lovejoy. No Roman numerals."

"That's because Peyton's a woman," Skylar murmured abstractly. "Damn, both your suspects are Lovejoys."

"Is this a problem?"

"Uh, yeah! They aren't just the most powerful family in town; they are the biggest business in town. No one can afford to offend them," she ended with a wail.

"It doesn't make them above the law." He knew that first hand. Of course, the situations he'd dealt with had to do with feudal rights and bloodshed. This time it had to do with reputations and a couple thousand dollars. The reasons might be different, but it would play out the same with him working for the victorious side.

"Are you kidding me?" Her voice rose. "Their relatives are the mayor, the sheriff, and the judge. Face it, they are the law."

"Skylar, I will take care of it." And this time he wouldn't even break a sweat. It was almost wrong having him against the Lovejoys.

"But—"

"I'm a pro at this, remember. I'll protect you." That was a given. He'd protected all of his sisters from schoolyard bullies, unfair bosses, and questionable men, although a few managed to slip by his guard. But he'd take a punch and throw a few if it meant keeping his sisters safe. Come to think of it, though, most of his scars and broken bones were because of his sisters . . .

"Thanks, Mike," Skylar whispered as her voice hitched with emotion. "I'm glad you're here."

Oh, great. Here came the mushy stuff. Hadn't he suffered enough? "Yeah, yeah, yeah. Tell me when you cook breakfast tomorrow."

"Again?" The snuffling vanished in an instant. "What's wrong with cereal and milk? Don't they feed you at the four corners of the earth?"

"Yeah, and they pay me, too." He wouldn't mention that in his last assignment he wound up in a crudely made hole for a prison with the occasional rotten fruit dropped down to him. That would go under the heading of Too Much Information. His sister didn't need to know about that side of his life, and he wanted to push it out of his memory. "Just because you're my sister doesn't mean you're getting freebies. You are paying me with home-cooked meals."

"Okay, fine. I'm going to bed now so I can get up bright and early to slave over a hot stove for you. Don't forget to forward the calls to your cell phone."

Mike growled. "The Answer Hotline was a stupid idea."

"How else was I going to explain your presence in the library after hours?" his sister asked. "It's a brilliant idea and you know it."

Right. Brilliant. Let's just see how brilliant when she took over the hotline. "Skylar, an old lady woke me up at four-thirty this morning to find out the weather."

Skylar coughed back a laugh. "You didn't hang up on her, did you?"

"I turned on the TV and got it off the morning news."

She chuckled. "That was sweet of you. I think you've missed your true calling."

He glared at the phone. "Don't mess with me. Night, Skylar." He disconnected the call before she called him sweet again.

Mike reviewed the paperwork until he was satisfied that it was a case of embezzling. He replaced the file folder and re-locked the cabinet, making everything look untouched. He turned off the library lights and walked down the green marble staircase that graced the main entrance. Mike let out a huge yawn and stretched his arms just as his cell phone rang.

"I'm going to kill my sister," he muttered as he grabbed the cell phone with one hand and checked his watch. Who was calling him this late? Don't these farmers go to sleep at sundown?

"Main Library's Answer Hotline," he answered tersely, wondering why they called it the main library when there were no others in the area. "This is Mike. How can I help you?"

"Hi, Mike," his most frequent mystery caller said. She sounded different. Relaxed. Slurred. "What's in a Jell–O shot?"

"Jell–O."

She laughed. The sound flashed through him like moonlight streaking through shadows. "And?"

"Vodka."

"Oh." His answer seemed to change everything. "As a rule, I don't eat or drink anything blue, but these cubes were so cute."

Concern niggled him. "How many have you had?"

"I don't know. Is that important?"

"It could be in the morning." He knew he was getting a call tomorrow on hangover remedies. She wouldn't enjoy any on his list.

Mike flinched away from the phone as throbbing music filtered the airwaves.

"Hey, Peyton, you're missing it!" a woman yelled in the background. "Macey's riding the cowboy!"

Mike's eyebrows shot up. Peyton? He listened intently.

The woman hastily covered her hand over the mouth-piece. "I'll be right there."

"Okay. Do you know you're in the wrong bathroom?" The background voice was muffled. Mike wondered if he was hearing it correctly.

"Business call."

Was he talking to Peyton Lovejoy? Mike rolled his eyes over the question. How many Peytons could there be?

"Thanks for the information, Mike. Good night." She hurriedly clicked off.

And it all suddenly made sense. Lovejoy's Unmention-ables' financial troubles. Peyton's secret double life. By day, she was a prim businesswoman. At night, she frequented the sex spots. Even in a small Midwestern town, that kind of life needed extra cash.

Mike clicked off his phone and shoved it in his pocket as he felt the call of the hunt surging through him. Peyton Lovejoy had just been promoted to his prime suspect.

She wouldn't know what hit her, but he was taking her down.

Two

Peyton whimpered as the afternoon sun glared accusingly on her face. She parked her sedan in the library's parking lot and flopped back on the seat. She hissed as incandescent stars of pain shattered violently across her skull.

Despite the air conditioner blasting cold air, it was still hot and muggy in her car. But she didn't have the energy to escape. She pushed her sunglasses higher onto her nose with clumsy hands. "I don't want to be here," she grumbled as she massaged her aching forehead.

The fact that she didn't have to be there seemed to make her hangover pulse with renewed energy. She could have stayed in bed and fended off the fatal hangover. No one would complain if she didn't show up for the Friends of the Library meeting. Owen could easily cover for her.

But it would take only one slip of her disciplined schedule to start an avalanche of chaos. She knew it would be all too easy for her to get someone to cover the next time, and the next. The old-timers in town had the uncanny ability of putting together two unrelated, unimportant events and discovering the truth. They would figure out in no time that the Lovejoy heiress didn't have a handle on the sinking business.

Despite her impressive resume, they would see she wasn't a natural leader.

She had to prove otherwise, and there was no time like the present. Peyton took a shaky breath. Her stomach churned in protest as she cautiously opened the door. The dinging bell made her wince as the summer heat rippled into the car. She glared at the keys still in the ignition and yanked them out, the hot metal searing her hand. Peyton quickly dropped the key ring into her purse and cautiously dipped her foot onto the hot pavement.

Almost there . . .

The seat belt jerked her back into her seat. Peyton gasped as the pain invaded her head and zoomed down. Her skin went from hot to clammy as her rebellious stomach threatened to heave.

It's going to be one of those days. Peyton concentrated on her shallow breathing. She wouldn't humiliate herself by retching in front of the library. She absolutely refused.

"Come on, Peyton." Shadows hovered over her open door. "You're going to be late."

Peyton slowly turned her head and peered through her sunglasses. Her cousin Owen and his wife, Samantha, hunched over the open car door.

The couple's perfect appearance made Peyton feel scummier. Owen belonged in those clothing catalogs that showed models on weekend jaunts to the country house. His boyish good looks didn't have a crease or wrinkle yet, just like his perfectly pressed chinos and designer yellow shirt.

As always, Samantha's appearance complemented Owen. Her long blond hair was pulled back in a sunshine yellow headband that matched the floral dress. She wasn't even breaking a sweat, though she wore opaque tights and closed-toe heels in the sweltering heat.

They're not normal, Peyton reminded herself. *Don't let it get to you.*

"Go on without me," she answered faintly. "I'll be right

there." She unsnapped her seat belt to give credence to her claim.

"Yeah, right." Owen didn't buy it for a second. He reached into the car and grasped her upper arm. Peyton reluctantly accepted her cousin's assistance and stumbled out of the car. "What's wrong with you?" he asked. "You look sick."

"Peyton, you shouldn't be driving if you're unwell," Samantha said. She reached forward and pressed her hand on Peyton's forehead. "You don't have a fever, but you do look pale."

"I'll be okay." She leaned on Owen for support and kicked her car door shut. "I'm not sick. The drinks at Jack's turned out to be stronger than I expected."

Samantha arched her delicate eyebrows. "You went to the male strip joint? What's it like?"

"Good Lord, Samantha!" Owen glared at his wife. "Peyton was too busy working on a deal to pay attention to her surroundings."

A vision of Bubba Joe's gyrating leopard G-string popped into Peyton's mind. A montage of sweat-slicked skin and tight muscles flickered before her eyes like an art film. Was there any business discussed last night?

"Of course." Samantha tucked her chin down and fiddled with the strap of her purse. "I'm sorry."

Owen sighed irritably. "Why don't you go on ahead? There's a lot of research you need to do for my speech to the Historical Society tomorrow."

"You're right." Samantha stepped back, her eyes downcast. " 'Bye, Peyton. I hope you feel better."

"Thanks. I'll call you later." She watched Samantha cut across the lawn before disappearing into the library. "She was only asking, Owen."

"I don't want her getting any ideas," he muttered. "One of these days I'll have that place closed down, along with that disgusting sex shop. They're trying to make a profit by turning our good women into sex addicts."

Peyton rolled her eyes behind her sunglasses. There were so many things in his statement that she would like to argue. Just not right now. Maybe when her head didn't feel as though it was going to shoot off.

Owen tugged her elbow and started walking toward the library. "Tell me how the meeting went."

Peyton decided to be nice and present the censored version. "Macey and her group are trying to kill me."

Owen laughed. "They can't be that bad."

Peyton didn't answer. They were that bad. How many women were physically removed from a strip joint? The owner of Jack's had blacklisted her. She, Peyton Lovejoy, head of the welcome committee at the country club, was forbidden to step into a male strip joint. She didn't think she could withstand the embarrassment. She knew Owen wouldn't handle the news well. Macey was anything but mortified. It was a badge of honor to her.

Her head pounded fiercely. "I'm ready to go back to bed."

"Don't worry. This meeting will be over fast. There's not much to talk about."

The meeting was just one item on her to-do list. She had piles of reports to go through at work, not to mention return a bazillion e-mails. And she had to do it all before going out with Macey again tonight.

"Peyton! Peyton Lovejoy!"

Uh-oh. That didn't sound like a breezy welcome. More like an I've-been-waiting-for-you kind of greeting a mother gives way past curfew.

"Save me," Peyton said under her breath. She saw Skylar Black walk out of the old stone and brick library building and approach her. There was a no-nonsense look about the acting head librarian. Maybe it was the brown hair pulled back into a tight French braid. Or maybe it was her tailored white shirt and pencil-slim brown skirt. It could be the dark eyes lasering in on her from behind the chic glasses. Whatever it was, the woman looked as if she was on a mission.

"Hi, Skylar. How are you doing?" Peyton managed a smile, although her face was going to crackle from the movement. She hoped the librarian wasn't going to make her day worse.

"Pretty good, thanks." The woman propped her fists on her hips. "I was hoping I could talk to you after the meeting." Skylar slid a look to Owen before pinning Peyton down with intent eyes.

"Sure. I'll search you out when the meeting is over." Just add another thing on her to-do list. At least it wasn't incredibly bad news.

"Skylar, you're needed at the main desk."

Peyton's body jerked to attention. That voice! The guy from the library's answer hotline was here! The rough, masculine sound tugged some invisible chord deep inside her, twanging the muscles low in her abdomen. Her nonexistent chest felt full and heavy. Damn, even the backs of her knees tingled.

Who knew his voice could pack such a punch? He barely even used it. Had she been missing out because she hadn't heard it up close and personal?

Up close! Peyton's eyes widened as she realized what that meant. No, no, no. She didn't want to see him and allow her fantasies to take on a disturbing, twisted reality. When she spoke to him on the phone, she forgot about him being a librarian whose nightlife consisted of answering trivia questions. What if Mike turned out to be a gnarled old man? Ick. Wait . . . What if he was gorgeous and she met him while she was still hung over? That's even worse! Oh, please don't let it be Mike.

Skylar glanced over her shoulder. "I'll be right there, Mike."

Mike. Of course it had to be Mike. Peyton swallowed heavily. *Okay, you know you're dying of curiosity. Just look. So what if all your fantasies about him die a sudden and painful death? It has to happen some time.* She looked up with feigned casualness and hoped her sunglasses hid most of her face. Her heart stuttered as she saw the man leaning against the main door.

The first thing she noticed was the long, tapered body that held a tang of raw masculinity. The snowy white T-shirt contrasted against his tanned, weathered skin. His jeans were faded to a pale indigo and clung to his lean, powerful thighs.

There was nothing elegant about him, but Peyton knew she was looking at the perfect specimen of a male in his prime. His muscles were sleek and compact. She sensed that despite his impressive height, he moved with stealth.

Without thinking, Peyton slid her sunglasses down the slope of her nose and greedily searched his face. His black, thick hair was cut close to his skull. His cheekbones were aggressive slashes set high in the primitive, angular face. Mike's alert, deep-set eyes missed nothing and swiftly snagged her gaze.

Peyton's blood tingled and zigzagged to her pulse points as she stared into his dark brown eyes. She couldn't look away. His eyes seemed to get darker. She felt as if she was falling into something deep and sensuous.

Oooh . . . Peyton swiped her lips with her tongue. *Let me dive right in.*

Peyton blinked. She blinked again and gave a small shake of her head, shoving her glasses firmly on the bridge of her nose. She couldn't believe she'd just thought that. Her chest tightened, wondering if she'd actually said it aloud. She quickly glanced at Skylar and Owen. No dropped jaws. No bugged-eye look. Whew. That was a close one. She'd been hanging around Macey too much.

"Oh, but before I do." Skylar waved Mike over. "I want you to meet Peyton and Owen." A look passed between the librarians. Peyton couldn't decipher the undercurrents. She didn't have time to dwell on it as she watched the man walk toward her with a lethal grace.

Peyton had the sudden need to run. Hard and fast, just as her pulse was doing that very moment. She didn't understand it. One minute she wanted to jump into him; the next she needed to escape.

What's up with that? Peyton wondered as her skin stung with awareness. *Awareness? Nah, more like sunburn. Heat stroke. Yeah, that's it.* What else did she expect as they chit-chatted under the blazing sun?

"Peyton, this is Mike Ryder, the newest member of our staff," Skylar said. "Mike, this is Peyton Lovejoy, the president of our Friends of the Library group."

Peyton hesitated before offering her hand. She knew she should have obeyed her first instinct the moment Mike grasped her fingers. His dark, callused hand swallowed hers, scratching her soft skin. Her wrist twitched, warding off the potent energy coiling around their joined hands.

She felt contained. Claimed. Peyton's forehead creased with a frown. It didn't make sense. It was just a handshake. One that had gone on for too long.

"Hello," she croaked out, looking in the vicinity of his shoulder and hoping her sunglasses hid the fact. "Nice to meet you." She discreetly tugged for freedom, but Mike continued to grasp her nerveless fingers. She zoomed in on his face. Her breath hitched in her throat.

Handsome didn't describe Mike Ryder. His face was too hard and had too many rough edges. Whiskers dusted the aggressive line of his jaw. Deep grooves bracketed his unsmiling lips. Tiny scars whitened by time marred his skin.

A tremor swept through Peyton. This guy had lived life. Hard. She looked into his eyes. The murky brown fascinated her. She wondered what he was hiding.

"And this is the treasurer of the group, Owen Lovejoy," Skylar continued. Peyton barely heard her.

"The fourth," Owen inserted.

Mike let go of her hand, his fingertips dragging against the center of her palm. Her nerve endings erupted with wild sensations. By the time he turned his attention to her cousin, Peyton felt like buckling with relief.

"Lovejoy." Mike gave him a firm handshake. He flicked a cursory look at her cousin, but Peyton sensed Mike didn't miss a thing.

"Ryder." Owen immediately removed his hand from Mike's and turned to Peyton. "We don't want to be late for the meeting." He gave a brief nod to the librarians. "If you will excuse us."

Peyton silently allowed Owen to escort her away. Later she would admonish him for his curt behavior. Right now she wanted to get away and regain her composure.

She walked up the stone steps and shakily ripped off her sunglasses before entering the shadowy recesses of the library. She exhaled, knowing that whenever she crossed the threshold, she would be shrouded with a sense of peace.

The cool air swept her heated skin as her eyes adjusted to the dark main entrance. She inhaled sharply, accepting the familiar scent of heritage and tradition. But this time she felt no peace. She was jittery and ready to burst through her skin. Heritage was as fragile as brittle paper. The tradition felt more like stagnant air.

Peyton rubbed the goose bumps on her bare arms. What was wrong with her? She usually looked forward to her trips to the library. It had been her refuge as a child, her hangout as a teenager.

But, then again, she'd never shown up with a hangover, Peyton thought as Owen maneuvered her toward the meeting room. Nor had she seen sex personified on the doorstep of the library before. That combination would steal anyone's peace.

The fine hair on her nape prickled. She had no doubt Mike had entered the library. Peyton fought the inexplicable need to look over her shoulder. She lost the battle and took a peek.

Mike was watching her.

She gulped and drew in another ragged breath. The slumberous dark eyes were murder on her refined poise. He closed the door behind Skylar, who talked to him in a hushed, urgent tone. His stark face showed no emotion, but his eyes gleamed. With interest? With knowledge?

He knows! Her stomach did several fierce loop-de-loops before freefalling as her intuition blared it across her aching mind like a neon light. *He knows!*

He knew she'd been calling him. She swerved her head back and stared at the floor in front of her. Her wide eyes burned like her popped neck. *Open the floor and swallow me whole.*

Stop panicking and start thinking! She bit the inside of her mouth. She wanted to pace. Instead she walked to the battered wooden table in the meeting room with her knees feeling as though they'd caved in.

Okay . . . okay . . . how could she explain her questions? Peyton's mind whirled as she absently put down her purse. Why was she so upset? Her questions weren't all that bad. They were undoubtedly bland and forgettable. She quickly reviewed her past phone calls, but her hopes dashed as she remembered every damning conversation. Oh, sheesh! She felt the sweep of crimson mottling her face.

"Peyton, are you going to be sick?" Owen took a prudent step back. "Because if you are, give me some warning."

"I'm fine," she rasped. She cleared her throat with a cough. "I'm fine." No good. The panic had seriously attacked her vocal cords. She looked around. "I need water."

"Hurry up." He made a show of checking his watch, probably just to use his new favorite toy. "You know how Miss Schultz gets if the meeting starts late."

"They can't start without me," she muttered irritably. "I'm the president."

Owen's lips pressed into a tight line. "That you are."

Peyton winced. "I'm sorry." She was careful not to mention her title with him, especially when she found out after the election that he'd wanted to be nominated for the position. "I don't mean to be so grouchy."

"Tying one on will do that," he said in a slightly raised voice.

"Ssh!" Peyton hissed, warning him with a glare. "I'll be right back." She looked around the meeting room, hoping none of the gossipmongers had heard. Deciding it was safe, Peyton quickly walked to the old-fashioned drinking fountain under the marble staircase.

You have to get a grip, she told herself as the icy cold water hit her lips. Her head pounded and she tried to ignore it. How was she going to handle this? She needed to be cool. Calm. Collected. After all, she was going to see this guy a lot. Why hadn't she thought of this before?

But she had. She wiped her lips with the back of her hand. She never gave her name when she called. She shouldn't be freaking.

Unless he recognized her voice.

She considered the possibility and wondered if she could pretend to have laryngitis every time she was in the building. Nah, there was no need. Her voice was unremarkable and so unlike a phone-sex operator's.

She needed a plan. She had to find out if (a) he knew, (b) he planned on doing something about it, and (c) how many people he had already told.

Every muscle froze as her mind turned over the possibility. The phone calls didn't exactly fall under privileged information. How long had he known Peyton was calling him asking explicit questions, and how many people knew about it?

That was the root of her anxiety. Dread mushroomed inside her chest. It wasn't the fact that she called the hotline with questions about sex and the wild life. It was that she *had* to call. She didn't want people to know that she was socially stupid and sexually slow.

Hi, my name is Peyton Lovejoy and I'm a nerd. A boring

one at that. Too bad there wasn't a 12-step program to change her into a scintillating wanton. It wouldn't help matters now. She eyed the drinking fountain and wondered at the chance of holding her head under the light stream and drowning herself.

Death by drinking fountain wouldn't look good in her obituary. Knowing her luck, the old-timers would think she was despondent from being blacklisted at Jack's, and that would be splashed over the headlines. Future genealogists would wonder why their boring ancestors couldn't die with dignity and style.

Wait a minute . . . Peyton's eyebrows perked up as her sluggish mind latched on to a fragment of her thoughts. Hold everything. . . . The corner of her mouth tugged up into a smile. A wicked woman would handle this with style. But what would she do exactly?

She needed to act scandalous. Sure, she reserved that masquerade for Macey and her associates, but what if she acted like one now? Peyton rubbed her hands and paced the floor under the staircase. It might actually work. Mike wouldn't be expecting it. She could easily get her answers using the element of surprise. The hard part would be acting wicked.

Could she act like a natural to the very guy who was giving her practical tips? In front of people who'd known her when all she wore were diapers? She cringed at the thought. That might be the clincher. She impulsively peered around the staircase and scoped out the lobby.

Mike was behind the main desk helping a girl with dark red braids. He ran the scanner over the entire backlist of Sweet Valley High books, assuring the young patron that they counted for the summer reading program.

Peyton looked around and listened. Most of the indistinct voices she heard were from the meeting room. There was no line behind the girl. Now was her chance to act like a woman with a lust for life but a secret allergy to audiences.

Her heart tripped a beat as she stepped out of her hiding

place. *It's okay,* she told herself. *No big deal.* She was only staunching any potential problems with her reputation. She dealt with worse situations in corporate boardrooms. Peyton tossed back her shoulders and strode past the staircase. It didn't matter if her business acumen was put to the test in those kinds of meetings. A test was a test.

She tilted her chin up as she made a determined line to the main desk. What if he did recognize her, but didn't care? Her foot shuffled against the floor. Then she'd feel like a fool. What if he insisted on letting her know in a subtle way? A nudge, nudge, wink, wink. The possibility spurred her on.

He didn't seem the type to be subtle. She wasn't sure what type he was. Peyton hadn't met anyone like Mike Ryder. And that put her at a disadvantage, since she knew he'd dealt with hundreds of women exactly like her.

Suddenly she stood in front of him. Peyton's mouth went dry as their eyes clashed. Her lips parted, but no sound came out. She had the oddest feeling of being stripped. Left vulnerable. She was grateful for the desk between them.

"Can I help you?"

"Uh, yes." Her mind went blank at his deep, seductive voice. "Do you have a . . . pencil I could use?" *A pencil? Oh, yeah. That was real smooth, Lovejoy.* She wanted to smack her forehead. A wicked woman could come up with something better. A cigarette. A vibrator. Anything but a pencil!

"Yep. Here you are." He retrieved one from a jar next to the computer monitor. "And before you leave . . ." he casually placed the pencil on a glossy brochure and slid it across the countertop to her clenched hand. Peyton looked down. The Answer Hotline screamed in bold red print right before her eyes.

Her next breath lodged in her chest. Her lungs shriveled as her heart hammered against her ribs. A buzzing sound filled her ears.

So that was the way it was going to be. Peyton slowly released the breath that began to hurt her breastbone. He was going to torment her with sly reminders. She wasn't surprised. Just disappointed.

"What's this for?" Her voice came out high like she'd been sucking a helium balloon. She couldn't bring herself to touch the incriminating brochure or the pencil.

"We're handing them out to all the patrons." He rested his forearms on the desk. "It's information about the library services."

"Oh." And . . . ? Peyton waited for him to unveil his knowledge. She couldn't look into his face. She focused on his arms. They were sinewy and bronzed from the sun. Why did she assume male librarians were pale and lacked muscle tone?

"Our newest one is the Answer Hotline." Mike reached over and pushed the paper closer to her. "Did you know we offer it?"

Was this a trick question? If her nerves weren't already tied in a knot, they were about to spring wildly now. "Yes-s-s."

"Right. Of course you do."

What did he mean by that? Peyton jerked her chin up and stared at him with wild eyes. His look gave nothing away. She waited for him to continue, her stomach twisting with dismay.

"Since you're with the Friends of the Library and all."

The twisting stopped. Was that it? Her brain immediately diagrammed the statement, looking for any possible innuendos. "Uh-huh," Peyton answered weakly.

A bony finger tapped her shoulder. Peyton yelped and jumped back.

"Ssh," Mike said as he straightened away from the desk. "You're in a library."

Peyton mumbled incoherent apologies and turned. She looked down at Miss Schultz. The lavender hair seemed particularly blinding today. Her wrinkled face held the same stern expression she'd used during her schoolteacher days.

"Peyton Lovejoy, where have you been? The meeting was

supposed to start three minutes ago." She tapped the miniscule watch on her wrist. "I cannot abide tardiness."

"Yes, ma'am," Peyton said as she stepped toward the
meeting room. She snuck one last look at Mike, but his back
was turned as he shelved the hold items.

If he knew she was the one calling the hotline with risqué
questions, he'd had ample opportunity to say something. But
apart from the professional courtesy . . . nothing. The indifference nettled her, but it was for the best. Because if he eventually figured it out, she'd have to think of something.
Something better than borrowing a pencil.

Mike waited until he heard the door shut. Only when he
knew Peyton was in the next room did his tension ease. He
stared at the book in his hand and slowly unclenched his
teeth.

Being a gentleman sucked.

His willpower was pushed to the limit with Peyton Lovejoy.
Were his reflexes blurring from lack of use? Or was it something more sinister?

Sinister? He snorted at the possibility. Peyton could never
be considered an archenemy. Although she definitely had
some diabolical features.

She had no idea how luscious she looked wearing a slip of
a sundress and not much else. The mint green color and delicate straps did little to cool the lust roaring through his veins.
He'd already figured out the quickest way of ripping the
dress off her slight, womanly curves and placing his mark on
her ivory skin.

He wanted to free her hair from the uptight braid. Mike
closed his eyes, knowing how it would feel to have his hot
flesh swept by her thick, brown hair. And to be taken by her
small, pink mouth.

Preferably right here, right now, on top of the main desk.
Her shrieks of ecstasy puncturing the silence would be a nice
touch.

Mike knew he should be appalled by his thoughts. And once he managed to walk without hurting himself, he might feel guilty. But he had pressing issues other than the one between his legs. Like why did her light perfume hit him with the impact of a killer left hook? He also wanted to know why the darkness attacking his soul retreated for one blessed moment when he saw her. And why, when he looked into her light brown eyes, did he feel a sense of homecoming?

"Psst." Skylar crept up to the main desk on exaggerated tiptoes. "Are you still mad at me?"

"Yes." With a conscious effort, Mike resumed shelving the hold items. He had no idea if he was cataloging them correctly. Not that he cared.

He needed to train his sister with a few basic rules. When he saw Skylar rush outside earlier, Mike intuitively knew she was going to screw up their work. It was too bad he couldn't lock his sister in her office. Knowing his luck, she would chew her way out and blab their plans to the first passerby. She was the type of rookie that you didn't want as a partner. The kind who disregarded commands like "stay here" and "keep your mouth shut".

"I was only trying to move things along," Skylar said without a trace of remorse. She walked around the desk and prodded his shoulder with hers. "I saw you talking to Peyton," she whispered.

"Uh-huh." He glanced in the direction of the meeting room and saw Peyton through the glass window of the closed door. She stood in front of her audience, appearing to be in her element. Her shoulders were thrown back, her chin tilted high.

But on closer inspection, Mike noticed how her brow crinkled. For a moment, she looked bewildered. Yet her stance was that of authority.

He almost missed the gesture of Owen writing something on his piece of paper and tapping it until Peyton looked down. Peyton blinked, looked up, and radiated with confidence.

"Yoo-hoo, Mike." Skylar snapped her fingers and then waved her hand in front of his face. "Earth to Mike."

"What?"

She exhaled impatiently. "Did you get anything from talking to Peyton?"

Yeah, a raging hard-on, but that went under the heading of Too Much Information. "No."

Skylar clucked her tongue. "Nothing at all?"

Mike ignored the comment but turned to his sister. "What are the chances of Peyton and Owen being in it together?" He tilted his head at the direction of the meeting room.

Skylar studied the cousins and gave the question serious consideration. "A good chance," she finally said. "Owen and Peyton are always together."

"Best friends?"

"Hmm." Skylar wrinkled her nose and shook her head when the term didn't fit. "Peyton might see Owen as a confidant, especially since he is the eldest cousin."

"Owen is older than Peyton? Why didn't he inherit the company?" From what he gathered about this cornfield town, they had very traditional, often backward, ideas. Having a young woman picked over an older male relative seemed strange by their way of thinking.

Skylar crossed her arms. "Official word is that he didn't want it."

Mike raised an eyebrow. Bull. He already had Owen Lovejoy the friggin' fourth pegged. The guy wanted it so much he could taste it. "And the rumor is?"

She looked around before leaning closer. "He wasn't offered the position," she answered softly without moving her lips.

"Why?" Mike considered a list of possibilities. Shady past? Excessively low IQ?

"He doesn't understand the needs of a woman." She pressed her lips together and nodded knowingly.

Mike narrowed his eyes. "Say what?"

"Take that anyway you want to"—Skylar held up her hand—"but I've seen his wife, and that woman ain't getting any."

"Skylar!" He couldn't believe he was having this conversation. With his little sister, of all people.

"Or she ain't getting done right."

He winced. "Thanks for the image that I hope to one day purge from my mind." He rubbed his eyes with the heels of his hands. "I think now would be a good time to explain two important terms for any investigation: Need To Know and Too Much Information."

"Oh, wait!" Skylar scurried around the main desk and headed for her office. "Let me get my notepad." She skidded to a stop. "Should I be writing this in code?"

Mike dragged his fingers down his cheeks. It was going to be a long vacation.

Three

"The library is now closed." And not a moment too soon, Mike decided as he turned off the antiquated intercom. If he talked to one more snotty kid or scatterbrained adult, the library would deal with more crimes than embezzling.

He flipped the lock to the front door. Standing in the doorway, Mike lifted his face to the sun still blazing in the evening sky. He took a deep breath and indulged in the pure summer air.

He heard a door creak behind him. "Okay, no one's lurking in the bathrooms," Skylar said.

Mike turned around. "Has that ever been a problem?" He couldn't imagine anyone wanting to stay in this mausoleum when there were wide-open spaces just outside.

"You'd be surprised what happens in this library," Skylar said as she leaned against the main desk. "The stories I could tell would scorch your eyebrows."

"I don't want to know." He studied his sister closely. The energy she'd shown earlier in the day was absent. "You look tired."

"I'm okay." She shrugged. "I have a lot of paperwork to catch up on. The last head librarian let a lot of things slide."

Mike grimaced. Paperwork. There was nothing he hated

worse. It must have something to do with all the instructions and deadlines. Which was why it came as a shock when he heard himself say, "I'll help you with it."

Skylar's eyes brightened. "You don't have to," she said cautiously.

And he didn't want to, but the head librarian job was very important to Skylar for some godforsaken reason. He would make sure she met every challenge to get the position. "Go lie down on the couch and take a nap. I'll close up here and get some food."

Skylar was already shaking her head. "No, I don't have time."

"We're going to spend hours doing paperwork," Mike pointed out, ignoring the dread eating away at his bones. "You need some rest or you're going to make mistakes."

She thought about it for less than a second. "Okay, a nap is probably a good idea." Skylar moved toward the employee lounge. "But don't let me sleep for too long."

"Not a problem." He grabbed a cart of children's books.

"And we still need to map our strategy for Operation Marple," she said before a giant yawn claimed her.

Mike froze. He willed his face to show no reaction. "Operation *what?*"

"Marple." Skylar stretched her arms above her head and yawned again. "As in Miss Marple. You know, Agatha Christie. You do read on occasion, don't you?"

Mike pinched the bridge of his nose. "You gave a name to . . ." He wasn't even sure what to call it.

"Every operation needs a name," Skylar insisted. "Oh, and we have code names. Yours is Watson."

"Watson?" Hey, wasn't he the assistant?

Skylar frowned. "That doesn't grab you? Would you prefer Sneaky Pie?"

He wondered if they were too old for him to dangle her headfirst above the toilet. It had been so effective in the past. "Go." Mike pointed to the lounge door. "Now."

"I'm going, I'm going." She disappeared behind the staircase. "Cranky."

Cranky. Yeah, he was cranky all right, Mike decided as he headed to the children's section. He had every reason. One minute he was driving an armored car chased by rebels. Now he pushed a cart of Dr. Seuss books. His colleagues knew him as Viper. His sister gave him the name Sneaky Pie.

Mike shuddered. How he'd survived a home with all his sisters was nothing short of amazing. It was no wonder he sought out the kind of job as a corporate trouble shooter. A job where men could be men.

He'd found the life of adventure he wanted. Images of his last mission whooshed through his mind before he could blink them away. The ominous shadows inside him threatened to bleed into his soul. He resolutely pushed them back. Maybe he got a little too much action. Now he wasn't sure what he craved.

An image of Peyton Lovejoy popped into his mind, but it wasn't how he remembered seeing her in the afternoon. Her silky brown hair fanned around her eager face. She lay naked on the main desk like a pinup girl. Her pert breasts made for suckling. Her hands reaching desperately for him, her body open and. . . .

Mike ground his back teeth as every one of his senses came alive. He knew exactly how it would feel to sink his cock into her softness. To be trapped in her wet heat as she climaxed violently, chanting his name.

That was a different kind of craving, he reminded himself as he savagely shoved the cart over the gaudy carpet. A craving that wouldn't be fulfilled. He had better sense than that.

Mike strode through the children's section and checked all the aisles. Since the section was right off of the lobby, he knew no one was still there. It was mind-boggling how much noise could come out of someone so small. He wasn't sure if he could handle being around all those kids. And the kids weren't too sure about him, either. If they didn't burst out crying from the sight of him, they would peek around the corner and study him solemnly. As solemnly as one could when sucking a thumb.

Deciding no ankle biters were left behind, Mike took the staircase two steps at a time. The second floor was silent. He checked through the reference section and returned the newspapers to the racks before he walked by each aisle in the fiction area.

The closing routine was a complete waste of time, Mike thought as he continued to the nonfiction section. Next time he'd just take care of the money and lock the door. Why did librarians think people wanted to stay here after hours? No one in his right mind. . . .

He stopped abruptly when he saw someone in the 300–400 aisle. Okay, he was wrong. There were people in this town that preferred the dusty crypt to tractor pulls and summer reruns on TV. Mike almost called out the closing announcement when he realized it was Peyton Lovejoy.

Mike's body clenched, ready to pounce. His instincts roared to make this woman his. *Don't even think about it.* His reaction was unsettling. He was never like this about women. Never.

What was it about this woman? Mike considered the question. She was perched on a metal stepping stool, her purse and laptop computer on the floor next to her. She wore delicate white sandals. The mint green sundress stretched tight across her legs and sweet ass. Her back was turned to him, bare and curved. He ached to outline each vertebra with the tip of his tongue.

Control. Stay in control. He focused on her hair caught in an uptight braid. When he was younger, he thought the only tempting thing about braids was pulling them.

Mike stared at her brown hair as he harnessed his rapidly growing need. Her hair looked thick and heavy. Silky soft. Luscious and probably fragrant with wildflowers. He frowned. Had braids changed in the past few years or was it just his tastes that had altered?

He felt the need to grab her braid, but it wasn't for a playful tug. Something much more possessive. His blood surged through his veins, demanding he stake out his territory.

Mike cleared his throat to alert Peyton before he did something stupid. She didn't look up from her book. He slowly walked to her, fighting back the call of the hunt. When he towered over her, Mike plucked the braid at the rubber band and pulled it gently. He thought that was very mannerly when he really wanted to wrap the braid around his hand until his palm cradled the back of her head. And then see how imaginative she could be in getting away.

Peyton looked up with a start, her brown eyes wide. The movement caused her braid to pull against his grasp. Realizing he was ready to give in to his wants, Mike let go of her rubber band. He stepped back and watched her eyes shut as a pink tide washed her face.

"The library is closed," he said gruffly. His voice ricocheted off the walls of the empty library. He didn't need the reminder of how alone they were.

"Sorry." She ducked her head. "I didn't hear the announcement."

How could she miss three announcements in a half hour? She must have some absorbing reading material. Mike glanced down at the book in her hand.

The Ultimate Slut Workbook.

Whoa! Excuse me? He gritted his teeth before he said anything. And step-by-step pictures, too. His teeth were definitely going to shatter. Every inch of skin tightened as it held back all of his red-blooded male impulses.

Peyton snapped the book shut. "I don't need an escort," she muttered prissily. She looked down and realized the back cover had a full frontal picture of the Kama Sutra position known as Dragons Facing the Mountain. She hastily flipped the book to the front, which depicted a barely dressed woman. The audacious title fit neatly between her widespread legs.

214 / *Susanna Carr*

Mike took the book from Peyton's unyielding hands. He knew he should play the librarian role and not mention her reading material. Anything less meant a speedy complaint landing on Skylar's overwhelmed desk.

He should shelf the book by the correct Dewey decimal system and leave in an orderly manner. If he didn't, he might not be able to pull back his shaky control. He didn't want to know the consequences of that.

More importantly, he should step back into the shadows so he could catch her embezzling. Making a mistake on whatever he was doing—and it sure as hell wasn't called Operation Marple—would be disastrous.

Yeah, he should do all those things, but when was the last time he had done what he was supposed to do?

Mike turned the book in his hand, wondering what the library was doing with it in its catalog. He silently studied the lovers as he inhaled Peyton's scent. The daring picture didn't do anything for him, but when his imagination superimposed Peyton and him in the embrace, his cock hardened fiercely.

"So you don't need an escort," Mike said softly. He looked up, his eyes advertising the ferocious interest he had in her. He didn't want to keep up with the gentlemanly pretense. Not while she gobbled him up with her eyes. "What do you need, Peyton?"

Peyton tensed and cast him a curious look. Like she wasn't sure if he was coming on to her or not. Like she just now realized she should have kept her distance. "I need to leave." She awkwardly rose from the creaking metal stool.

Mike leisurely flipped through the pages. His head jerked at one colored picture. Hmm. He'd heard about that position, but he didn't think it was physically possible. "Do you want to check this book out?"

"No." Her voice sounded strangled. He wondered if she would brazen it or skulk out of the library, never to return. Peyton did neither as she made a sudden grab for the book.

Mike easily slanted it out of her reach, although he

wouldn't mind wrestling her for it. "You sure about that? Why not?" He continued browsing the pages, acting as if it was normal for him to tease her. He didn't indulge in flirting, but it was different with Peyton. He wanted to watch her reaction. Wanted his body to thrum with anticipation.

"I don't need—" She straightened her shoulders and looked at him unflinchingly. Mike noticed she did that when she was unsure about something and trying to hide it. Pretty soon that chin was going to go sky high. "I don't have to."

"Memorized it already?" He held up the book and pointed at a vividly explicit picture. "I personally don't recommend diagram four." Although he might try it again if she was his partner.

Just like clockwork, her chin tipped up. She folded her arms across her chest for good measure. "You shouldn't be talking to me like that."

And you should be running. Why aren't you? "Yeah, why not?"

"It will cost you your job," she announced in a doomsday tone. All that was missing was the thunder and lightning to punctuate her threat.

He nodded. "True, but you know what? There are a lot of things I shouldn't do. Like pulling braids . . ." He thumbed the pages. "Stealing kisses."

He felt her gaze focus on his mouth. His lips tingled, and he knew of only one kind of balm to take away the burn. "No, you shouldn't," she finally said.

Didn't she realize that every "shouldn't" she said made him want to show why he should? She couldn't understand, being someone who craved rules. Or did she? "When was the last time you did something you knew you"—he looked up— "shouldn't?"

Peyton swiped her tongue across her lips. Mike wanted to chase it with his own, right after laving the nervous pulse beating wildly at her throat.

"Like reading this book." He set it on top of an encyclopedia series. The slick book seemed inappropriate with the orderly row of thick, scholarly volumes. Almost irreverent.

Her gaze followed his hand. "I have every right to read that book." Her voice dropped off to a mumble as he stepped closer.

"Like doing what they described," he said softly. Mike kicked the stool out of the way. Neither of them paid attention to the screeching wheels careening down the row.

Her back bumped against the bookshelf. Mike flattened his hand against the solid post. His other hand gripped the shelf next to her elbow. Her scent drove him wild. He knew it flavored her skin, and he wanted to taste every inch. Then go back for seconds.

He leaned closer. His mouth was above her ear. "You know you shouldn't want to do it with someone you barely know," he whispered.

Peyton hunched her shoulders protectively, watching him, fascinated.

"A stranger." His breath stirred the wisps of hair around her ears. Her eyelids drooped. She parted her lips, softly panting with expectation.

He dipped his head lower. His mouth was above hers. "A stranger like me."

Mike withdrew slightly, but it was too late. He was trapped in the coil of desire of his own making. Peyton surged forward and kissed him.

The contact struck him motionless. His muscles tightened as the blood roared through his ears. Raw energy swept through, snagging at the dark shadows, weakening them. He felt pure. Alive. Desperate for more.

Mike roughly curled his tongue along the edges of her mouth. Peyton's lips were soft, naked, and willing. Her voracious kisses matched his.

He leaned into her, greedy for her heat. He was hot, but with a consuming fire. Her heat created something more powerful. Mike wanted a part of that. His hip collided with hers as his cock pressed against her stomach.

Peyton didn't push against him. Later Mike would realize that her guerilla tactic was far more effective than a straight-forward battle. But he couldn't think of anything at that moment other than how she mewled and softened against him, drawing him in.

Mike deepened the kiss, already addicted to the taste of her. She welcomed him into her mouth, gasping with delight as his tongue dominated hers. He wanted to devour her, but he knew she would shatter under the full force of his lust.

She surprised him by sucking his tongue into her mouth. Deep. Any plans of gentleness fled as he felt the pulling sensation straight to his swollen cock. He braced himself, the sensations pushing past the edge of pleasure.

With his shaky hand, he coaxed her jaw for more. He knew it was asking for trouble. One more kiss and he would end it before he overwhelmed Peyton completely.

Her pulse skittered under his hand. It matched his own. He stroked the length of her throat. His fingers tangled with the delicate strap of her sundress.

Mike refrained from snapping the thin rope. He shoved it over her shoulder, promising himself he would stop. His fingers trailed the gentle slope of her breast. The cotton sundress no longer fended him off.

He plucked her hard nipple with his callused fingertips. She gasped as her nipples tightened. Mike cupped her breast. It was soft. Perfect. He squeezed, and her shivers reverberated inside him, answering a deep need. His control collapsed. There was no holding back. He had to find out how perfectly she fit him.

Oh, my God! I am being felt up! The apex of her thighs throbbed, her hangover a distant memory. *Me! Peyton Lovejoy! In the public library!*

Was there a discreet way of shoving her breast into his mouth? Hmm . . . it might be too late for discretion. After all, she was already topless. Well, partially topless. He'd figure out her enthusiasm soon enough.

She shrugged the strap off of her other shoulder, feeling bold. She was ready to tackle Mike like an Amazon warrior. It was also somewhat scary. She had no clue how she'd gotten in this situation. No idea about the rules of conducting public sex.

Peyton removed her hands from the bookshelf and pressed them against Mike's shirt. His heat shimmered through the white cotton. She felt the sculpted muscles of his chest. Smoothing her inquisitive hands over his ribs, she knew the T-shirt had to go.

She leaned into him, yanking at his shirt until it came free from the low-riding waistband of his jeans. Peyton trembled with delight as her hands touched his hot bare skin. He smelled of soap, heat, and man. Lots of man. And all of it for her.

Who knew this happened when you played hooky. She was so thankful she'd followed her impulse to ditch the office and work on her laptop at the library. And she thought that was being naughty! She had no idea.

She threaded her fingers through the crisp hair of his chest. His heat zipped up her arms. Her fingernail caught in a dark whorl and scraped his taut nipple.

With only a guttural groan as her warning, Peyton was back against the bookshelf with a clatter. The volumes behind her slanted and fell with a thud as Mike wrenched the bodice of her dress to her waist.

They looked silently at each other. His eyes were smoky with desire. His face was sharp with need. All she could do was stare at the challenging glint in his eye as her raspy breath echoed around them.

Mike bent down, and Peyton anticipated a sensual onslaught. Instead he swirled his tongue around the pale pink aureole of her breast. He licked her flesh round and round. The circle became smaller. Slowly . . . slowly . . . smaller.

What? Peyton nearly screamed the word as needles of longing pricked her breasts. Now he was going to tease her? She wasn't going to stand for that. She—

The thought evaporated as he covered her nipple with his hot, moist mouth. She grabbed his shoulders and dug into his muscles as the needles of want pierced her skin.

And then he bit down.

A cry ripped from her throat as a blanket of goose bumps covered her skin. He didn't bite hard. Just a nip to feel the edge of his teeth. The edge of him.

She parted her legs as he bunched the hem of her dress above her knees. Peyton needed him so much. Her heart pounded in her ears. Her core clenched the emptiness, ready to sheath his length.

He cupped his hand over her damp heat. She felt achy. Peyton wished he would rip her panties away. She bore down, riding against the heel of his hand. It wasn't enough. Not nearly enough.

Mike rubbed the pad of his thumb over her engorged clit. She shuddered as her legs twitched. He pressed firmly. Her arms lashed out as she grabbed the shelves before she slithered to the floor.

He pushed her legs wider. Peyton gripped the shelves for dear life as his jeans scratched her inner thighs. He grabbed her bottom with his hands and cradled her against his erection. Her dress draped over their intimate juncture.

Mike held one hand at the small of her back. He speared his other hand under the folds of her dress and found her clit again. Tiny convulsions wracked her muscles. Her head flopped back, banging into the crowded shelves, causing a noisy avalanche of books.

For a moment, Peyton felt disoriented. Where was the floor? She decided not to find out and held on to the shelves. She gripped Mike's waist tighter with her legs.

She found anchor by focusing on Mike's face. His was stark with need as his callused hand trailed the softness of her thigh to her waist. His forehead crinkled with a frown as his fingers hooked over the hem of her cotton panties.

Please, please, please, she silently begged. *Don't tease me now. Rip them off. Tear them into shreds.*

The man had no psychic abilities. His frown deepened as his fingertips grazed the silk ribbon and lace embellishment of her underwear. He paused for what seemed like an eternity, rubbing his knuckles against her quivering abdomen.

Mike squeezed his eyes shut. He drew back and gently unhooked her legs from his hips.

"What are you doing?" she asked as he smoothed her dress over her shaky legs.

"That book isn't going to prepare you for the likes of me," he said roughly. He stepped away so he couldn't touch her. Or perhaps so she couldn't touch him.

"Don't flatter yourself," came the instinctive defense. Book? What book? Her breasts stung, her muscles strained for completion, and her nerves screamed for more. Who cared about a book? "What are you talking about?"

"You think this is what you want. A quickie, with a stranger. In public is even better."

"You don't know what I want." The problem was, did she? Other than him, inside her, to the hilt so the pulsing would stop. She didn't have time to wonder about it as she hurriedly pushed her straps up onto her shoulders. The cotton fabric rasped against her sensitive nipples.

"I know you're not ready for dealing with me."

"And who are you?" She scrambled for her purse and laptop. Every move felt ungainly. She wanted to get out of there while she had some dignity. "I thought you were a guy who jumped at any opportunity." It wasn't true. She sensed he wasn't like that, but she wanted to say something that stung.

He rubbed the back of his neck with a tense hand. His

nose flared with annoyance. "I'm trying to act like a gentle-man."

"It doesn't suit you. And gentlemen don't suit me." The moment she uttered those words, she realized it was true. Something had happened here. Whether it was Mike or the illicit moment, the wild woman inside her was unleashed. And she wasn't about to lock her back in. "I'm looking for a man. Someone a little uncivilized. Someone a little wild. Excuse me." She walked away, each step ringing with pur-pose.

"You don't know what you're getting into," he called out.

"No, Mike." Peyton was excessively proud that she con-tinued walking without looking back. "You don't know what you just missed out on."

Four

It was the underwear.

Peyton smacked her hand down on the side of the bath-tub. Scented bubbles spattered her face, and she wiped them away, realizing where she went wrong. Her panties had somehow offended Mike and halted their encounter.

Why couldn't he ignore her clothes? Peyton slid deeper into the tub, sighing as the hot water lapped away the tension in her shoulders. At the very least, he could have ripped them away. Unless they were really a mood killer.

And here she had been wondering why Lovejoy's Unmentionables had so many financial problems. If their customers received the same reaction during lovemaking, it was amazing they'd been in business this long. She needed to have Macey's work more than she realized.

But what was it about her underwear? It was white. It covered what it was supposed to. Hmm . . . Peyton frowned. That could be the problem right there.

There had to be something more. But what? It was cotton with lace and ribbon. The style was feminine. Ladylike. Girly.

Peyton's groan echoed in the bathroom.

So *not* sex-against-the-bookshelf panties.

Her head clunked against the tub. She considered clunking it again. Well, she couldn't correct her mistake. And it wasn't really her fault. The advice was always clean underwear in case of an emergency. Nowhere did it say sexy underwear in case of getting naked in front of a man like Mike Ryder.

Peyton shifted in the large tub. The water swirled around her, but it lost all of its soothing qualities. Her skin felt tight. Her nerve endings buzzed with anticipation. It was as though all her senses were ready to pop out of a cake, but someone super glued the top.

You're not ready for someone like me . . .

Oh, puh-leeze. Peyton rolled her eyes at the memory. She was more than ready. Couldn't he see that? She was eager. Who did he think he was? Passing judgment on her because of her panties.

What would a wild woman wear? Probably nothing at all. Peyton pressed her lips together and shook her head. Uh, no. She knew she wasn't ready for that yet. She could go braless without a problem, but that was a what's-the-point decision since she was one step up from a training bra.

But she had to forgo the usual ribbon and lace. She was a wild woman now. Peyton pumped her fist in an attempt to charge up her spirits. She had to dress wild, inside and out. The clothes made the woman. The underwear made the woman.

Grandmother Lovejoy wouldn't agree. The founder of Lovejoy's Unmentionables had many unyielding beliefs. One became the company's unofficial mission statement: make the customer feel good. Grandmother never equated sex and her product. Function and comfort, definitely. Even quality and possibly beauty. But never, ever sex.

Which was why Peyton didn't have anything remotely sexy in her underwear drawer. Or her closet, for that matter. She might have to improvise. Especially tonight when she took Macey and her gang to the pool hall.

Tendrils of anxiety pulled at her stomach. This would be her first visit to a pool hall. Why did Macey want to go? She didn't seem the sporting type. Unless she was hunting for trouble. "Oh, give me strength," Peyton muttered.

What did one do there? She didn't know how to play and hoped it wasn't required. The less she did, the less likely she'd make a fool of herself.

She needed a strategy. First things first: what did one wear? Peyton wished she knew whom to ask. Her gaze flew to her cell phone lying on top of her powder blue towel. She could always call . . .

No. Forget it. Her foot tapped against the edge of the bathtub. She wasn't going to call Mike. That jerk. Leaving her high and dry while he got all high and mighty. "You're not ready for the likes of me . . . ," she mimicked.

Who was the one who started it? He probably had sex in the stacks with any woman who stayed past closing. Peyton's eyes widened. The mounds of bubbles crackled as she sat straight up.

She didn't like that idea at all. The possibility that it had nothing to do with her. It was all a matter of being at the right place at the right time.

Peyton hugged her knees to her foam-encrusted chest. No, she decided. That wasn't it at all. Mike had some rough edges, but he wasn't on the make. He was too busy trying to become strong again. His eyes said it all. He was alert to his surroundings, but withdrew inside himself to heal a deep wound.

Peyton shook her head at the fanciful idea. The guy was not some battle-scarred warrior. He was a librarian, for crying out loud.

Which was probably why she was shocked he made a pass at her. The stereotypes of librarians were ingrained into her psyche. But that didn't explain why she found it thrilling.

Peyton's mouth curved into a smile. It was amazing being naughty. And for once it felt natural. She wasn't waiting anxiously for his next move. She didn't worry about timing and when it was appropriate to undo his belt. She went with what felt right.

She didn't feel all right at the moment. She was on edge. And it was all Mike's fault. How would he like it if she got him all hot and heavy and left him like that?

Peyton shot another look at the phone.

No . . . she shouldn't.

Her train of thought was scandalizing. Her skin tingled with the idea. But she wasn't going to do it. She wasn't going to call Mike for some dirty talk.

Why not? The mischievous voice whispered through her mind.

Lots of reasons. Peyton ticked them off with soapy fingers: (a) she didn't know how, (b) she would get caught, and (c) . . .

She couldn't come up with another good reason. Well, there had to be a (c). She didn't know it yet. Reason (b) was a given . . . although . . . how could she get caught? No one knew she was calling. Mike had no clue.

No. Peyton shook her head. It was a bad idea. She still didn't know how. It was a bad, bad idea. But then, she was trying to be a bad girl. She grabbed the phone and hit the speed dial before she could talk herself out of it. She had to call him anyway. Just to find out about pool halls.

"Main Library Answer Hotline. This is Mike. How can I help you?"

His voice bolted through her, twanging her muscles with awareness. "Hi, Mike. What is the proper etiquette at a pool hall?" She rubbed her fingers over her collarbone, hoping to soothe the erratic jumping of her pulse point. Instead the evocative citrus scent wafted over her.

He paused for a second. "There is no proper etiquette."

There had to be. Even Jack's had rules. They may not consider them rules. Call them customs, traditions or habits, but they were rules. Maybe she wasn't asking the right question. "Well, what does one wear?"

"Full body armor."

Her hand stopped. "I beg your pardon."

"Don't show any skin," he advised tersely. "Wear some-thing with long sleeves and a high neck. Baggy jeans. Yeah, you can't go wrong with baggy jeans."

That couldn't possibly be correct. Macey didn't go any-where that had a strict dress code. Unless she was prepared to break it. "Are you sure about this?"

"Yes."

He seemed adamant, but it didn't sound right. And she knew he hadn't taken the time to look up the answer. It might be unwise to take fashion tips from a guy. A guy li-brarian, at that. "All right." She decided to let it pass and ab-sently stroked her wet skin from shoulder to shoulder. "What's the object of the pool game?"

"It's very complicated." His tone was withering. "Don't play with the regulars. You know what? You're better off going somewhere else. Like miniature golf."

Peyton snorted and quickly covered her faux pas with a cough. "Uh, why can't I play with the regulars?"

"You'll get hustled." He said it as though it was already a done deal.

"Interesting," Peyton said softly. She'd never placed a bet before. Not even for the raffles at work. No one expected her to participate. "You better tell me the rules."

He let out a long, irritable sigh. "I have to find the book."

"No problem," she said brightly and leaned back into the bathtub.

"Why are you going to the pool hall?" he asked, his voice and soft footsteps echoing in the library's lobby, "if you don't know how to play pool?"

Peyton shrugged. "Just looking for some fun." She swept back a lock of hair from her face. Water dribbled from her arm and down her chest.

"Fun." Mike's disapproval was loud and clear.

There he was getting all high and mighty again. She

wanted to tweak his attitude. "Not just any kind of fun," she added. She hoped her statement was filled with innuendo.

"I can imagine," he said dryly.

Whew. She didn't have to spell out the insinuations. All thanks to his coarse imagination. Peyton smiled and smoothed a droplet of water into the slope of her breast.

"Okay, found it. Hold on." She heard the ruffling of pages. "Pool. This game of skill is an evolved form of croquet."

Peyton rolled her eyes toward the ceiling. She was going to a pool hall, not a garden party. "I don't need the history, but thanks anyway."

"Yeah, right," he said. "You usually want all the background information. Are you sure you don't want to take notes?"

"Yes, I'm sure." Was he teasing her? She couldn't be sure. "What equipment do I use?" Her splayed fingers trailed down her breast.

"There's a table."

Duh. She knew there was a table. She could picture the soft green velvet crushing underneath her naked back as Mike claimed her with wild abandon. Overwhelmed her with hot pagan sex. Took her with—

"A cue stick, rack, and balls."

Peyton blinked and jerked out of her fantasy. "Uh . . . that sounds simple enough," she said hoarsely. The tingling of her breast connected with the dull heaviness of her womb.

"It's not."

"I think I can handle it." Her slick fingers slipped to the tips of her breasts. She remembered the sweet intensity when Mike captured her nipple between his teeth. The tender force was bliss. Her breasts ached for the sensation. Peyton squeezed the rosy peak between her finger and thumb. She exhaled shakily as ribbons of pleasure streaked through her veins. She pinched harder. The sting set off fireworks under her skin. Peyton closed her eyes and let out a soft moan.

"What kind of game are you playing?"

Peyton's eyelids fluttered open at Mike's gruff voice. Her stomach seized up as her face flushed red. How did he know what she was doing? She tried to stall as she thought of a convincing lie. "E-excuse me?"

"What game?" He paused waiting for an answer. "8-ball? 9-ball? Snooker?"

"Oh." Her shoulders sagged with relief, and she placed her hand over her jumpy stomach. "8-ball, I guess."

The pages crackled. "A pool table is four and half feet wide and nine feet long."

Peyton inhaled deeply, reining in her impatience. She didn't remember Mike sharing this much trivia. Ever. Why did he have to start now?

"It's covered in polyester and wool," he continued disinterestedly.

She rubbed her stomach. It quavered as she listened to Mike's husky voice. "I thought it was velvet."

"Nope. The table has six pockets. Four corner pockets, one at each corner of the table. The two side pockets are located—"

"Don't tell me." Her hand drifted lower. "At the sides." Peyton let out a deep chuckle. The sensuous quality of her voice surprised her.

"At each long side in the center," he corrected. He went on at a rapid pace. "A pool table also has rails that border the edges."

"Uh-huh." The side of her hand skimmed her pelvis bone right before she speared her fingers through the wet curls between her legs. She pressed her lips closed and smothered a moan.

Mike paused for a moment. "You use them to balance your hand to make rail bridges," he said roughly.

Rail bridges? That didn't make sense, but Peyton was beyond caring. She cupped her sex. The pressure from her hand didn't soothe the throbbing. It intensified. "Okay," she said shakily.

"Near each end of the table, there is a small white circle called a spot."

Her finger nestled in the folds of her mound. She gasped. "Spot."

"Yeah," Mike growled and cleared his throat with a cough. "Just a second. I've got another call waiting."

Call waiting? Peyton frowned with incomprehension. The words twirled in her mind. Call . . . "No!" she shouted.

"What?" Mike asked, startled.

Please, don't be finished. Although she was ready to move her phone onto Vibrate, it would be a poor alternative to Mike's sexy voice. "You can't!"

"It'll take a second," Mike promised.

"They'll call back. I need this information *now.*" She was not above begging at this moment.

"Hold, please."

Mike covered the mouthpiece with a shaky hand, tilted his head back, and took a deep breath. Peyton's soft gasps and moans in the back of her throat were killing him. He wanted to be there with her. Cover her wet body with his. Pleasure her beyond all reason. Watch her come. Again and again.

Mike exhaled slowly. He needed to end the call. He should have after her first gasp. Why didn't he? Because he was a sucker for punishment? He wanted to finish what they started earlier today?

Or was it because he knew he screwed up and this was a second chance. He didn't want to waste this opportunity. Peyton Lovejoy might be mad as hell at him, but she wanted him enough to indulge in phone sex.

He rolled his shoulders and grabbed the book he was reading. He was a grown man and could control this phone call. Master his body's responses. Master Peyton's responses, but that wouldn't be much fun. A renegade image smashed into his mind. One of Peyton naked with her emotions and reactions. Mike took another deep breath and placed the phone back onto his ear.

"I'm back," he said. He heard Peyton's escalating breathlessness and the rolling of water on the other end. "Where was I? Oh, yeah. All you do is set the cue ball on the head spot when you start the game." There. Now he could tell her to have a nice day and hang up. But he wanted to know what she would do to keep him on the phone.

"I'm not worried about the table," she said in a wispy voice. "I'm worried about"—water slapped against porcelain—"the stick."

He swallowed. "What about it?"

"How"—her breath hitched in her throat—"do I hold it?"

Mike looked for the passage in the book. "The cue stick consists of three parts." Mike closed his eyes. "The tip, the shaft, and the butt."

A soft mewl escaped from her. "And how do I play with it?"

He winced as his cock hardened. Mike leafed through a few pages. "Take the cue stick and stand close to the table. Your legs should be lined up perpendicularly to the edge of the table."

"As opposed to what?" she mumbled. "Horizontally?"

He imagined Peyton horizontal on the pool table. She looked good. "Part your feet a shoulder's length distance."

He heard the soft lapping of water and imagined her spreading her legs. "Okay."

"Distribute your weight equally between both feet."

She murmured incoherently, "Got it."

"The knee closest to the table should be bent slightly."

"Bent? Ah . . . yes," she hissed.

Mike heard the swish of water. The irregular breathing. "The back knee remains straight," he said calmly, ignoring the blood roaring in his ears.

"O—oh!—kay."

Molten lust pooled in his groin. He squinted at the blurry pages in front of him. "Lean toward the table."

"Mm? Mm-hmm," she murmured over the sound of sloshing water.

"Hold the butt of the cue stick with your . . . dominant hand. His mind had a perfect image of her ladylike hands grasping his length.

"Yes . . ." Wonder suffused the word.

Mike clung to her pleasure. It was pure. Glorious. If only he could watch her eyes light up with satisfaction and feel the warm flush of her skin.

"Tell me more," she said between gasps. "More."

"Place your nondominant hand on the pool table, palm down. It should be five to ten inches away from the cue ball." He didn't even know what he was reading anymore. He didn't think Peyton knew or cared, either.

"Uh-huh."

The rhythmic slap of water sent his racing pulse into overdrive. "Raise your thumb slightly."

Peyton cried out. "Ohmigod—Oh . . ."

"Lay the shaft of the cue stick between your thumb and the side of your hand." His knees bowed. He was desperate for her touch. Desperate for her.

"Okay." Peyton's voice rose.

Damn. He lost his place. He wasn't going to hunt for it. Nothing mattered other than Peyton's climax. "Slide. The. Stick."

"Ooh." The keening cry caught in her throat. "What now?" she asked urgently.

"Slide it back and forth."

"And side to side?"

"No. You want it to slide"—he grimaced—"smoothly."

"So all," she panted, "I have to do . . . is rub the shaft along my hand?"

The book fell from his grasp. Mike slapped his hand on

the nearest bookshelf and sagged against it for support. "No, you still have to hit . . ." He couldn't remember the words. "Hit . . . the ball."

"How?"

The torment in her voice almost destroyed him. She was so close to finding paradise. If only he was right beside her. He would do anything to give her the ecstasy her body craved. "Pull back the cue stick with your arm."

"Yes?" The rollicking water muffled her question.

He inhaled raggedly. "Aim for the center."

"Yes—uh—y—"

Mike heard a loud splash. "And strike."

"Ye—!" Peyton's shriek ended abruptly as the connection went dead. He heard nothing except his shallow breathing. Mike removed the phone from his ear, holding it as if his life depended on it. His knuckles were stark white.

He slowly flipped his phone closed, careful not to crumple it in his hand. He inhaled sharply, determined to gain control over his body. If the breathing trick didn't work, he would crush his phone into dust.

Did Peyton Lovejoy think he was stupid? Probably. Would she have pulled that stunt otherwise?

He needed to think about her duplicity. That should make his cock go limp. How did a woman who was embarrassed at being in a strip joint practically rip off his clothes the next day? And why couldn't she ask him about the hotline, but then call him while she was in her bathtub.

Mike winced. Don't think about the bathtub. Stop thinking about how the water went from splashing to crashing against her naked, aroused body.

He had to stop thinking about it. He needed to figure out these two images Peyton presented. One that needed to read *The Ultimate Slut Workbook* and one who masturbated while on the phone.

Mike clawed the shelf and rested his head on the edge of the case. Just before the connection went dead, he heard her come. Soft mewls and gasps to something more guttural and primitive. His bad knees almost caved in when she came while listening to him. She climaxed violently. Just as he imagined she would.

Damn, he was hard. His cock was ready to shoot off of his body.

And he couldn't act on it. He was undercover as a gentleman. A gentleman didn't blow a sting because he wanted to haul his prime suspect from the bathtub and take her on her tile floor. Now. Right now.

A gentleman didn't know what he was missing. He was no gentleman, but no one could deny his professionalism. He would be patient and wait for the right moment while the target went to a pool hall with a climax afterglow.

To a pool hall filled with bikers.

Hell. He savagely kicked the bookcase and strode off, ignoring his cock straining against his faded jeans.

"Skylar!" he bellowed as he took the stairs. Forget the embezzling and the masquerade. Forget the time he already put into this investigation for his sister. Peyton was walking into trouble. He didn't care if she was a thief; he wasn't going to let her go to a pool hall unprotected.

His sister appeared at her office door, holding a carton of Chinese take-out. "What?" she asked, her mouth bulging with food.

"I'm leaving."

She stuffed the chopsticks into the carton. "I knew it. I wondered how long you could handle the idea of paperwork." She frowned at his grim expression. "What happened?"

"You don't want to know." He tossed his cell phone onto the main desk. "You're in charge of the Answer Hotline tonight."

Skylar's face lit up with excitement. "Is it about Operation Marple?"

"For the last time," he bit out as his jaw felt as if it was going to shatter, "it is not called that."

"Whatever. Are you going to do a stakeout? You need food for that. Oh, and backup. Wait for me." She took a step deeper into her office.

"Good night, Skylar, and don't follow me." He glared at her.

Her bottom lip pouted. "You're not coming back tonight?"

"Not if I can help it." He strode out of the library, ignoring his sister's next comment about him seriously needing to get laid. Right now he wanted to make sure a certain Peyton Lovejoy didn't get laid. Unless it was right underneath him.

Five

Peyton wondered how she'd gotten herself into such a mess. It had probably happened when she ignored that inner voice screaming, *Are you insane?* Yeah, that was most likely it.

She cautiously looked around the pool hall again. Fortunately there was no suggestive music. Her nerves could only handle so much. Her ears still rang from the snippets of vulgar conversation. She had a vocabulary list she needed to ask about when she called the library's hotline again.

That was, if she made it out of the pool hall alive. She was lost in a sea of tattooed and pierced men. She had been bumped, grabbed, pushed, and pinched. Her eyes stung from the stale cigarette smoke and dim lighting. Her nose was on strike after inhaling sour beer and unwashed bodies.

"Hey, babe." The low, menacing rasp cut through the boisterous voices. Peyton slowly looked over her shoulder and saw the bald man glaring back. Man? Beast was more like it.

She looked into his deadened eyes, and every alarm in her body rang. She hunched her shoulders protectively. "Yes?"

"Get the fuck off the table," he growled.

She lurched forward. "Sorry." Peyton tugged down her cut-off shorts. Mistake number 74 of the night. The man's cloudy eyes followed her movement.

Now was not the time to linger. Peyton bolted and searched for her group. There was safety in numbers. Not much, but more than she had right now. Peyton gathered her courage and walked deeper into the bowels of the pool hall. The neon beer signs and weak fluorescent lighting cast an eerie glow on all the leather, denim, and chains. Peyton's anxiety shot up another level when she saw that Macey had latched on to the most dangerous looking biker she'd seen. The greenish tattoos decorating his face were enough to give her nightmares.

Peyton decided it would be safer to approach Macey's associates, who played pool nearby. She didn't want to join in the game, but maybe she would be invisible around these women.

Or maybe not. She watched the blond associate lean down until she was almost lying on the table. The woman jutted her bottom out, and the black leather miniskirt rode up the curve until everyone in the establishment knew she wasn't wearing underwear. Peyton took a step back. This wasn't the kind of game she wanted to play or win. Even if she was partially dressed.

Peyton looked down at her outfit and sighed. Once again she hadn't dressed correctly. She had thought she looked hot. She'd sacrificed a perfectly good pair of jeans and made them into cut-off shorts. The white tank top she wore to sleep during the summer completed the outfit.

That was mistake number 3 of the night. She'd cut the shorts a little too high and uneven. And the way she was getting double takes made her wonder if there was any indecent fraying she should know about.

Macey and her group had seemed almost surprised by her outfit choice. Had they expected her to show up in a Chanel suit or something? Being able to surprise Macey gave Peyton a temporary boost of confidence.

Her positive attitude had died instantly once Peyton saw that Macey and her associates wore leather miniskirts with slinky shirts. The styles advertised what the women were after, but the fit was pure haute couture. Yet it wasn't the fit or the style that turned heads. These women oozed sexual confidence. Peyton didn't think she had anything to ooze.

Peyton slammed back into the present, tensing up as she felt a shadow draw over her. "Buy you a drink?" a nasal masculine voice whispered too close to her ear.

She stepped back and looked at the man who wore a grimy baseball cap that hid his eyes. All she could see was wisps of lank blond hair and the bottom half of his pale face. The small mustache was nothing more than fuzz, accentuating the man's thin lips.

"No, thank you," she said politely. She neither wanted to offend nor invite conversation. Thanks to the explicit picture airbrushed on his T-shirt, complete with a politically incorrect caption, she knew more about him than necessary. Peyton motioned at the almost full beer bottle she'd been holding for the past hour. "I already have one."

He tilted his head, revealing his slender nose and squinty eyes. "You look familiar. Do you come here a lot?"

"No." She wanted to make a face. What kind of pick-up line was that? True, no one had ever tried to pick her up before. All of her dates and boyfriends met her through friends and family members. They didn't need to come up with something memorable.

"I got it." His eyes squinted even more, if that was possible. His lips curled in repugnance. "You're that Lovejoy heiress."

The accompanying snarl to the label didn't bode well. "My name is Peyton," she replied courteously.

He purposely ignored her offer of a handshake. "Yeah, yeah. That's right. Peyton," he repeated as if it were a swear word.

Peyton dropped her hand. "And you are?" she asked with a determined polite smile.

"Hank." He made a loud hacking sound before he spat

tobacco juice on the floor. Peyton dodged the brownish glob before it landed on her shoe. She had a feeling it wasn't an accident, but she wasn't going to call him on it.

As hard as she tried, Peyton couldn't place him anywhere at Lovejoy's Unmentionables. "And you work . . . ?"

"I don't work for you," he said emphatically. "But most of my family does. Like my cousin Bubba Joe."

The name set off warning bells in her head. It was too coincidental for him to mention that specific employee. "I know Bubba Joe," she replied serenely when she felt anything but.

"Yeah, I heard." The gleam in his eyes indicated he'd gotten an embellished version of the events. She had a flash of horror that people thought she had given a public display of her fellatio skills instead of Macey.

But now wasn't the time to worry. She needed to set this guy straight. Peyton arched her eyebrow. "I beg your pardon?" She let the ice seep into her voice. Politeness wasn't going to work this time.

Hank ran his tongue against his teeth. "He told me you were at Jack's last night. Were there until they had to kick you out."

That's it? Or was that just the teaser? She wanted to push him away, but she also wanted to know the rumors. What could possibly have been said that Hank couldn't stand the sight of her? "So?"

"And here you are now." He gave her a once-over that made her skin crawl. Hank's eyes grew bigger as he stared at her nonexistent cleavage. Peyton wanted to whirl around and cross her arms over her chest.

She took an instinctive step back while her mind ordered her to stay her ground. Her heel hit something solid. Peyton winced as she realized she bumped up against one of the support beams. "What are you insinuating, Hank?"

He dragged his eyes up to her face. "Huh?"

Peyton's back teeth clicked in irritation. "What are you trying to say?"

He pursed his lips, and the mustache momentarily disappeared. "Nothing. Just noticing." His gaze flicked back to her tank top. "Noticing you've been partying a lot."

Oh, so that was it. She knew courting Macey in this manner would raise eyebrows, but Peyton wasn't prepared for an in-your-face attack. She wanted to launch her defense, but why bother? Hank didn't want a debate. He felt he had the right to say she didn't deserve a life outside Lovejoy's Unmentionables.

And the sad thing was, there was very little in her life but the company. But no one cared about that until it looked as though she was no longer chained to her desk. She might have controlling stock and a position of authority, but everyone in town felt they owned a piece of her.

The overwhelming demands clawed at her. Anger shot through her, and she lashed out. "What about you, Hank? Are you here for fun or for health reasons?" She glanced at his beer bottle. "You're taking that for medicinal purposes?"

Hank glared at her. Apprehension curled along her spine. "Don't you like using fancy words? Fits." He took a swig from his beer bottle. "And, yeah, this here is for my health. My mental health."

Peyton wanted to recommend Hank visit someone who offered prescription-strength along with anger management classes, but decided she'd already said too much. She would let him have his say and get it out of his system. That was probably safest.

"You see." Hank leaned back on the heels of his worn boots. "I don't have an inheritance coming my way. I have to work for my money."

That pricked under her skin. Did people think she wasn't working? "And what do you think I'm doing?"

He made a slurping sound with his tongue against his

teeth. "Partying." His eyes wandered down the length of her body again.

"Is that what you think?" She folded her arms across her chest. She knew that was a bad maneuver in the game of body language, but she couldn't help it. Peyton shifted her stance to project assertiveness rather than defense.

"Yep, that's what I think." Hank took another swig from the amber-colored bottle. "Your fancy ways and fancy degree mean squat. No one thinks you've got what it takes to turn this company around. So why don't you just quit?"

At that very moment she wanted to, more than the moments she woke up every day ready to tender her resignation. It was one thing to keep trying to do a better job every day, every hour, every decision. It was another to face the challenge when no one thought she was capable of succeeding.

"Do you see anyone around who is qualified to take my place? Are you interested in the job?" She scoffed at the idea.

"Shouldn't take too long to find someone. Any man could do the job right. Anyone but you." He jabbed his finger at her. "We need someone who's not afraid of hard work."

Peyton saw red. No one had the right to say she wasn't working hard. "Keep your ignorant assumptions to yourself." She turned away.

Hank grabbed her upper arm and wrenched her back to face him. "Who are you to call me ignorant?" He took a step forward, pressing Peyton against the support beam.

Peyton squeezed her eyes shut, regretting the slip of the tongue. She grimaced as Hank's fingers bit into her arm. She considered her alternatives. Knee in groin or smashing her beer bottle over his head. Both choices offered the possibility of hurting herself more than him.

Peyton wondered if swooning into a dead faint was her best move when the atmosphere suddenly changed. The pool hall grew quieter. Danger crackled. Hank seemed to realize it and shifted. Peyton cautiously cracked open an eyelid and

looked around. She sagged with relief when she saw Mike
Ryder standing at the door.

Mike stood at the threshold, scanning the crowd, his arms
loose against his sides. For a small town, the number of pool
halls was surprising. It rivaled the amount of taverns and
churches. But the search didn't quench his determination. It
fed it. The quiet growing anger was an extra bonus to his
mood.

He spotted Peyton right away. She was in the far corner
against some creep, but the lady was hard to miss. Relief
kicked him in the gut. An unfamiliar emotion followed up
with a one-two punch.

Mike scowled as he realized her position. How the hell
had she managed to get cornered? Didn't she know basic
self-defense?

He gave the cretin a you're-already-dead glare. The man
showed some display of brain cells and wisely slunk away
from Peyton. Mike then got an eyeful of her outfit.

Son of a bitch.

Mike's balls crawled into his stomach at the sight of
Peyton's shorts. The soft denim hugged the curve of her pe-
tite hips and showed off a lot of smooth, bare leg that made
a guy dream about wrapping them around his hips.

But it was her tank top that did him in. The soft white
fabric clung to her breasts, unable to conceal the shadows of
her dusky pink nipples. What the hell was the heiress of an
underwear factory doing running around town without a
bra? And around here, of all places. The lady had a death
wish coming around here looking like that.

There was only one thing he could do. Stake his territory.
By the way she was looking at him, it shouldn't be too difficult.

He strode through the smoky pool hall, his eyes intent on
Peyton. He knew all the exits and what could be used as an

impromptu weapon. He swiftly classified each man he passed. The bystanders, the troublemakers, and the deadly ones with trigger tempers.

"Mike!" Peyton looked up at him, relief and excitement mingled in her brown eyes. "What are you doing here?"

Mike cupped the back of her head with his hand and hauled her against him. His fingers speared through her loose brown hair. She gasped as he kissed her ruthlessly.

Her soft lips didn't put up a fight. They invited him to linger. Mike wanted to do exactly that, but he had to prove his claim first. He tilted Peyton's head farther back and felt her muscles tauten as her balance faltered.

Don't fight it. He hoped she understood what he was doing. *Don't push away. Not unless you want more trouble coming your way.*

Peyton didn't push him. Her fingers grappled at his shoulders before she melted against him. She opened her mouth wider as he forged his tongue.

She tasted of velvet and promise, with a hint of beer. Her heat seduced him. Mike's surroundings hazed over, and the noise level blurred. He wanted to sink deeper into her inviting mouth, but that would be trouble. He couldn't ignore what was going on around him.

He pulled her away reluctantly. She looked dazed. Turned on. She looked at him as if he was some knight in shining armor. If that didn't turn *him* on.

She blinked, her eyelashes fluttering like butterfly wings. "Good to see you, too," Peyton muttered under her breath.

Mike felt the corners of his mouth tug up. It had been a long time since he felt like smiling. He was rusty at it, so it might look like a grimace of pain.

"Realized what I'm missing out on," he drawled, his heartbeat like a jungle drum.

Her chin tilted up. "Maybe it's not available anymore."

Mike shrugged with more confidence than he felt. "To others. Not to me."

She started to argue, but thought better of it and looked away. Mike's confidence skyrocketed just as Peyton's face shuttered to nothing. In a split second she presented a polite smile. The quick transformation fascinated Mike.

"Peyton, where have you been hiding this one?" A woman slithered by. Her attitude shrieked big city. She eyed every inch of him with slow deliberation.

"You'd be surprised what you can find at the library," Peyton responded.

The woman laughed. It was a practiced laugh that was supposed to turn heads whether she was at a cocktail party or a baseball game. "Hi, I'm Macey Bonds." She held out her manicured hand.

"Mike Ryder."

Macey clasped her other hand over his. "Do you play?"

He got the message, but it went right over Peyton's head. "No, I'm here for Peyton." Bluntness was the quickest way to deal with this woman.

"And you're dragging her away." Macey withdrew her hand. Her smile took on a wary edge. She must not like being read so easily by a stranger. "That's okay. It's cool. See ya, Peyton."

"I-I-I'm . . ." Peyton stuttered as Macey walked away without a second glance. "Mike, I can't leave."

He grasped her wrist. "Yes, you are." He was already living on borrowed time. If any trouble happened, she would discover he wasn't some mild-mannered librarian. Or a superman, for that matter. Once his true colors were shown, Peyton would wisely run in the other direction.

She dug her heels and tried to yank free. "I happen to be with these women."

He didn't feel like arguing. He'd rather kiss her stupid and carry her out of this place before she came to. But he had a feeling gentlemen didn't do that. They probably had a discussion and compromised. Ugh. "But you'd rather be with me," Mike said, sensing that didn't sound New Age and sensitive.

She was about to rip into him, but took a deep breath instead. "I'm not denying that," she said as she pulled from his grasp, "but I'm here on business."

He gave her a look. If that was her business attire, he wanted to see what she wore on casual Fridays.

Peyton placed her hands on her hips. "I am. Macey Bonds is the hottest name in lingerie these days. I'm trying to work out a deal with her, but you are interrupting."

"I apologize." He gave a mocking bow and placed his hand on his heart. "Act like I'm not here. Please, go on and conduct business."

She straightened her shoulders. "Thank you, I will." She twirled away.

"And good luck getting Macey away from that biker," he called after her.

She stalled. Mike's mouth kicked up knowingly. But she hadn't given up yet. He needed to go in for the kill.

He stood behind her, placing his hands on her upper arms. He had the crazy urge to envelope his body over hers. Soak up her heat and give her everything his body had to offer. "I bet he bites," Mike continued gruffly. "And I wouldn't be surprised if he had rabies." He flashed another look at the guy. Rabies was the least of their worries.

"Okay. Fine." Her shoulders slumped, and she leaned into him. Mike's fingers flexed, refraining from caging her with his arms. "I guess I can't conduct any business right this minute. But I'm not leaving." She stepped away from him and turned, her eyes flashing with defiance.

Mike knew that Peyton was back to business now that she had a bodyguard for the night. She knew he wouldn't let anything happen to her, and he sure as hell wouldn't leave her. He decided he could concede just a little. "The tables are full. Let's go play pinball."

Her forehead pleated with a frown. "I haven't played before. You wouldn't by any chance know the rules to it?"

Mike rolled his eyes. What was it about rules with this

lady? "It's simple. But what would be better is for us to ditch this place."

She shook her head vigorously. "I can't leave them here."

"Sure you can. They won't care." He now understood that Peyton was torn between her personal code of conduct and the desire to head straight home and bolt the door. Mike thought it was yet another example on how manners didn't make much sense.

"No." Her eyes sparked with determination.

"All right." He gave a frustrated sigh. "Pinball it is." He placed a proprietary hand on her back and escorted her to the wall of pinball machines. Mike noticed how Peyton kept close to him, especially when they walked by a few steroid-pumped bikers. He liked it too much.

"Okay." He leaned his hip against one machine and dipped his hand into his jeans pocket. "Here's some change."

"Uh, no." Peyton stared at the pinball artwork. "Not this one."

Mike glanced at the picture of a busty woman with curvaceous legs crossed in a classic pinup fashion. The white panties peeked under the skirt, and the see-through shirt displayed everything in loving detail.

"The picture doesn't matter." He wasn't going to let them play at the other machines. That would make them easy targets with limited ways of getting out in case of an ambush.

"Oh, really?" She motioned at the blinking lights under the glass. "Then why do I get extra points if the ball bumps into her cleavage?"

"Do you want to play pinball?" He surveyed the pool hall again. The machines placed them at a disadvantage. The position exposed Peyton while creating a blind spot for any oncoming problem. "Here, I'll show you how it's done."

Mike moved to shield Peyton's back. He brushed up against her ass as he stood directly behind her. Bracketing his arms on either side of her, trapping her against him and the machine.

Peyton inserted the coins and straightened until her body was flush with his. She showed no reaction to their close proximity, but rather murmured her surprise as the pinball danced with bright colors. Her bare arms rubbed against his as she sought the flipper buttons. His mind buzzed from the touch of heated silk. By the time she slid her hands under his for the flipper buttons, Mike didn't know if he would survive the game.

And then Peyton nestled into him. His entire body lit up like the damned pinball machine. She rested her head against his chest with such an unspoken trust that it made his heart stutter. It was difficult to say who was supporting whom the way her back meshed with his abdomen. Her ass cushioned his cock perfectly. It took every shred of willpower not to buck against her softness.

He questioned his decision to literally back her. Was this the wisest move or an excuse to touch this exasperating woman? He didn't like the idea of his strategies being based on anything other than expertise. Mike didn't want to regret accepting the blind spot. He pulled the pinball knob harder than necessary.

"Oh!" Peyton exclaimed as the silver ball zigzagged over the pinup girl. She leaned forward and pushed the buttons with abandon. The bells and flashing lights didn't hold Mike's attention. He swallowed a groan as Peyton slanted her hips back and forth. Every move made him crave more.

"You're doing great," Mike said as Peyton double flipped and missed the silver ball. He wasn't going to think of what their entangled and bumping arms reminded him of. He wasn't going to consider how his hands swallowed hers. "You're a natural."

Peyton chuckled and shook her head in disagreement. She pulled the knob with gusto, the sharp move almost sending Mike over the edge. He clamped his hands over her hips. His hands shook slightly against the rough denim.

Her hips swayed, and Mike's fingertips were white as he

endured the pleasure-pain of Peyton's intimate moves. He imagined bending Peyton over the flashing machine and shucking off her shorts. Sinking into her and covering her body with his while the machine continued to tilt and whirl.

Mike shook the tempting fantasy out of his mind and glanced around. He did a quick survey as he mentally flailed himself with self-disgust. Once again he'd allowed his cravings to override his duties. When was the last time that happened?

Mike abruptly ended his surveillance as Peyton ground into his groin. Again and again and again. Her body slapped against his as she tried desperately to keep the silver ball from going past the flippers.

"Let's ditch this place," he growled in her ear. He couldn't take it anymore. He wanted her all to himself.

The silver ball slid past the flippers as Peyton shivered with awareness. She hunched her shoulders and curled into his chest. "I told you, I have guests here."

He nuzzled into her neck, inhaling her dewy skin. He gave in to temptation and pressed his tongue against the pulse point of her throat. "Your friend left."

She jerked away from him. "What? When?" Peyton turned around, and searched with desperate eyes. It was apparent that Macey and her rabies-infested biker were gone.

Peyton extracted herself from his embrace. Mike didn't put up much of a fight, deciding leaving the pinball machines was for everyone's good. He strode to where Peyton stood with the other women. "Where's Macey?" he heard her ask.

"Left." The blonde didn't look up as she made a weak shot. The balls clacked listlessly around the green felt. "Always wanted to do it on a Harley."

"At top speed," the redhead added.

"You're kidding me, right?" Peyton looked at the woman, then swiveled to face him to get verification. Mike shrugged. It wasn't completely unheard of.

"Nope, I'm not kidding." The blonde leaned over the

table to make a shot. Her breasts threatened to split the seams of the skimpy silk halter top.

Mike draped his arm around Peyton's waist. He was too unwilling to break off contact. "Come on, we're leaving."

"Bye, Peyton." The redhead blew on the cue stick and stirred up a cloud of chalk.

"But, but . . ." She locked her knees. Mike ignored her wants this time and successfully escorted her out of the hall. He didn't understand how Peyton planned to salvage the night. That was sheer determination if he ever saw it.

"Where do you want to go?" He directed her to his car, a nondescript rental two-door sedan. He felt a kinship with the automobile. They were both wolves in sheep's clothing.

"I don't know."

Mike's anticipation plummeted. Did she still want to be with him, or were his bodyguard services no longer required?

"You decide."

"Nope. I asked you. Want to do it on a Harley?" he teased, and motioned his head to the motorcycles lined up next to the pool hall.

"At top speed? No thanks. That's not on my list of fantasies."

Mike's eyebrows shot up. "You have a list?" He hadn't expected that. But now that he thought about it, she was the type to put it on a spreadsheet.

She closed her eyes as her face pinkened. "I probably shouldn't have said that."

"What's on your list?" He wanted details. He wanted to know how many fantasies were listed and if they could try them all before the sun came up.

She shook her head silently and kept her eyes focused on the door lock.

"The library with a stranger?" he ventured as he opened the car door for her.

She glared at him and refused to answer. Peyton moved for the passenger seat.

He blocked her way. "You better tell me."

She looked down at her feet. She chewed her bottom lip. "Well, there is one place. But it's dumb." She looked everywhere else but at him. "Really juvenile."

That intrigued him. He expected something dripping with lace and candlelight. "Tell me. Where do you want to go?"

She swiped her tongue along her bottom lip and abruptly looked straight at him. He could see the excitement, the determination, and the fear rolling in her brown eyes.

"Okay, Mike." Her chin and shoulders were military straight. "Take me to the Gates of Hell."

Six

"I see it!" Peyton pointed at the thicket of trees. "That's the pitchfork."

Mike pressed his foot against the brake pedal and stared through the windshield at the burnt, hollowed-out tree. "That doesn't look anything like a pitchfork."

"Of course it does," she disagreed with a smile. How was it that every smile hammered a chink off the heaviness in his chest? "Maybe you're not looking at the right tree," she suggested. "Do you see the trunk and two branches forking up?" She flexed her fingers in what Mike assumed was a pitchfork motion.

"I see a dead tree stump." He also saw that this excursion had become a pilgrimage. If he had taken her straight to his apartment, they would have already experienced sexual enlightenment in one hundred and one different ways. "Are you sure we're looking for a pitchfork?"

"Yes, I know that for sure. The pitchfork is the thirteenth and final gate." Her voice hummed with excitement. Peyton's eagerness hadn't dimmed since they started the bizarre scavenger hunt. It amazed him what people in a small town would do for entertainment.

"I'll take your word for it. Which way do we turn?"

"Um . . ." She studied where the headlights illuminated. "Right?"

He turned right on the skinny dirt road and considered how she gave the direction. "You don't know?"

"I know," she assured him, trying to get a better view of the surroundings. "I've heard about this place enough times from my friends."

"Wait." He slowed the car down to a crawl. "You've never been here? Not even when you were a teenager?"

"No." The smile faded, and he didn't know what to say to get it back.

He maneuvered the car over bumps and potholes until they reached the clearing. Driving to the edge of the hill, Mike parked the car and turned off the ignition. The view overlooked a vast expanse of farmland, a patchwork of dusky blues, grays, and black. The summer night cast the sturdy barns into shadows and almost hid the thin ribbons of road. He couldn't hear anything but rustling leaves and chirping crickets.

The hot breeze whispered through the trees next to them and rippled across the cornfields. The black sky stretched around them like a velvet cocoon. Nothing got in the way of the majestic sweep of stars or the silver moon. There were no competing neon lights and no buildings blocking the view.

This was no hell. He should know. But he also knew enough to remember this place couldn't be heaven. After all, they were looking at yet another cornfield.

Maybe he'd been in this small town too long, because the endless farmland didn't bother him as much. He wouldn't be opposed to considering this place as the gates of paradise. Of course, he might need some convincing. Over and over.

Mike turned the headlights off and focused on Peyton. She had that look about her. This moment represented something to her, and she was going to savor every second.

Did it matter if he was here, or would any guy do? Nah, Peyton could have left the pool hall with anyone. She wanted him. Whether it was because she thought he had gentlemanly tendencies was another matter. Mike ignored the stab of guilt. "And you guys call it the Gates of Hell because . . . ?"

"Some college kids named it decades ago." She nervously cleared her throat. "It kept their nosy siblings from stumbling onto this Lover's Lane. The gates have become something of an urban legend. You know, people who didn't believe in the gates' power came to a grisly end. Most teenagers don't even know this place exists."

Mike leaned back in his seat and watched her lapse into silence. She tucked her long brown hair behind her ear. She looked out the windshield, but her body buzzed with expectancy. He didn't know if she was going to jump him, jump out of her skin, or out of the car. She shied away as he reached out with one hand and hooked his finger around a wayward curl. Mike slowly wrapped the ends around his finger, his hand moving closer to her neck.

Peyton bolted into action. He felt the sharp tug of her hair, but she didn't acknowledge the pain. She unbuckled her seat belt with fumbling hands. "Come on."

Mike released her hair as she launched over the head support. He feinted to the left as her foot came whizzing by his head. "What are you doing?" He cautiously glanced in her direction and watched her bare legs whirl.

"Isn't it obvious?" Her voice sounded close to the floor of the car. "I'm going to the backseat. Oomph!" She landed in an untidy heap.

Mike felt the corners of his mouth twitch. The last time he was in the backseat was probably right before he understood the merits of comfort and luxury. "Are you crazy?" he asked as she righted herself into a sitting position.

"Nope." She crossed her legs and patted the seat next to

her. Her welcoming, seductive smile was worthy of a siren. Mike didn't try to resist.

"I'm too old for this," he muttered as he opened the driver's door.

Peyton laughed and watched him push back the driver's seat. Her eyes gleamed with hungry anticipation as he edged his way into the back. "You said you'd take me anywhere," she reminded him.

He slammed the door closed. "Yeah, but I was thinking of somewhere both of us could have plenty of room." Stealthily moving on his hands and knees, Mike pursued her to the other side of the car.

"This has lots of space," she announced. The edge of bravado blurred as she slid into a reclining position.

He hovered above her. His knees pinned her legs. His forearms rested against her shoulders. Mike paused, wanting Peyton to feel the full effect of her cage. "I was thinking more in line of my bed. Or your bed."

She swallowed. "Beds are boring."

He lowered his face until their foreheads grazed and their hot breaths mingled. "You haven't been in my bed."

He brushed his lips against hers. Leisurely tasting when he really wanted to dive into the pleasures. Ease the torment of his body right now.

Her eyelids fluttered closed. Mike suckled the bottom lip until she sighed and parted her mouth for more. He wouldn't let her lead the lovemaking this time. Mike sank the edge of his teeth into her plump bottom lip. Peyton gasped and swiftly closed her mouth in reflex.

Mike kissed the sore spot on her lip, eliciting a frown from her. He wanted to keep her guessing when to expect gentleness or tender force. Anything that made her relinquish all control.

He knew she wanted a raunchy encounter, but wasn't going to give it to her. Sex, yes, but not one of those fuckfests where details were unimportant. He wasn't going to give her a memory in which only the position and location mattered.

Peyton had other ideas. She grasped his face with eager hands and surged her tongue into his mouth. His body clenched as he greedily claimed her offering. The audacious act ignited the sharp need in him. It ate at his control.

Maybe he was going too gentle and slow. He slipped his head from her grasp and nuzzled her neck.

"Mike," Peyton murmured, pulling at his hair. The needles of pain enhanced the everlasting fire licking his blood.

"Hmm?" His mouth rested at the base of her throat. He inhaled the scent of her. The combination of citrus, sex, and all woman made his head buzz.

"I want you to . . ." Her voice trailed off as he meandered down past her shoulder. "I want you . . ."

"You want me," he teased before circling the tip of his tongue around her nipple. Her breath hitched as he sucked the peak through her shirt.

She cried out and writhed under him. His mouth pulled and then stopped to see what she would do. Her writhing increased. Her hands clawed at his skull. He kept his mouth just above the wet spot on her shirt.

She tossed and thrust. "Mike, I—"

He moved his hand onto her other breast and squeezed the hard nipple between his fingers. The move took Peyton by surprise. Her hands flailed out and hit the car door.

"Ow," she muttered. She shook the pain from her battered hand.

Mike raised his head. "That's what you get for going into the backseat."

Peyton stuck out her tongue in response. Mike caught it in his mouth. As he devoured her kiss, he shoved up her tank top. His hands, shakier than he would have liked, cupped her naked breasts.

Her softness undid him. It scorched his hands and sizzled

up to his arms. He was losing power over his own reactions. Mike retreated from her mouth and yanked her tank top over her head. Her body arched against his.

Okay, now this was heaven. Her body was bare and open for him; the darkness and moonlight created fascinating shadows on her pale curves. Her eyes gleamed with frank sexual need. Her mouth was branded by his touch.

"Hey." She motioned with her arms caught in the shirt.

"No, you're perfect just like that." His voice was husky with stark need.

"Why?" She sounded worried.

"Ssh." He placed his palm on her breastbone. "Give it a try. You might like it."

"Then you're next." Her eyes widened as he unsnapped her shorts and whisked away her clothing. She kicked them off before he suggested she keep her feet bound.

Mike returned to her mouth once more, gentleness forgotten. The sight of her body destroyed him. He wanted to give and receive pleasure inside her. The purgatory was too much.

He trailed his fingers down her pelvis before brushing his fingers against her curls. When he speared his hand between her legs, she wrenched her mouth away and moaned.

His fingers rubbed against the slick folds. She parted her legs, silently asking for more. Peyton roughly kissed him as he slipped a finger inside her moist heat. She gasped and bucked against his hand.

He teased her with a relentless rhythm, enjoying the tremors in her body as his body begged for release.

"I want you in me," she whispered raggedly. Her body clenched against his fingers. Her body tensed and quivered as she mewled in the back of her throat.

Her expression sharpened. Her hips pitched back and forth. Mike pressed his thumb against her swollen clit, and a piercing cry escaped her rounded lips.

Mike watched with growing fascination as she climaxed.

He continued to caress her as the power unfurled in her body. It flushed her skin, stripped Peyton to her very core, her very essence. It was a glorious sight. Need flailed and stung his body.

"Now." Urgency threaded her wispy voice as the after-shocks pulsed through her dewy body. "I want you now."

Mike reached for his back pocket. The realization that he didn't have any condoms hit him with an unwelcoming wallop. "I can't," he bit out, his shoulders sinking in disappointment as his cock hardened with fierce anger. "I don't have anything to protect you."

"So what?" Her legs wove around his, ensnaring him more.

"No." The word dragged out of him. He wanted to throw away caution, sink into her, and find nirvana.

"But I need you in me." She tormented him with the roll of her hips. "Please."

"No." This was agony. Hell.

Her brow furrowed above her closed eyes. "Don't leave me like this again."

"I won't." He wanted to guide her through all the pleasures of paradise. Have her link the pleasure with him and only him. His fingers stroked her wet heat. "Damn, I knew you'd look like this."

"Hmm . . ." She arched against his hand and murmured with delight.

Mike felt his nostrils flare as he decided to strip away her last barrier. "When you were in the bathtub."

Peyton's eyes flew open as her lungs shriveled up. "How did you—when did . . ." Her strangled voice came out in a whisper.

Mike placed a gentle hand on her bare stomach. He held her fast as his other hand continued creating magic. "I've known since last night."

Last night! "You didn't say anything."

The edge of his mouth kicked up. "And miss out on your orgasm?"

Her entire body blushed. The heat alone singed her. "Let me go." She awkwardly grabbed the hem of her tank top and pulled it down.

He sighed deeply and let her escape. "Why?"

How could he ask her that? Peyton scurried into a sitting position and searched through the dark for her shorts. "Why didn't you tell me that you knew?"

Mike sat down and stretched his arm on the back of the seat. His foot deliberately dragged her shorts and panties onto his side of the car. "Because you already knew."

"I did not!" She crossed her legs as she stared at the heap of clothing. She could make a grab for it, but that would leave her in a more undignified mess than the one she was in right now. She wasn't going to get anywhere near those unless Mike was good and ready.

"Who are you kidding? You knew."

Peyton wiggled uncomfortably on the seat. Okay, maybe deep down inside she had been aware this morning that he knew. Perhaps she'd accepted his silence too readily. And it was quite possible that she hadn't pushed the issue so she could enjoy the anonymity.

"You should have told me." Peyton folded her arms in front of her chest. Her breasts still felt heavy.

Mike shrugged. The gesture was in contrast to his heated gaze. "Would you have called me with all those sexual questions?"

She hunched her shoulders. "Absolutely not."

"Would you have masturbated while on the phone?"

"No!" Sheesh, did he have to be so blunt?

He leaned closer. "Would you have come as you listened to my voice?"

Peyton looked away and pressed her lips shut. How could she explained what happened? "I hadn't planned on doing that."

"Are you sure?" he murmured as if he knew her better than she knew herself. At the moment, it was a scary possibility. "It's easier to let your inhibitions go when you think you're having anonymous sex."

Irritation flashed through her with a streak of vulnerability. She'd had enough of his arrogant psychoanalysis. "You might think you know how my mind works, but—"

"I do. You wanted to punish me for stopping this afternoon." He reached out and grabbed her at the waist.

She ineffectually batted at his hands. "Put me down this instant," she demanded, her voice thick instead of acerbic. Her eyes widened as he set her down and her bare bottom straddled his jean-clad thigh.

"You wanted to be wicked." Mike's all-seeing eyes were too close to hers. "But you didn't want to deal with the consequences."

She should have stopped his assumptions with a few choice words. If only she could come up with a defense, but she was busy controlling her body's responses as his hard thigh pressed against her sensitive flesh.

"You wanted to have me without letting anyone know." Mike's hands caressed the length of her bare legs, sending a sparkling shower of awareness across her skin. "Including me."

Peyton winced. Okay, when he put it that way, it sounded bad. "I'm sorry. It won't happen again."

"Shame." His hands clasped her hips. Heat billowed as her womb tightened with anticipation. "It drove me wild."

"It . . . it did?" She, Peyton Lovejoy, had the ability to make this man go wild. It was hard to believe. The knowledge shifted something inside her, releasing a warm, golden glow.

The heat in his eyes shone in response. "I went to every pool hall looking for you," he admitted. "Hearing your soft cries wasn't enough. I wanted to watch you."

She swallowed as he moved his legs, the rough denim rubbing against her soft skin. The friction was unbearable bliss.

Her tongue flicked the edge of her suddenly parched lips. "Watch. Me."

"That's right." He rocked her hips gently. She slowly rode his leg. Ribbons of white heat formed in her pelvis and spread through her legs and chest.

"Was it everything you imagi—" She stuttered to stop. She couldn't believe she just asked him that. It was too revealing.

"Oh, yeah, and more." The crook in his smile was devilish. "But I couldn't come with you. Again." His face sharpened with desire. "You knew all I could do is listen to you come."

"Come for me now," Peyton ordered softly as her fingers tore at his jeans. She dragged his zipper down and carefully revealed his penis.

Peyton did her best not to blink or gasp. She didn't want to give Mike any indication of her limited experience. But she had never seen a man that big or thick and pulsating with masculine energy. It was magnificent.

If only she could have him filling and stretching her. She shuddered with a fierce craving.

Mike stifled a groan. "Touch me," he said roughly. It wasn't a plea or an order, but a combination of both.

She grabbed him at the base of his thick penis. She felt the power shimmering underneath the veined skin. She wanted to capture that power, make it a part of her.

Peyton held him tight and dragged her hand upward. Her other hand grasped the root of his penis and followed the first.

Mike's fingertips bit into her bare buttocks, his insistent palms encouraging her to ride faster. He threw his head back, the veins bulging from his neck the same way cords of veins throbbed from his penis.

"Peyton." He inhaled sharply as her thumb swept against the weeping tip. Mike clenched his eyes shut as she coated his length with his moisture.

The heat inside her burned brighter. She was desperate to feed the heat until it consumed itself. Giving Mike the ultimate pleasure would do that. "Tell me what you want," she offered, tightening her grip on him.

He turned his head, fighting the oncoming climax while inviting defeat. "More of this." He ground her into his leg. Her muscles greedily accepted the deeper move.

She swayed against him, gasping as the sensations gathered in her core and blazed hotter. "You would rather have this"—she squeezed the tip of him—"than being in me?"

His hips rose from the seat. He opened his eyes into slits and growled. "Don't."

"This"—her nails scored the underside of his penis—"instead of buried inside me."

"I'm warning you." She felt his body tremble. He was on the edge like her. She wanted to unleash his power.

"Buried deep . . . and tight." She clenched him hard.

"Peyton!" Mike's hoarse shout dissolved as he thrashed under her hands.

It was silent in the car, but the air around them hummed. "You should have told me that you knew," Peyton chastised. "You are the only one who knows, right?"

"I don't kiss and tell." Annoyance burred his words. "Your reputation is safe with me."

"I didn't mean—" A metallic sound captured her attention. "What is that noise?"

"The car next to us."

Alarm trickled down her spine. "When did they show up?" She casually glided off his leg. She was going to be blasé about this. She wasn't going to freak out.

Mike's eyebrow rose. "Around the time I was screaming your full name and social security number."

She acknowledged his sarcasm with a closed-mouth smile and peered out the window. "Oh, no! I know him." She ducked down and pressed her body against the backseat.

"So?" Mike asked as he zipped up his jeans.

"He's a major stockholder for Lovejoy's Unmentionables!" she squawked. "Wait a second . . . he's not married to her." She frowned and shook her head. That didn't matter at the moment. "Quick, help me find my clothes before they see me."

"Like they would say anything?" He calmly reached down and handed her the pile of her clothes.

She snatched it from him. "It's different with me," she explained hurriedly. "People expect a lot more." The argument at the bar was still fresh in her mind. She followed the rules laid down for her, and it wasn't enough. Imagine what the townspeople would say if they discovered she veered off the path!

Mike watched her dress. "What do you want for yourself? Other than meeting people's expectations?"

Peyton looked at him, momentarily lost. She shook her head. "It doesn't matter right now."

"Maybe it should."

She didn't have time to explain that she didn't have that kind of luxury. All she wanted to do was get out of here. And why wasn't he even trying to get ready? "Where are my shoes?"

"About this shirt." Mike hooked the strap of her tank top with a proprietary finger. "You're never wearing it in public again."

The command scraped at her. Her eyes narrowed with annoyance. "Why not?"

His finger trailed down her breast. "Because I can see everything you have to offer."

Did he mean—? "Nooo." That was impossible. She'd checked her appearance at every angle before leaving the house. Granted, the lighting in her closet wasn't the best, but . . .

"Yes." He lazily outlined the aureole of her nipple with unsettling accuracy. The peaks of her breasts budded at his touch.

Ohmigod. Her stomach felt as if it fell into an endless hole. All those guys at the pool hall had seen her like this. She cringed as she remembered Hank's eyes glued on her chest. "I just walked around town looking like a . . . like a . . ."

"Like the picture on the pinball machine?" His slanted smile was sinful. "Yep."

Seven

"A, b, c, d, e, f, g," Mike sang softly as he tried to remember what went after "k." After shelving books for hours, his mind had finally collapsed into mush.

"Ahem."

He sighed and shoved a book into an opening. "I don't want to hear it, Skylar."

"It's not often I get to hear you sing," his sister said indulgently.

"Shut up," Mike advised.

"It's so . . ." Her voice went up another octave.

"Don't say it."

"Cute."

He glared at her. "You're living on borrowed time."

The threat had no effect. Skylar leaned against the bookshelf and crossed her ankles as if she had all the time in the world. "It's interesting."

Mike ignored the unspoken prompt. He picked up a book from his cart and studied the spine as if it fascinated him.

"About two weeks ago, you were on edge."

He searched along the shelf, wondering when Skylar would get the hint that he wasn't listening to her.

"Now you're relaxed."

He ran his fingertip along the shelved books. Like hell he was relaxed. This small town got on his nerves. The library gave him the hives. His sister drove him nuts.

"Rejuvenated."

Okay, maybe rejuvenated. Maybe. All Peyton had to do was smile and he was ready to take on the world.

"Mellow."

He dropped the book as the word jabbed him in the gut. "Hold it right there. I am not mellow."

"Yes, you are."

"No, I'm not." He couldn't afford to be. Mellow would get him killed in his line of work. Was that why his last assignment had gone bad?

"Are, too."

"Am not." He suddenly felt closed in. Back to the dark, eerie abyss. Where he fought to escape. Fought to keep control of his mind since he couldn't control his surroundings. An environment that stank of gun smoke, jungle, and blood.

"Too."

"Not," he rasped. Mike held up his hand as his mind pushed away the tendrils of the memory. "Define mellow."

"Relaxed. Pleasant for a change." Skylar shrugged. "Those rough edges are beginning to soften."

He swiftly cornered Skylar before he realized what he was doing. "I am not getting soft." He pointed his finger in her face. A fine tremor swept his hand.

Skylar batted him away. "Just a minute ago you were singing the alphabet. You're lucky I interrupted or "Mary Had a Little Lamb" would have been up next."

He clamped his hands on her shoulders. "I am not getting soft," he repeated.

Skylar frowned and studied his face. "There's nothing wrong with that. I think it's great. This town is doing wonders for you. You should think of retiring here."

Was his sister put on this world to torment him? "I am

never going to retire or settle down. I am never going to live here, and I never, ever, will soften. Got it?"

"Okay, Mike." She patted his shoulder. "Whatever you say."

He raked tense fingers through his hair. "Once this embezzling case is put to rest, I'm outta here."

She snapped her fingers. "Speaking of Operation Marple." Skylar ignored his long-suffering sigh. "I was just talking to Peyton Lovejoy."

Every muscle in his body twanged. So much for feeling rejuvenated. "Yeah?" he asked and took a step back.

"I called her about a Friends' project."

Annoyance swept through him. "Skylar Ryder . . ."

"Ugh." She made a face. "It's Skylar Black now, remember? I've been married and divorced, which is more than I can say for you."

"You can throw your pathetic personal life into my face, but it won't divert my attention." The bunching of his shoulder muscles relaxed. He was regaining control again. Over himself. Over his sister.

Skylar put her hands on her hips. "At least I have a personal life."

"I think the verb tense you're looking for is 'had', and your tactic isn't working. You should have told me that you were contacting Peyton."

"No, I didn't have to. This is regular business. They host a book sale every August. While we were discussing it, I *casually* mentioned that they seem to be doing a lot of events, but less money was coming in from previous years."

This was Skylar's idea of interrogating? "What did Peyton say?"

"She'll follow up on it." Skylar shrugged and rolled her eyes. "Kind of lame answer, huh?"

What did Skylar expect? Maybe he could repair the damage. "Did she sound surprised? Defensive?"

His sister pursed her lips as she considered the questions. "She looked concerned."

"Looked? She was here?" And she didn't seek him out? What was he thinking? That she had to make an appearance whenever she was on the same street? Not that the idea didn't have merit . . . Damn, he had it bad for her.

"Yeah, she still is." Skylar motioned with her thumb toward the staircase.

"Where?" And why did he care? He'd like to think it was to follow up on his sister's questionings, but that was a lie. Where was his drive to help his sister get out of this mess?

"How should I know?" Skylar said. "She was talking to Samantha Lovejoy next to the drinking fountain a few minutes ago."

"I'll be back." He abandoned the cart without a second glance. "I'm taking my break."

"What are you going to do?" she whispered fiercely. "Interrogate Peyton?" She yanked his arm. It didn't do any good as her shoes squeaked against the floor while he pulled her along with him. "I don't think it's a good idea."

He stopped and plucked his sister off his arm. "I know what I'm doing. I'm a pro." He had to start acting like it, even if it meant distancing himself from Peyton Lovejoy. The knowledge worsened his mood.

Skylar let out a growl and shoved her hands in her hair. "I need a vacation."

"Hope it'll be better than the one I'm having."

"I should get going," Samantha said suddenly. She took a step back, her fixed gaze widening on the staircase behind Peyton. "I need to run some errands before Owen's breakfast meeting tomorrow."

Peyton turned to see what had grabbed Samantha's attention. Her breath hitched when she spotted Mike. He moved down the steps with the unhurried confidence of a veteran gunfighter. Displeasure intensified the harsh features as his cold gaze sliced across the lobby. She pitied the poor sap he was after.

Peyton felt the shadows swirling around him. She recognized how much the darkness was a part of Mike. It could shroud and protect him or it could cloak and smother. Peyton respected its power and knew better than to try to erase the shadows, but she wanted to help Mike tame his dark side.

Mike stepped onto the main floor and glanced in her direction. The hungry gleam in his eyes matched the voracious heat streaking through her. Her heart banged against her ribs as he approached her. "Peyton," he said in a low growl that made her press her thighs together, "we need to talk."

She blinked with surprise. About what? Wait. *She* was the poor sap he was after? Her thigh muscles unclenched.

His words revolved around her head. *We need to talk.* Those four words from a man made any single woman cringe. Her stomach gave a sickening flip. He was dumping her. Already. That had to be some kind of world record.

Peyton dipped her chin as she valiantly tried to hang on to the semblance of a polite smile. She wanted to act indifferent. No, she really wanted to wail at the injustice. It wasn't fair! She wasn't ready to break up. She hadn't started on her wish list. She hadn't even gotten Mike naked. Peyton ruthlessly squashed the pang of regret. *No, it's fine,* she decided. *His loss.*

She jutted her chin out and turned to Samantha. "I'll . . ." Peyton frowned at the empty space and belatedly realized that the woman had already left. Peyton didn't blame her. Mike could be intimidating when he was in a good mood.

Returning her full attention to Mike, she caught his silent appraisal. The muscle in his jaw popped as his gaze slowly inched up from her heels to the scooped neckline of her sheath dress. Pleasure flared under her skin, lingering along her curves. Her breasts felt heavy as Mike's focus zoomed in. Peyton bit her bottom lip as her nipples tightened.

Mike's weathered skin stretched against his stark features. He hadn't touched her, but his unabashed lust sent a quiver down her spine. Had it been any other man, she would have shot him dead with an icy glare. But this was Mike Ryder. An aroused Mike ready to pounce and she didn't want to obstruct any immediate ravishment. Quite the opposite, Peyton decided as she put her hands on her hips and rolled her shoulders back.

Mike looked directly into her eyes. She almost dropped to the floor as she saw his raw need. Peyton didn't doubt that he was one step away from taking her breast in his mouth. Right there, right now. And that was the best idea she heard all day.

Maybe she had been reading his mood all wrong, because he didn't look ready to dump her. She didn't know all the rules of sexual relationships, but she'd bet a guy wouldn't dump a woman he still wanted to take against a wall.

And the way he looked at her made her feel wanted. Sexy. She could ask for anything and he would do whatever it took to give it to her. She was tempted to test her newfound power, and maybe that concerned Mike. He needed to be in control and draw up the parameters of the relationship.

Peyton smirked at the possibility and felt his gaze follow the line of her mouth. The buzz of feminine power was nowhere near as addictive as Mike's touch. She wanted to feel both, and if she was a wicked woman, she could have it all. But wicked women didn't follow men's rules. Not unless they were asked really, really nicely. She couldn't wait to see Mike's persuasion skills.

"So, what's going on?" she asked huskily.

Mike shook his head as if to rid himself from the seductive spell. "Not here." He placed his hand on her back. Peyton stumbled, her nerve endings going haywire from his guiding touch.

He opened the Employees Only door and escorted her inside a dark room. Peyton wrinkled her nose at the overwhelming scent. It was similar to the reassuring smell of the library, only concentrated. "What is this place?"

"The archives." The door closed with a thud as he flipped on the weak lights. "Mostly German documents from the first settlers."

"Wow." She set down her purse on a nearby desk. "Kind of creepy."

"Yeah, it's the same way in full sunlight." He pulled out a chair. "Sit."

Peyton hesitated. No way was she going to be treated like an errant schoolgirl in the principal's office. Not that she would know what that felt like.

"I'm fine here," she replied as she perched on the edge of the tidy desk. The hem of her dress rose up her thighs. Silk rasped against silk, the sound amplified in the hushed office.

Mike's gaze traveled along the length of her leg. "There are a few things I need to ask you," he said distractedly.

"You don't need to," Peyton said, crossing her legs and hoping she didn't topple off the desk. "I understand."

"You do?" He reluctantly dragged his attention away from her creeping hemline. "What do you understand?"

Peyton shrugged expressively. "That while you're not looking for a long-term commitment," she said, swinging her foot, "you do want mutual exclusivity."

"Uh-huh." Her dangling shoe seemed to have a mesmerizing effect.

"And although you don't have any claim on me, you do have some requirement on what I wear. Does this pass inspection?" She held her arms out wide.

Her heart lurched when Mike reached out and trailed his fingertip along the neckline. The pulse in her throat jumped as he continued the unhurried journey to her shoulder. He hooked his finger around the fragile strap that peeked from under her dress.

"At least you're wearing a bra," he murmured, tucking the wayward sliver of satin back into place. Peyton swallowed awkwardly. She wanted him spellbound, but somehow she was getting caught instead.

"And you want sex," she ended in a rush as Mike caressed her collarbone with the side of his thumb, "but where there's a lot of space. Preferably in a bed." She paused, wondering how she was going to pull off the seduction. It was exciting in a terrifying sort of way. "You do know there's more to sex than what can be done in a bedroom, right?" she mocked. "I mean, consider all the possibilities we have right here."

Mike flashed a shrewd look. "Such as?"

"Sit down and find out," she answered. Peyton tried to say it in a whisper worthy of Marilyn Monroe, but she felt she was failing. If he rejected her obvious come-on, she really would go drown herself in the drinking fountain.

His eyes gleamed. With interest or amusement, she wasn't sure. "Okay," Mike said, curling his foot around the chair leg and dragging it to him, his gaze never leaving her, "but I know nothing's going to happen."

"What makes you think that?" she asked, trying not to sag with relief. She slid off the desk, her legs shaky.

"Because I'm sitting at"—he checked the metal nameplate—"Ima's desk. In the library. Filled with people."

She wished he hadn't made a list of everyone who could find out about her illicit moment. Her mind now felt as frenzied as her pulse rate. "So?" She grasped the armrests and leaned forward until her eyes were level with his. The moment her gaze connected with his, the chaos inside her stopped. She had a very clear idea of what she wanted no matter what.

"You freaked out at the Gates of Hell because someone might have seen you," Mike reminded, his Adam's apple bobbing as he gazed at her neckline.

Peyton tilted her head. "Maybe I decided I want to ignore the rules with you," she whispered into his ear.

He gave a disbelieving grunt. "Yeah, right."

She boldly palmed the hard ridge of his jeans and felt his

penis jump. Okay, Peyton thought, that step worked like it was supposed to. She moved quickly and took his mouth with hers. Dipping her tongue past his lips, she initiated the kiss before she lost her nerve. She wanted to do this more than she wanted her next breath, but she didn't know if she could pull it off.

Mike dueled her tongue with languor. Desire, warm and wet, trickled down her body, saturating her muscles until she felt weak with need. Peyton knew he would take control of the kiss. She needed to surprise him and act on how she felt, library patrons be damned.

She slipped her hands under the hem of his soft T-shirt. His skin felt hot. She felt his muscles bunch as she splayed her fingertips across the defined contours of his stomach.

Peyton withdrew her mouth from his and knelt between his sprawled legs. She ignored the discomfort of the cold floor as she reached for his button fly. Mike stilled. His nostrils flared as his tension crackled in the silent room. "Peyton?"

"Hmm?" she asked as she unbuttoned his jeans and slowly lowered the zipper. Parting the denim, she exposed the white cotton. She rubbed his length and watched Mike battle for control over his own responses. Wild eagerness skipped through her veins. She was too impatient to tease him and carefully freed his penis.

Her lungs contracted as she cradled his length with both hands. His scent was primal male. Gripping him hard, she trembled and swelled as she imagined his penis deep inside her. She lowered her face and swiped her tongue over the tip.

Mike's groan was music to her ears. She glanced up and saw his dark eyes glitter as ruddy color suffused his cheekbones. Peyton kept her eyes locked with his as she lapped and laved. He tasted hot and intense. His chest rose and fell with each lick and nibble.

After tasting her way from tip to base, Peyton journeyed back to his engorged head and pursed her lips around him.

Mike unclenched his hands from the chair. His fingers sank into her hair as she drew him into her mouth.

"Pey-*damn*." He bunched her hair into his fists. She heard her hair clip scatter across the floor. His hips jerked as she held him captive with her mouth. One hand gripped the base of his penis while the other fondled his testicles.

Mike's head dropped back. "I'm going to—" he muttered darkly.

She gripped him harder with her mouth. Her cheeks tingled, her jaw ached, and she wanted more. She felt insatiable. Vibrant and alive. All powerful. All woman.

Mike bucked against her mouth. He shuddered, his eyes squeezed tight as he roared with pleasure. His pulsing echoed with the throbbing between her thighs.

Peyton slowly released him. "Ssh!" she teased with a satisfied smile. "You're in a library."

Eight

Mike's hand hovered over the computer mouse. The emptiness of the library scraped at his nerves. He hesitated before deleting the e-mail from his boss, but he couldn't ignore the request to return. Or the fact that he wasn't ready to go back.

He wondered what it all meant. Was he reluctant because his last mission had failed, or did he believe he was getting as mellow as his sister suggested? Why did the challenge of claiming Peyton in the middle of this cornfield sound more exciting than chasing adventure around the globe? Because the life and the woman were exotic to him, or because he felt a connection he was unwilling to break?

The ring of the phone blistered the heavy silence surrounding him. Mike was glad for the distraction and for the first time eagerly answered the phone. "Main Library Answer Hotline. This is Mike. How can I help you?"

"Hi, Mike." Peyton's voice wafted over him like a soothing, warm blanket. "I was wondering about something."

"Yeah?"

"How does one ask a male librarian out on a date?"

Heat surged through his bones. "Very nicely. Flashing skin helps."

"That's difficult to do over the phone," Peyton said with

amusement, and Mike could picture her smiling. "Can I just say I'm naked while I'm talking to you?"

His imagination went wild. "No," he said gruffly, "because I know you're lying."

Peyton laughed. "You know me too well."

He couldn't deny it, but he knew better than to agree. "I'm waiting for you to ask me out."

"I know this is short notice, but would you like to come by my place tonight?"

"Can't," he answered, both relieved and disappointed. "I'm working. But you can come over to the library. It's closed." He flinched in surprise as he made the offer. Where the hell did that come from?

"All right," Peyton said hesitantly. "I'll be there soon."

"See you then." Mike quickly hung up the phone before he made any more suggestions.

Peyton halted in the middle of the library entrance and peered up the marble staircase that led to blackness. "Wow," she said reverently. "It looks different."

Mike closed the main door with a thud. "Yeah, better."

Peyton tilted her head back at him. "You're not a people person, are you?"

"What was your first clue?"

"I'm surprised you work in a public library," she said as she slowly turned in a full circle. The shadows made the familiar setting mysterious. Almost glamorous.

Mike shrugged off the comment and leaned against the main desk. "I'm surprised you're not out terrorizing the town."

"That's tomorrow."

"You let Macey loose for the night?" His tone clearly questioned her wisdom. "Do you think the town is ready for it?"

"I'm sure she's all tied up somewhere. That woman—" The phone rang. "Someone else calls the hotline?"

"You thought you were the only one?" Mike asked as he reached over the desk.

"I think I'm jealous," she teased.

"Shouldn't be. You give me the best questions." He placed the phone to his ear. "Main Library Answer Hotline. This is Mike. How can I help you?"

Peyton's pulse kicked from the words. Her body was conditioned to Mike's husky greeting like Pavlov's dog. She quickly turned away and moved toward the steps before he caught a glimpse of her tightening nipples.

"Doc, Happy, Sneezy . . ."

Peyton's heart turned over. The tender patience in his voice made her melt, probably because the patience was the core of who Mike Ryder was. It was definitely one of the reasons she fell in love with him.

Her foot slipped off the step. Love? She clutched the copper handrail as she repeated it in her mind over and over.

She gasped as the knowledge hit her in the chest. No, she couldn't fall in love. Peyton walked briskly up the steps. It didn't fit in the scheme of things. It, it—(a) she barely knew him, (b) she didn't have a clue how he felt . . .

Okay, she reasoned with herself when she approached the landing, technically it didn't matter how he felt. Her feelings weren't based on his. And even if he hated her guts, he wouldn't use her feelings against her.

Because that's the kind of guy he was. He had a code of honor that was unshakeable. Maybe she did know him, she mused as she cautiously stepped into the darkness, uncertain where she was going. Maybe she was falling in love with him.

Darn it. She wasn't ready for that.

"Hey, Peyton," Mike called up. His voice boomed around her, and she instinctively moved deeper into the shadows. She felt vulnerable. Hiding wasn't going to help her. She needed to brazen it out.

"Peyton?" A hint of warning sharpened his tone.

New plan. She'd hide here until the brazenness showed up.

"I was going to microwave some popcorn. Do you want some?"

Popcorn? Peyton mouthed the words in disgust. No, she most certainly did not. She wanted to show Mike how much she loved him without making herself completely vulnerable. She really wanted to strip him naked, make him breathless with hot, sweaty love, and feel him pulsing inside her. Popcorn wasn't going to get the job done.

Peyton tucked her hair behind her ears and straightened her shoulders. Now wasn't the time to wait for her brazen attitude to show up. It was time to take control of the night.

She shakily moved away from the shadows. Her footsteps reverberated in the lobby. Glancing down, Peyton saw Mike leaning against the huge newel post. His knowing look made her realize that popcorn was never on the menu.

A frisson of caution zigzagged down her spine. Mike always seemed to know what she was feeling. He knew her next move before she did. If that didn't freak her out! She needed to do something unpredictable.

She looked at the wide marble banister. No, she wouldn't . . . Peyton smiled. And that would make it the perfect move.

Peyton perched on the banister. She flinched at the cold marble as her thin sundress twisted against her legs. Raising her hands, she slid down the staircase at warp speed.

Her eyes widened as she careened downward. Peyton let out a squeal when she realized she was no longer in control. She couldn't jump off without hurting herself. If she stayed on, she'd slam into the newel post. The very big, very solid newel post.

Peyton squeezed her eyes shut. She had to jump and land in a dignified manner. One . . . two . . .

Oof! Peyton collided against Mike's chest. Her face buried deep within his soft white T-shirt, her heartbeat thudding loudly in her ears. She inhaled his warm, masculine scent before she sighed with relief.

His hands circled around her waist. She felt protected. Cherished.

She also sensed that the stunt had made her look idiotic instead of wild. A blush sizzled from her face. "I always wanted to do that," she said softly, pulling her face away from his chest. She couldn't look him in the eye.

"What stopped you before?" Amusement laced his voice. He caressed her waist with his callused fingertips.

Peyton shrugged, ignoring the rippling effect of his touch. She couldn't tell him the truth. That sliding down staircases was against the rules, and for a very good reason. That answer didn't jive with the wicked woman image. "Too many other things I wanted to do," she muttered.

"What do you want to do now?"

She tilted her chin, her gaze level with his mouth. "You." She looked up into his eyes. "Now."

His harsh features tightened as emotions flickered through his eyes. Feral and conquering. Pain. Desire. And finally surrender right before he crushed his mouth against hers.

Mike tasted the wildness that spurred Peyton on. He knew he could lose control with her and she would be primed. He also knew that the rougher, the baser the mating, the more she would relish the sex. She was on a hunt for a good time. And he was the prey.

The throbbing urgency of his cock told him not to question his fantasy coming to life. His troubled mind suggested he was picked because he was there and he was never accused of being a gentleman. His heart dropped when he realized it was just a matter of sex for the thrill of it.

He had no right to judge, but damn if it didn't hurt. He had only himself to blame. He'd told her how to be a wicked woman, and his actions had unleashed a man-eater. If he wanted her without getting destroyed, he needed to keep his emotions checked.

Mike ripped his mouth away from hers. His lungs felt ready to explode. He gazed at her wanton beauty, and his resolve slipped.

He turned her to look toward the ascent of the staircase. Away from him. The primitive longing clearly stamped on her face called to the wild beast inside him. Mike knew better than to set free his dark side.

Peyton sat astride, her flimsy sundress bunched around her bare thighs. Mike straddled the banister behind her. The bite of the newel post in his back tempered the softness of her ass against his hard cock.

Mike reminded himself that softness didn't belong in the moment. She wanted wild, untamed sex. She wanted to fuck.

He grasped her hip with one hand and held her fast. He speared his other hand through her brown long hair. Moving her head to the side, Mike latched onto the curve of her throat and sucked.

Peyton mewled and instinctively tried to pull away, but Mike wasn't finished branding his woman. She gasped when he released her, the feminine sound ricocheting inside him. He felt grim satisfaction at the angry red mark declaring his possession.

"Mike," she moaned as she moved to face him. Mike's battered heart couldn't risk a full frontal assault. His fingers tightened against her hip, caging her as he pulled her back against his chest. She slammed against him, her tangle of hair slapping his face.

Mike grabbed the folds of her dress and shoved them to her waist until he revealed her sheer panties. He wanted to unwrap her like a present. Slowly peel her clothes off her body and taste the flesh he revealed. Caress, kiss, and savor her. But she'd been looking for casual sex since she first called the hotline. He'd give it to her. He'd rather it be from him than any hicks from this town.

The thought of another man touching Peyton just about killed him. Mike grasped her breasts with more force than he intended. She writhed and moaned under his hands, arching her back, making him break into a sweat.

Mike cupped her sex. She was so hot, so wet. So ready. He stroked her clit through her damp panties and squeezed her breasts with his other hand. The lobby vibrated with Peyton's whimpers. He swallowed a groan, determined not to say anything. Words weren't expected during a good time, and the ones dancing across his tongue like hot pepper would reveal too much.

Peyton stretched her arms and laced her fingers behind his neck. He knew he was in danger of getting trapped in her pleasurable web. She brushed her lips against his unshaven jaw. "Mike." The plea gave a seductive rasp to her voice. "Enough teasing."

Mike stopped himself before he took her mouth with his. He was too susceptible and could get lost in her kisses. He lay her face down until her breasts flattened against the banister. She clutched the edges with her hands as he yanked down his zipper. He grabbed a packet from his pocket and quickly slid on a condom.

Shoving her panties to the side, he eased the tip of his cock against the entrance of her core. For a split second, Mike questioned the depths of his self-control. He knew she wanted him to rut like an animal, and his body craved the same. But he didn't want to hurt her with the raw urgency swirling inside him.

He slowly entered Peyton, pausing as her body struggled to accommodate his size. His muscles shuddered with her responsive groans. She felt hot. Tight. Damn good. His hips thrust and swung into her.

Mike tried to maintain the steady rhythm. It was a miracle

he hadn't attacked like a starving beast. He felt swollen, thick, and ready to explode as she countered his thrusts with the sway of her hips and the dip of her spine.

His balls crawled into his stomach as her husky sighs filled his ears and clouded his mind. When he felt her tighten, he knew he didn't have the willpower to hold off his innate response. His control shattered at her first scream. Ripples of her orgasm convulsed around his cock, and he pushed harder. He closed his eyes and gritted his teeth, desperate to stave off his release, but it was a lost cause.

A starburst of power stormed his body. He held on to her as he plunged into her slick heat. The marble edge stung against his thighs, but it didn't stop him. With Peyton's broken words urging him on, nothing could slow him down. His release roared through him, swiping his next breath, the next beat of his heart.

He collapsed against Peyton as he pulsed into her. With a soft grunt, she accepted his weight. Mike greedily swallowed air and listened to her banging heartbeat that matched his. God, what he wouldn't do to make Peyton Lovejoy his for life.

Peyton stirred underneath him. "I love you," she whispered.

Mike's heart jolted. It was something he wanted to hear, but it hurt so much because he knew it wasn't true. She didn't love him. She loved what he represented: a good time. And like all good things, it had to end. Now. Before it destroyed him.

Dread hit Peyton like a fist when she realized Mike heard her words. The tension in his body meant he didn't welcome the news. She braced herself, wondering if he would ignore it or purposely misconstrue the meaning.

Mike briskly disentangled himself from her. "Don't confuse a good orgasm with true love," he said, unhooking his leg from the banister.

She flinched as her exposed heart cracked from the cold words. "Don't talk down to me," she countered in a wobbly voice. She shifted and determinedly looked at his remote face.

To her surprise, Mike was the first to break eye contact. "You don't know what you're talking about," he replied, holding out his hand to help her down.

Peyton ignored his offer of assistance and jumped off the banister unaided. "I didn't expect you to respond the same way," she said calmly. She felt anything but calm.

"Yeah, you did." The rasp of his zipper seemed to punctuate his statement. He headed for the men's restroom without another word.

Maybe wished for, but never expected, she decided as she adjusted her clothes. She'd never expected for someone like Mike to fall for her. She knew how life worked, but she wished that just once the rules were broken for her.

When Mike walked back into the entry, he seemed surprised that she was still there. She belatedly realized he had given her an opportunity to leave. "I didn't mean to scare you," she muttered as she walked to the main desk to get her purse.

His eyes glittered with warning. "I don't scare that easily."

Peyton raised her hands in mock surrender. "Hey, sorry I said anything." It was difficult to say anything as the pain of rejection clawed her. "Next time I'll keep my mouth shut."

"There won't be a next time."

Ouch. Peyton couldn't stop wincing. What happened? The night had offered so much promise, and it was quickly becoming a disaster.

Mike closed his eyes for a brief moment. He looked weary. "I'm going to give it to you straight."

Peyton questioned the chances of surviving Mike uncensored. It didn't look good. "What's going on?"

His smoky gaze ensnared hers. "You wanted a good time and I gave it to you."

She narrowed her eyes. "I hope it wasn't too much of a

sacrifice." He was trying to push her away. She needed to find out why, but digging deeper would hurt more.

"You don't get it." He raked his fingers through his hair. "I let you break my focus. I'm a professional. I know better."

"Focus?" Peyton enunciated the word with disbelief. "On what?"

"My job."

She glanced around the quiet, empty library. "No offense, but just how much concentration is needed in answering phones?"

"I meant a different job." The muscles bunched in his jaw. "I'm not really a librarian."

She paused, waiting for some elaboration, but none came. "Am I supposed to be floored by this confession?" Peyton didn't know where her snippy comments were coming from, and she was sure she would regret them.

Mike scowled. "What's that supposed to mean?"

"You don't seem to fit in here." She rubbed her arms, trying to ward off the cold that originated from deep within. "The other librarians seem to know more."

A ghost of a smile played on his mouth. "Skylar will be thrilled to hear that."

"So?" She shrugged. "What's this job of yours?"

"I'm a corporate troubleshooter. What that means is—"

"Yeah. I know what guys like you do." And the moment he revealed his true profession, Peyton could picture him driving bullet-proof SUVs and using weapons with lethal efficiency. "You are a mercenary with stock options."

Mike glared at her. "I protect businessmen in areas of unrest."

She rolled her eyes at the correction. Her pain was quickly congealing into something hard and brittle. "That must look great on your resume, but it doesn't explain why you're here."

"Skylar is my sister."

Peyton drew back in shock. No. Way. The two were so diferent. "Skylar Black is really"—she frowned—"Skylar . . . Ryder?"

"Used to be." Mike walked around the main desk. "My mom thought it had a certain lilt. My sister thinks otherwise."

"What did she have to do with this?"

"She's trying to become head librarian."

Peyton was trying to understand, but none of it made sense. "By filling the staff with relatives?"

Mike rested his elbows on the desk. "She was concerned about the money coming in. There's some suspicious activity. She called me for help."

"And the suspicious activity?"

"We uncovered the embezzling."

Peyton stood still. Wow. She couldn't believe it. She knew all the librarians, and none of them would take money.

"The money is coming from the Friends of the Library."

Surprise took her breath away. No, he was wrong. Her stomach flipped with dismay. Peyton's lips parted, but she couldn't get a word out.

Mike leaned closer, his eyes level with hers. "And I think you know about it."

That jump-started her vocal cords. "What?"

"Or have something to do with it."

She stared at his face. He really meant it. He thought she was a criminal! "Of all the nerve—you think I'm stealing?"

"You're president of the group." He ticked off the points with his fingers. "You have access to the money, and you're living a double life that requires extra money."

Peyton's mouth fell open. "I'm leading a what?" She placed her fists on her hips.

"You heard me," he replied, unruffled by her outburst. "Where's the money, Peyton?"

"I don't know! I'm not a thief."

"Then Owen is."

Peyton inhaled sharply and flexed her fingers before she did something stupid. Like punch a mercenary. "He isn't. He wouldn't dirty his hands."

Mike pursed his lips as he considered her statement. "And you?"

"I don't steal!" she yelled back. The echo blistered her ears. Her body shook with anger, and she knew it was too late to pull back and hide behind her ladylike façade. "I'm leaving." She grabbed her purse.

Mike propped his chin with his hand. "Don't do it on my account."

Peyton pushed the door open before turning around. "You don't believe I stole the money. I know you don't, otherwise you wouldn't have told me about your investigation." She felt some satisfaction as Mike's face darkened. "If you got freaked out about the love thing, all you had to do was say it."

"Goodbye, Peyton," he said tersely. "I hope you had the good time you were looking for."

"It's not goodbye yet," Peyton said as she swung the door closed. "I'll let you know when it is."

Nine

Peyton turned the light on at her office desk and propped her chin on her fist. It was official: there wasn't an ounce of wickedness or wildness inside her. If there were, she would drop everything and leave the mess for someone else to clean. She would go back to her bed, take the week off, and stay at home with a freezer full of ice cream.

She rolled her eyes at the thought. She couldn't even pout like a scandalous woman. A scandalous woman would jump on a plane to an obscenely expensive spa. In fact, that kind of woman might not come back at all. If she did, it would be with an incredibly gorgeous boy toy at her side.

Peyton wrinkled her nose. Forget the boy toy. She didn't want one. She'd return it to get an exchange for someone that had more experience. More depth with the occasional rough edge. Someone she could rely on. Someone like Mike.

She groaned and clunked her forehead against her desk. She had to stop thinking about Mike Ryder. He wasn't interested in her, and she wasn't going to try to change his mind. She had more urgent things to worry about, like Lovejoy's Unmentionables.

Peyton straightened her shoulders and settled in her chair. She studied the spreadsheet again, wishing for a miracle.

Every number indicated that she had to get a deal from Macey Bonds immediately. It didn't matter that her instincts were having a temper tantrum over the idea. She had no other choice.

She had to be honest with herself, Peyton decided as her eyes began to smart with unshed tears. She had alternatives for the family business, but they were all difficult for everyone involved. None of the choices was going to make her welcome around town. She'd be blacklisted in more places than Jack's. Like the next family reunion, for instance.

Tears welled against her lashes at the thought. She knew she shouldn't care what people thought, but people's opinion of her was the only power she had. It was the reason she'd inherited this business. It was why every committee wanted her.

It was why Mike got close to her. So he could strip the good opinion away and reveal his interpretation of who she was. Peyton's bottom lip trembled as the first tear dripped down her cheek.

Maybe Mike was right; maybe she was a fraud. She'd thought her business background and creative ideas would wow everyone. She'd thought being a wicked woman would get the business deal from Macey. Now she wondered if she'd caused more trouble for everyone.

Peyton froze when she heard footsteps. She sniffed and quickly wiped her eyes. Owen walked by as she finger combed her long hair so it hid the hickey on her neck.

"Owen?" she called out to him. "What are you doing here so late?"

He popped his head around her door. "Hi, Peyton. I didn't realize you would be here. What are you working on?"

"A little bit of everything." She leaned back in her chair. "The business. Macey. Friends of the Library."

"Again?" He folded his arms across his chest. "Is Skylar bothering you?"

"Well, not really . . ." Peyton didn't know how to bring

up the embezzlement accusations. Even if she laughed it off, her cousin wasn't going to take it very well.

"Do you want me to handle her? Be the liaison?"

Peyton grew very still. How handy that would be for him. "No, no," she said casually as her senses went on full alert. "You're on more committees than me. It wouldn't be fair."

"It's not a matter of fairness." Owen flicked off a piece of lint from his sleeve. "You can't handle it. I can. What's the big deal, anyway? Family helps family."

Peyton searched his face, her heart thudding in her ears. She saw nothing out of the ordinary. It seemed like a genuine offer. She felt like a rat for questioning it.

"Thanks, Owen." She smiled weakly. "I might take up your offer, but not right now. My schedule should get better once Macey leaves town."

"Suit yourself." He shrugged and headed for the door. "But if you decide otherwise, let me know. Night, Peyton."

Peyton mumbled her response. She screwed her eyes shut the moment Owen left. She couldn't believe she'd questioned his motives. Owen was her cousin! She'd known him forever, and he had never done anything remotely illegal.

But she questioned what she knew because Mike suggested it. Peyton dug her fingers into her hair, but the stinging pain didn't erase the shame she suffered. She was so stupid to listen to that . . . jerk.

She picked up the phone. This time, he was going to listen to her, whether he wanted to or not. Her fingers flew over the buttons before she had a chance to think twice.

"Main Library Answer Hotline. This is Mike. How can I help you?"

Oh . . . boy. Peyton belatedly realized it wasn't such a good idea to call. Considering how his husky voice made her heart flutter, it was obvious that she needed intervention from the hotline. "You've helped me plenty," she informed him brusquely. "Thanks to you, I almost made one of the biggest mistakes of my life. Way to go."

"That was a comment," Mike said coolly. "This is the Answer Hotline. Was there a particular question you needed answered?"

"Yes," she replied and stuck her tongue out at the receiver. "A jerk masquerading as a gentleman gave me a hickey. I want it off and I want it off now. Despite what was said in high school, brushing it with a plastic comb or using toothpaste doesn't help. Concealer isn't hiding it, and I'm not about to wear a turtleneck in the summer."

"What's the problem?" Mike sounded bored. "The mark isn't territorial."

"Liar." She growled the word.

"It's more like a scarlet letter. Something a wicked woman would be promoting." A flash of anger pierced through his indifference. "Why hide it when you can flaunt it?"

Peyton didn't trust herself to speak. Her hands shook as she slammed the phone. She picked it up and slammed it again. Hard. Just in case he didn't get the first message.

Mike winced as the slam blistered his ear. He firmly returned the phone to the cradle, wondering why being an ass didn't come easily anymore. But he wasn't going to apologize. This was the best way. So what if the slam echoed the loneliness he felt? He'd lived with the feeling before. He'd get by.

He heard Skylar fiddling with her papers on the other side of the desk. Mike inhaled deeply and clung to the last shred of his patience. He schooled his face and turned to face her.

Her smirk set his teeth on edge. "What. Is. So. Funny?" Mike used his scariest voice. The one that made recruits blubber. It should have the same effect on his sister so she would back off.

"Nothing." Her smile grew wider.

Maybe his sister was missing the self-preservation gene. He hoped that was the case and not the possibility that he'd lost his edge. "Good. Now, where was I?"

She leaned forward on her elbows. "You and Peyton having a fight?"

Mike tensed. "What makes you think it was Peyton?" He reviewed the phone call and knew he hadn't said her name.

Skylar wiggled her eyebrows. "Because I know of the little archive encounter," she answered in a sing-song.

Mike closed his eyes briefly. Terrific. Peyton was going to die of embarrassment and add another sin to his list.

"Really, Mike," Skylar continued, sounding spookily like their mother. "Can't you take her somewhere nice?"

"She doesn't want anywhere nice," he muttered.

Skylar's expression turned dreamy. "She just wants you." She flattened her hands upon her heart. "Aw. That's so romantic."

He snorted. "No, it's not. She wanted to do some slumming." Shit. Mike winced, wondering if it was too late to eat his own tongue.

She dropped her hands. "Say what?"

Yep. Too late. "This isn't a Need To Know situation."

"How is dating my brother slumming, I'd like to know! That's it." She slapped her hands on the desk and shot out of her seat. "It's her and me, after work, in the library parking lot."

"Easy, Skylar, easy." He was too old to be associated with a rumble in the parking lot, no matter how entertaining it might prove to be. "My motives weren't that pure, either."

"You're in love with her." His sister returned to her seat. "How is that not pure?"

His skin suddenly felt hot and stretched tight. "I'm not—"

Skylar bestowed an annoying superior smile. "You are."

"Can we finish this discussion some other time?" he asked, rubbing the back of his neck. He needed to get out of this office, this building. But that would tell Skylar much more than she needed to know.

"Sure." She primly folded her hands and looked him dead

in the eye. "You were trying to explain why Peyton wasn't the prime suspect anymore." Her straight face was so perfect, it bordered on exaggeration.

Mike scowled. "It has nothing to do with how I feel about her."

"Hmm." Her mouth was suspiciously zipped.

"I think Owen Lovejoy is the culprit," he continued, struggling to concentrate on the job at hand. "He has the motive, means, and opportunity."

"And Peyton?"

"Overworked." He shrugged, wishing his body didn't go into full alert the moment he heard Peyton's name. "She depends on her cousin to handle a lot of stuff."

"So what you're saying is that Peyton's just an innocent bystander?"

Oh, God, here it comes. "Shut up."

"Peyton and Mike sitting in a tree, K-I-S-S-I-N-G," Skylar sang off-key, bopping her head to the beat. "First comes love, then comes marriage, then comes baby—"

Fragmented pictures flickered through his mind unheeded. Images of making Peyton his, now and forever. Of waking up next to her and knowing his day would be filled with love and his nights full of passion. Of Peyton growing big with his child. But none of those events would happen. Mike felt the color drain from his face.

"Oh, Mike." Skylar clapped her hand over her mouth. "I'm sorry. I didn't mean to hurt your feelings."

Mike knew exactly what he had to do. He couldn't let Peyton slip away from him. He had to show her that a good time could last a lifetime.

Skylar grasped his hand and yanked hard. "Mike, come on. Don't be mad at me, please. You know how I am. I never know when to stop teasing."

"That's true," he said distractedly. "Now shut up. I'm concentrating on a plan."

"A plan for what?"

A rare smile tugged his mouth. "For getting Peyton back."

"Yes!" Skylar pumped her fists. "Woo-hoo! I knew it! You were never one who would settle for unrequited love. So"—she rubbed her hands with anticipation—"you need any help?"

Mike's eyes widened with alarm. "No."

"You might need it," she added in wheedling tone.

"No," he repeated firmly.

"Come on, please!" She clasped her hands in prayer. "Operation Cupid is going to be complicated."

He shot a beseeching look toward the ceiling. "I don't believe this."

Ten

What am I doing here? Peyton stumbled to a halt, colliding with Macey's associates. When they said they wanted to go to a sports bar for the sexy bartenders, Peyton assumed she was going somewhere familiar. Normal.

There was no way this was a sports bar unless the Olympics recently instated sex. She was furious at herself for not questioning Macey's insistence. The establishment's name of *Score* should have at least tipped her off.

And the lingerie tycoon had been adamant to celebrate immediately after they reached a deal. It didn't matter if the contract wasn't signed. To Macey, it was an excuse to party.

"What do you want to drink?" Macey's redheaded associate shouted over the ruckus.

Peyton wouldn't be surprised if the place recycled drinking straws. "Iced tea."

The redhead shared a confused look with her blonde coworker.

"Long Island tea?" the blonde corrected.

"No, iced tea." She reluctantly removed her navy jacket to battle the steamy heat. The ecru shell blouse began to stick to her skin.

"Okay, whatever." Macey shrugged, appearing cool and

chic in a mannish shirt and hip-hugging black trousers. "I'll be right back."

Peyton sat down on the rickety chair and cautiously looked around the smoky room. She instinctively crossed her arms when she noticed every game and machine had an explicit theme. And here she thought that pinball machines crossed the line of good taste.

Gingerly leaning back in her chair, she quietly listened to the associates grade the men in the bar. Peyton did a quick survey. The men prowled around like animals in heat. Not one looked interesting. Not one reminded her of Mike.

A sigh escaped past her lips, and Peyton closed her eyes. *Forget about him.* She needed to get out of this funk. No, she needed to get out of this bar.

She opened her eyes to see Macey return with the drinks, drawing attention with her swagger and take-on-the-world smile. Peyton didn't know how the woman did it. Macey didn't care what people thought of her. She went for broke and she lived life.

Absently sipping the weak tea, Peyton wondered why she couldn't do the same. Where did she go wrong? Well, for starters, she'd accepted her inheritance and was about to lose it all because she didn't trust her own judgment. She acted like someone she wasn't to get a business deal she didn't really want but needed. She had fallen in love with a guy who thought she was a thief and broken up with him before she could get him naked.

Her shoulders sagged in defeat. Yeah, that was pretty much it.

"Come on," the blonde said as she rose from her seat. "It's about to start."

Peyton jolted from her morose thoughts. "What is?"

"The tournament," the blonde said over her shoulder.

She rolled her eyes. Whatever. Peyton stood up, hooked her purse strap firmly on her shoulder, and followed. She couldn't imagine what the tournament was about, and she wasn't going to try. At this point, she didn't care if it turned out to be flabby guys wrestling naked. Just as long as she didn't sit at the table alone, she was fine.

Peyton followed in Macey's wake, feeling dull and insipid in comparison. It wasn't that she wanted to be like Macey. Yes, the woman was successful and lived with intent, but Peyton didn't want Lovejoy's Unmentionables—or her—to be based on sensuality.

She wanted to be measured by her achievements, not her bustline. Peyton wanted to be sensual without her personality being based on it. She wanted to be herself, if it meant quietly browsing the stacks in the library or getting wild with Mike.

As for Lovejoy's Unmentionables, she wanted the company to maintain its quality reputation while updating its image. After all, they might manufacture girdles, bras, and underwear, but they didn't sell sex. They sold items to make a woman feel good. It had nothing to do with what others felt about her.

Peyton paused as the thoughts snagged in her mind. Her pulse quickened. There was something there she wasn't seeing. Something important.

"Here, you go first." Macey ushered her toward the bar. A husky man hoisted her on top of the bar. Peyton saw a few other women standing next to her. Macey's associates managed to push their way to the other end of the bar.

Peyton looked over the sea of men. Where was the tournament? She couldn't see anything set up. She peered at the other side of the dark room.

A high metallic sound screeched through the speaker system. "All right, boys and girls," said the jovial announcer, but Peyton couldn't see anyone with a microphone. "It's time for the Wet T-shirt Tournament."

She frowned. What are they talking about? *Wet—*

The crowd whooped their approval.

T-shirt—

She automatically shielded her eyes as a spotlight blared on her.

Tournament.

She looked down and saw hundreds of hungry male eyes staring back.

Her stomach flip-flopped. *Kill. Me. Now.*

Nuh-uh. No way. No how. No. No, no, no. She wasn't going to do this.

She wasn't going to be seen as a sex object instead of a person.

She especially wasn't going to do this because she wasn't wearing a bra!

Peyton turned to Macey. "Um, I-I think I'll pass."

"Oh, come on," Macey replied with a trace of annoyance. "It's good, clean fun."

"For who?" Peyton retorted just as the redheaded associate got hit with the water spray from the bartender, who clearly enjoyed his duties. The woman preened as though she was born for the moment. An outline of her bra appeared from underneath her sodden dress. The redhead used some amazing muscle techniques that made her breasts move. The crowd went wild.

Peyton's jaw almost hit the floor. "How did she do that?"

"She used to be a stripper," Macey explained matter-of-factly.

The next contestant squealed as she got soaked. She definitely wasn't wearing a bra. Obviously intimidated by the bionic breasts next to her, the local girl shimmied her hips and inched her T-shirt higher.

"No taking off shirts," the voice from the loudspeaker commanded. The men groaned in protest, but the emcee didn't yield on the rule. "Any contestant who does so will be disqualified."

Disqualified? Peyton's attention perked up. She gripped the hem of her blouse with her fingertips. Wait. What was she thinking? This was ridiculous. All she had to do was quit. To heck with what people might think of her.

She lifted her hands in surrender. "I'm out of here."

Macey turned to face her, inadvertently blocking her way. "Why?"

Peyton pressed her lips together and crossed her arms. It was past time to say how she really felt. "Because (a), I shouldn't have to increase my sensuality rating so that you guys will do business with me."

"It's the nature of the industry," Macey yelled over the crowd.

"No, it's not." She shook her head. It wasn't about the industry, or the culture, or even the times. It was about choices. "And (b), I don't think being adventurous or fun means having to have sex."

Macey squinted as if she had been thrown a brainteaser. "Then . . . why bother?"

"And (c)," Peyton continued, determined to say it all now, "I don't think underwear has to be skanky to be sensual."

"Excuse me?" The crowd was chanting over a contestant, but Peyton could hear Macey just fine. "Did you say skanky?"

"Sensual means just that." Peyton held her hand out, splaying her fingers. "The five senses. And your designs offer it, but for the person who sees the clothes. Not the one wearing them."

Macey was outraged. "You're giving *me* fashion advice?"

"No." Peyton flattened her hands on her hips. "I'm telling you that I made a mistake. I'm going to all these places that make me uncomfortable just to establish a good business relationship. But it's not much of a relationship if I'm compromising my principles."

"Principles." Macey spat out the word as if she had just tasted something past the expiration date. "Well, that's a fine time to tell me. If you don't like sex, you're not going to like making my designs."

"I like sex plenty. With the right guy."

Macey impatiently tossed her hands in the air. "Honey, there ain't no such thing as the right guy. Or, Mr. Right, Mr. Right Now, or even Mr. All Right." She turned to face the crowd, thoroughly disgusted.

"There is such a thing," Peyton insisted. "And that's when I feel wild and wicked and sexy. That's the only time that it means something."

Macey's eyes widened, and tension invaded her shoulders. "And I'm guessing your Mr. Right is that guy who followed you to the pool hall." She tilted her head in a cautionary gesture.

Peyton frowned, befuddled. She looked where Macey indicated, her gaze slamming into Mike Ryder's angry stare. "Oh . . . fudge."

"That's one way of looking at it," Macey said. "He's pissed."

Pissed? Trust Macey to downplay trouble. He was like a deadly snake ready to strike. Peyton felt her knees wobble, knowing she couldn't escape fast enough. "What is he doing h—?" She gasped as the ice cold water splashed against her.

Mike couldn't decide. Did Peyton Lovejoy keep refusing to wear a bra as a silent rebellion to her family's business or just to drive him insane?

Probably both, Mike decided as he cut through the cheering crowd. Peyton appeared stunned. He'd felt the same way when her secretary had told him where she'd gone.

He reached the bar, and Peyton looked down at him, frantically blinking the water from her eyes. "Mike. What are you doing here?" She yelped as he grabbed her from behind her knees. She landed on his shoulder with a whomp, and he headed back for the door before she could catch her breath.

"Hey, Peyton," Macey hollered, "are you sure this one is a Mr. Right?"

Mike almost smiled, but he was still too furious to actually do it. So, Peyton thought he was Mr. Right. He still had a chance with her.

She slapped his back with her purse. "Put me down right now," Peyton hissed.

Not gonna happen. The way he saw it, he was doing her a favor hiding her breasts with his shoulder. She would undoubtedly disagree.

Peyton cuffed the back of his head with her purse. He gritted his teeth when something sharp and heavy hit behind his ear. What the hell did she have in that thing? "You're making a scene," she accused.

Was this the part where he was supposed to care? Because he didn't. Guess he was never going to learn how to be a gentleman. Good thing gentlemen didn't "suit" her.

She tried to kick him. He anticipated the move and blocked it before she pierced his liver with her pointy shoe. Mike decided to lay down the law before she showed any homicidal tendencies. He patted her ass, warning her to knock it off. He wouldn't mind letting his hand linger on her sweet curve, but Peyton tensed under his warning touch.

"Jerk," she muttered under her breath.

Yeah, that was his Peyton. She really knew how to give a tongue-lashing.

"Just so you know," she said with pseudo-sweetness, "this is topping my most embarrassing moments, all of which, coincidentally, involve you! I was not this humiliated when you caught me with the slut workbook, or even when you found out that I was masturbating on the phone."

Mike ignored the bouncer's double take as Peyton listed her most embarrassing moments. He walked around his car and opened the driver's door before dumping her into his seat. Without a word, he scooted her to the other side and sat down.

Mike was prepared to use the autolock, but Peyton settled into her seat. She put on her seat belt and crossed her arms.

And then seethed. Ah, Mike thought as he gunned the engine, he loved it when women gave him the silent treatment.

Peyton kept up her attitude as Mike drove to her house. He sensed her surprise that he knew where she lived. She had to be real mad at him to remain quiet.

From the corner of his eye, Mike saw her surreptitiously removing the keys from her purse. Just as he expected, Peyton waited until he parked before she jumped out of the car and made a run for it. How she managed to get to the other side of her front door before he got there only proved two things: he had underestimated her and there was a high probability that he *was* mellowing.

Peyton yelped when she saw him and slammed the door against his foot. Mike pushed it open with ease and walked inside. After a cursory glance around her small house, he was relieved to see she wasn't a neat freak.

"Thank you for driving me home," Peyton said through clenched teeth. "You can leave now." She pointed at the door.

Mike's gaze traveled her dripping wet shirt and navy skirt that skimmed her hips in all the right places. "We have to talk."

"I have nothing to say to you." She stabbed her finger at the door again.

He stuffed his hands in his pockets. "First you need to change," he said gruffly.

"Oh." She plucked at her blouse. "Does my appearance bother you?"

The wet material rippled across her chest, creating a series of X-rated fantasies. Mike suddenly found it difficult to swallow. To breathe. His cleared his throat, which felt as tight and heavy as his cock. "Yes."

She stiffened, and he could feel her tension from across the room. "Why?"

He wasn't going to speak his mind. Peyton knew he was

uncivilized, but she didn't need to know just how untamed he could be. "Do you have any idea what you look like?"

Her defiant expression crumbled. "Yes." Her bottom lip quivered. "I'm finally getting the idea." She staggered to the sofa and collapsed face-first.

Mike stared at her and then glanced around the room. Hell, what just happened here? "Peyton?"

"Go home." She raised her arm and floppily pointed to the door. "Just leave."

Did she think he would do that? She had a lot to learn, Mike decided as he strode toward the sofa. "What idea?"

"That I look stupid." Her reply was muffled.

"Uh . . . no." She made his head buzz, his heart race, and his cock throb. He was the one who could barely string two words together in that kind of condition. "Peyton, you got it all wrong."

"I know. That's the whole problem," she wailed.

She lifted her head. His chest squeezed at the sight of her tear-streaked face. It hurt more than the time he punctured a lung. Mike didn't know what the problem was, but he would do anything to fix it.

"I got everything wrong," she admitted. "I thought I could save Lovejoy's Unmentionables. Wrong. Then I decided that Macey Bonds was the answer to all my problems. Wrong! Then I thought acting like a wanton would get me the deal. It did, but at what cost? Look at me." Her voice raised an octave. "I look like a moron."

Mike crouched down in front of her and met her teary gaze. "No, you don't."

She shyly tucked her chin before burrowing her face into a sofa pillow. "I'm tired. Upset. Wet."

He stroked her mussed hair. It felt warm and soft under his callused hand. "You're sweet and sexy," he corrected.

"Stop trying to cheer me up," she said in the pillow. "It won't work."

"I'm not that nice," he reminded her, threading his fingers in her long tresses. "If I thought you were doing something stupid, I'd tell you."

He heard her dainty sniff. "That's true."

"The wet T-shirt contest was stupid," he said, and watched Peyton's head nod in quick agreement. "Hanging out with Macey is stupid." Peyton kept nodding. "Getting mad at me is stupid."

Peyton stopped in mid-nod. "Oh, I should have seen that coming." She shot an accusing glare at him.

Mike let his hand fall from her. He had to say everything before he lost his nerve. "I don't think you're a thief."

She drew back, hesitant to accept his confession. "You did."

"At first," he admitted, "but then I met you. And that stuff I said about you involved in the embezzling? I know you wouldn't do that. I lied. I'm sorry I hurt you."

"You don't know anything about me," Peyton said sadly. "It's all been an act."

"Believe me, I looked hard enough that I could see through the act," Mike said. "It didn't take long to tell that you are loyal and hardworking. You're also kind of goofy and follow the rules too much, but I love that, too. I love everything about you."

Her lips parted in surprise. Mike's heart pounded in his ears. "Yeah, I . . ." Damn, now wasn't the time to choke. "Love you."

Peyton's eyes glowed. "It'll get easier saying that with practice."

He claimed her mouth with his, but before he could deepen the kiss, she broke away. "No," she muttered and held her hands up, "this isn't going to work."

Mike groaned with frustration. Maybe he should have gotten some advice from Skylar and followed Operation Cupid. Oh, God, what was he thinking?

"You may say you love me, but you don't want to." She sat up. "You made that perfectly clear."

Mike straightened to his full height. "I messed up. I . . . I was"—he rubbed the back of his neck—"scared."

That got Peyton's attention. "You were?"

He looked away. "Do we have to talk about this? Now?" He knew he could spill his guts to Peyton. He trusted her and knew he wouldn't regret saying anything. He could probably tell her anything from his dreams to his nightmares, but it didn't make sharing any easier.

"Yes." Her tone held a bite of steel he hadn't heard before. It was comforting. Arousing. "What are you scared about?"

"I'm more . . . scared"—he despised that word—"of losing you. I don't think I could live with myself if I did that." Mike waited, but was greeted by a silence that scraped at his nerves. "Say something."

She rose from the sofa and stood in front of him. "You haven't lost me."

"Close," he muttered. His hands bunched and flexed at his sides. He wanted to kiss the hell out of her. But everything felt unfamiliar. Dangerous territory. One move and he could put everything at risk.

Peyton captured his gaze with her knowing eyes. "You're not going to lose me," she promised gently. She hooked her arms around his shoulders and pressed her soft curves against his hard body.

He wrapped his arms around her. He couldn't pull back. His self-control was slipping fast. "What do we do now?"

Peyton arched her eyebrow. "You're asking me for advice?"

"No," he replied hoarsely. "Just asking for some input."

The corners of her mouth twitched. "Follow your instincts."

His hands slid down her back to the gentle slope of her hips. "My instincts are leading me to your bedroom." He cupped her ass.

"Yes, finally!" Peyton wagged her eyebrows suggestively. "Then do it. Take me to bed."

Eleven

Peyton gazed out the passenger's window as her hometown stirred around her on the sleepy summer Saturday. She tilted the cell phone away from her ear as Macey ranted. She had not been looking forward to this particular conversation, but it had to be dealt with immediately.

Mike reached over and rested his large hand on her leg. She immediately took comfort in his strength, and her heel stopped tapping against the floor mat. "Calm down, Macey," Peyton said on the phone.

"You're bailing out on me," the other woman accused.

"No, I'm reconsidering." She curled her fingers over Mike's scarred knuckles. "I still want to do business with you." *Only my way,* she added silently. *My rules.*

"Even though my designs are too *skanky* for your tastes?"

Okay, she probably should have used some restraint on her vocabulary. "Do you want my honest opinion or not?"

"Not." Macey paused and sighed loudly. "Maybe. It would be a refreshing change."

"That's because all your groupies know 'yes' is your favorite word," Peyton teased before she resumed her business persona. "Now this is what I propose."

"I can't wait to hear this."

Peyton's confidence waffled under Macey's sharp sarcasm. She hesitated, and felt Mike's hand move. Looking down, she saw his thumb stroke her knee. "We manufacture the items that work within Lovejoy's Unmentionable's mission statement. Anything that makes a woman feel good. Off the top of my head I'm thinking the whole cami set collection and the bras with matching panties."

Macey was silent for a moment. "Exactly how does this help me?"

"You want quality stuff, right? Have us do the job we're best equipped for." Peyton tried to sound confident, but she couldn't stop the jitters. She was going for broke, and it didn't feel exciting. It felt nauseating. But she couldn't play it safe this time. Her only backup was her instinct and Mike's belief that she could do it.

"Then what am I supposed to do about my other production needs?"

"I know a couple of manufacturers who might be able to do some of your collection. But they specialize and can't do it all." She felt as though she was bombing. About to crash. Kaboom and splat. No way could they peel her off the pavement after this spectacular failure. Her eyes stung. "Let's meet in my office Monday and we'll get into more detail," she breezily offered.

"You mean I have to stay in this hick town longer?"

Peyton's chest tightened. Wait. That wasn't a flat-out no. Macey was willing to hear what she had to say. Her hopes soared. She squeezed Mike's hand before flashing a big, fat smile to everyone on Main Street. "Aw, you don't mean that," she told Macey.

"Yes, I do," she replied with feeling.

"There's inspiration in every corner of this place." Her voice went up a notch as Mike's hand inched up her leg. She clamped her thighs together. "Go visit a farm." She heard his choked laughter at the suggestion.

Macey huffed with disbelief. "I don't think so."

"But you're"—there had to be something around here for Macey—"missing a farmer's daughter outfit in your catalog." Wow, that was scary. She didn't remember noticing that. Maybe there was something to be said about flying without a net.

"I am? How can that be?"

Peyton heard paper shuffling and pictured Macey looking for her latest catalog. "See, this place will do you good."

"Gawd," Macey stretched the word into several syllables, "you are way too cheerful. You must have gotten lucky last night."

A secretive smile played on her lips. "See you Monday." Peyton ended the call and turned to Mike. "Thanks for letting me use your phone."

"No problem." He pocketed the small electronic. "I knew yours was ruined from the infamous bubble bath."

Peyton made a face and ignored the blush streaking across her skin. "It's going to be difficult to explain that to my phone company." She frowned when he turned the car into the library parking lot. "You got me out of bed because you had to work? But you don't even work here. What gives?"

Mike turned off the ignition and paused. "There are a few things I have to do," he said finally before he got out of the car and walked over to her side.

"And then you have the day off?" Peyton asked as she scrambled out of her seat. "Maybe we can do something later." Anticipation fluttered inside her. She had that list of fantasies they hadn't even touched.

"If you'll want to," Mike answered cryptically and escorted her inside the building. She barely had a chance to greet Skylar at the main desk before he hurried her into the empty meeting room. "Stay here. I'll be right back."

Peyton didn't have time to utter a word as he left the room, softly shutting the door behind him. Why did she have to be here, the one place in the library that didn't have books? She shrugged and opened her purse. When the time was right, she would find out what had him preoccupied.

She was sitting at the wood table, scribbling and scratching out numbers on the back of an envelope, when Mike returned. "That was fast," she said.

"What are you doing?" he asked as he rounded the table.

"Trying to come up with some ideas to increase Lovejoy's cash flow," Peyton said as she gathered her stuff. "With the lack of money coming in, I have to make some really tough decisions."

Mike sat on the edge of the table. "I'm proud of you."

She ducked her head, the praise taking her by surprise. "You're backing a fool," she muttered as she closed her purse.

"Never." He curled his fingers under her chin and tilted her face until she met his gaze. "I'm always on the winning side," Mike reminded her.

Skylar walked into the meeting room, saving Peyton from explaining that all winning streaks end. Mike let his hand drop before standing behind Peyton's chair.

Peyton rose from her seat when she saw her cousin and his wife walk in. Owen was dressed casually in chinos and a pink polo shirt while Samantha's dress reminded her of delicately spun cotton candy. "What are you guys doing here?" Dread seeped in her bones when Skylar shut the door and leaned against it.

"I have no clue," Owen responded haughtily. "I received a message from Skylar to be here when the library opened."

Oh, no. "Mike, please." Peyton turned and warned him silently with pleading eyes. Mike didn't understand how things worked in this town. A stranger couldn't go accusing a highly connected local guy of a crime without suffering repercussions. "This is ridiculous."

There was no trace of tenderness in his face. "If it is, then I will take the blame."

It was going to be a disaster. "You have it all wrong," she insisted.

"What?" Owen interrupted. "What's wrong?"

"Someone is stealing from the library through the Friends of the Library fund." Skylar cut to the chase. "We think it's you."

Peyton whirled around. "Not we," she clarified. "Skylar and Mike."

"Me? Owen Lovejoy the fourth embezzle?" He shook his head with disbelief and chuckled. "You are out of your mind."

"Did you?" Mike asked, showing no signs of sharing Owen's sense of humor.

Her cousin stopped smiling. "No," he answered irritably.

"Did you know embezzling was going on?" Peyton winced at Mike's rapid-fire interrogation. It could only get worse.

Owen shot a scathing look at Mike. "Who are you to question me?"

Peyton walked away from the table before Mike could leap over it. While her cousin understood the way things worked around town, he had no idea about Mike Ryder's code of conduct. "Owen, you don't have to listen to this." She cupped his elbow. "Why don't you and Samantha leave? I'll deal with it."

"No one is leaving until we get this settled," Mike announced as he strode toward Owen. That coldness in his voice made her skin prickle. Peyton noticed no one was questioning his authority anymore.

"Leave him alone," she said. "He wouldn't do such a thing."

Mike's nostrils flared. "Stop defending him."

"Yes, Peyton," Owen said as he shook off her hand. "I'm quite capable of defending myself. I don't need to hide behind a woman."

"Owen!" His words had the same effect as a slap. Peyton slid a look at Samantha, who hunched her shoulders and was blocking out the conversation. "I'm only trying—"

"Why would I steal from the Friend's fund? I'm on the board of all the local charities. Much more prestigious ones."

"Do you embezzle from them, too?" Skylar piped up from where she remained standing by the door. Samantha, standing beside the librarian, flinched from her bluntness.

Owen glared at her, his eyes narrowing into slits. "I don't steal."

"Glad to hear it," Mike said. "Now back it up with proof. Let's start with looking over the Friend's checkbook." He crossed his arms. "Do you have a problem with that?"

"I don't have it on me." Owen gave a cursory pat to his pockets. "I never do. You'll have to ask Samantha where she keeps it."

Realization crashed through Peyton's troubled mind. She could almost hear the pieces falling together like tinkling shards of glass. Mike shimmered with tension, and Peyton knew he'd come to the same conclusion.

"It's more important for me to be at the meetings to make the decisions," Owen explained, jutting his chin out. "Samantha has the time to—"

Peyton and Mike turned to Samantha. The woman dipped her head in shame and covered her face with shaking hands.

Half an hour later, Mike silently watched his sister lead Samantha and Owen out of the meeting room. He didn't feel victorious nor as though it was a job well done. He felt weary.

When the door closed with a snick, Peyton pushed away from the shadowy corner. Mike was keenly aware that she had been there for the entire showdown. He couldn't figure out if she was upset about her relatives, uncomfortable about being there, or just trying to avoid his silent support.

"Skylar was very generous," Peyton finally said, unable to look him in the eye.

"That's my sister. She should have been tougher." Mike walked toward her. She looked lost and alone, and he needed to show her that wasn't true anymore.

"I still think it was wrong of you guys to take the law into your own hands," Peyton complained, "but I understand it." She rubbed her arms as if she caught a chill. "If Samantha went to jail, it would have destroyed her. Repaying the money and doing community service at the library is much more just."

"Probably. Or maybe Skylar knew the sheriff's daughter wasn't going to get a police record," he added cynically. Mike reached for Peyton, but she turned away. He didn't think it was an accident. Cold fear gripped him.

"She might prefer some jail time than going home with Owen," Peyton murmured as she cast a worried glance at the door. "He took it personally."

Mike placed his hands on her rigid shoulders and gently massaged her tense muscles. "Yeah, it has to be hard discovering that your wife embezzled money from your charity so she could buy things from the sex shop you hate."

Peyton leaned against his chest. He swallowed a sigh of relief. He moved his arms to hold her close and share his strength. But she didn't want any of that and broke free.

What was he doing wrong? "Peyton, I'm sorry." He splayed his hands out, helpless and hating the feeling.

She turned around, confused. "That you thought Owen did it? Don't apologize to me about it."

Mike stepped toward her, but she turned away again. Damn if he was going to chase her all over the room. "I'm sorry you hate me because of it," he said, fear and frustration burring his words.

She stumbled to a halt. "I don't hate you."

"Could have fooled me. Ever since I proved what Samantha did, you've been keeping your distance from me." Her guilty flinch boosted his fear. "I had to fulfill my promise to Skylar by revealing Samantha's actions."

He saw Peyton take a deep breath before she faced him. "And you did it. So now what?"

He was definitely missing something. "What are you talking about?"

"You had your showdown with the bad guys." She made quotation marks in the air with her fingers. "You saved the town. Rather, the library. Do you go riding off in the sunset next?"

Realization hit him like a sucker punch. She thought he was leaving her. He was pissed she would think that of him, that he would take her love and walk away. But then, he'd never given her any reassurance. "Oh, now I get it. You're waiting for me to leave," he claimed, knowing he was dead wrong but wanting to get a rise out of her. "You had your fling and you want to get back to your normal life."

Peyton looked at him as if he was an idiot. "Hardly." She stalked to the table and grabbed her purse.

"Good." He crossed his arms and braced his feet. "Because I'm staying."

Her purse slid from her fingers and hit the floor. "You are?" The hope flickering across her face warmed his heart.

"Yep. Before Owen came in here, I e-mailed my boss and resigned. Effective immediately." And it felt better than he expected.

"No way." She gripped the table edge and leaned against it. He saw her chest rise and fall as she tried not to get too excited. "What are you going to do?"

"I need to find a job." He didn't know who would hire a retired troubleshooter with bad knees. No way would he work for Lovejoy's Unmentionables. "A place to live. I wouldn't want you to marry an unemployed homeless guy."

Peyton's mouth moved before she uttered a sound. "Marry."

"Yeah." He approached her, his eyes steady and confident on her stunned face. "We're getting married."

"You haven't asked me," she pointed out.

He set his hands on either of her and leaned in, inhaling her scent. "Why should I? I know the answer."

"Very funny," she answered primly. "Come on, Mike. I can't consider marrying you until I get a proposal."

He leaned in further, surrounding her. Trapping her between the table and him. Peyton grabbed his T-shirt with her fingertips so she wouldn't fall. "So," he asked, his mouth a kiss away from hers, "do you wanna?"

Her eyes gleamed as she pressed her lips tight, refraining her laughter. "A proper proposal."

"I'm not much into being proper." He swooped down for a kiss, but captured the mischievous corner of her mouth as Peyton dodged.

"That's part of your charm. Now get down on your knee." She pushed at his chest, but it didn't budge him. "And beg." She relished the word.

He did neither. Mike cradled her face with his hands and looked into her eyes that mirrored his love. "Will you marry me?" he asked, his voice husky with emotion.

Peyton's glow dimmed. "Are you sure that's what you want?" she asked in all seriousness. "My life is here."

"I'm beginning to see why you like this place." And he did. He still wasn't too sure about the cornfields, but the town had everything his soul had been craving.

Her hands crept up his shoulders, and she laced them behind his neck. "Being married isn't going to be as exciting as your former life."

"You're right," he agreed. He wrapped his arms around her and held her tightly. "It's going to be more of an adventure with you at my side."

Peyton's blush fascinated him. "And I'm not a wild woman," she confessed.

"You are. When we're alone." He brushed his mouth against hers, his body shuddering with impatience. "Because you know."

A frown creased her forehead. "Know what?"

"That you can have your wicked way with me."

Please turn the page for
an exciting preview of
THE IRISH DEVIL
by Diane Whiteside.
Also available this month from Brava.

Donovan & Sons was busier than usual, with men working hard to load a series of wagons. Viola's eyes passed over them quickly, seeking one particular fellow clad in a well-tailored suit. He could be found occasionally in a teamster's rough garb but only when driving a wagon. His clean-shaven face was always a strong contrast to every other man's abundant whiskers.

Her eyes lingered on a dark head above broad shoulders, tugging hard on a wagonload's embracing ropes. The right height and build, but red flannel? Then the man turned and Donovan's brilliant blue eyes locked with hers.

Viola gulped and nodded at him.

His eyebrows lifted for a moment, then he returned her silent greeting. He strode toward her, still gentlemanly despite his dust. She was barely aware of his men's curiosity.

"Mrs. Ross. It is an honor to see you here." Her grandmother would have approved of his handshake but not his appearance. His black hair was disheveled, his clothing was streaked with dust, his scent reeked of horses and sweat.

And his shoulders looked so much more masculine under the thin red flannel than they ever had in English broadcloth.

She swallowed and tried to think logically. She was here to

gain his protection, no matter what distractions his appearance offered.

William smiled down at Viola, curious why she'd come to the depot. Probably for money to return back East.

"May I have a word with you in private, Mr. Donovan?"

Poor lady, she sounded so awkward and embarrassed. "Certainly. We can use the office," he soothed, and led the way across the yard. "Would you care for some fresh tea or coffee?"

"No, thank you. What I have to say should not take long."

She must want a seat on the next stagecoach out of town, if the conversation must be fast. Buy her that ticket and she'd be gone in a day. Bloody hell.

William ushered her into the small room, bare except for the minimum of furniture, all solid, scarred, and littered with paperwork.

She accepted the indicated seat but was wretchedly nervous, almost fidgeting in her chair. He wanted to snatch her up and swear the world would never hurt her again, then hunt down Charlie Jones and his fool wife. William closed the wooden shutters on the single window, filtering out much of the light and noise from the bustling corrals, then settled into his big oak swivel chair.

"What can I do for you, Mrs. Ross?" He kept his voice gentle, his California drawl soft against the muffled noises from outside.

She took a deep breath, drew herself up straight and tall, and launched into speech. "May I become your mistress, Mr. Donovan?"

"What? What the devil are you talking about?" he choked, too stunned to watch his language. He knew his mouth was hanging open. "Are you making a joke, Mrs. Ross?"

"Hardly, Mr. Donovan." She met his eyes directly, pulse pounding in her throat. "You may not have heard, but my business partner sold everything to Mr. Lennox."

He nodded curtly. He must have been right before: she

needed money. "I met Mr. and Mrs. Jones on their way out of town. I won't be doing business with them again," he added harshly.

"Quite so. But my only choices now are to marry Mr. Lennox or find another man to protect me. I'd rather be yours than an Apache's."

"Jesus, Mary and Joseph," William muttered as he stood and began to pace. *Think, boyo, think. She deserves better than being your woman.* Heat lanced from his heart down his spine at the thought of her in his arms every night. Marriage? No, she'd never agree to a Catholic ceremony. "There are other men, men who'd marry you," he pointed out hoarsely.

"I will not remarry. Besides, Mr. Lennox blocked all offers other than his."

"Son of a bitch." The bastard should be shot. "What about your family?"

"They disinherited me when I married Edward. Both families refused my letters informing them of his death."

How the devil could a parent abandon a child, no matter what the quarrel? His father had given everything to protect his children.

William's gut tightened at the thought. Condoms were helpful but not a guarantee. If she stayed in his bed long enough, the odds were good . . .

"You could become pregnant," he warned, his eyes returning to her face. Blessed Virgin, what he wouldn't do to see Viola proud and happy, holding his babe in her arms.

"I can't have children."

"The fault could be in the stallion, not the mare," William suggested, his drawl more pronounced. And this stallion would dearly love to prove his potency where another had failed.

And we don't think you will want to miss
IMMORTAL BAD BOYS.
Here's a taste of Rebecca York's story,
"Night Ecstasy."
Available next month from Brava.

When a striking redhead walked in, he was lounging comfortably at a table near the door. She'd dressed casually, in dark slacks and an emerald green knit top.

As she stood looking around the room, he gave her a little wave.

With a slightly hesitant smile on her face, she crossed to him.

"Taylor?"

"Yes."

"I'm Jules."

"Nice to meet you," she said in that low sexy voice that he liked as much in person as over the phone.

They shook, and he also liked the firm strength of her hand. His own hand was large and warm. One thing he'd been amused about in his reading was the notion that a vampire had to be cold. In reality, he had control of his own temperature, just the way he had control over a partner's mind when he was drawing blood. And since he walked through the world of men, he kept his own body at a steady ninety-eight-point-six.

He was aware of her tantalizing woman's scent drifting

toward him. And of the way she licked her lips with an endearingly nervous gesture.

He cleared his throat. "What can I get you?"

"Chardonnay."

He ordered from the bartender, then ushered her outside onto the cement deck overlooking the river, just as a tourist paddle wheel boat went by. In the warm night, there were few people outside, and it wasn't difficult to find a corner table.

He crossed his legs at the ankles and stretched them out beside the table, trying to look a lot more casual than he felt. He'd rarely been more attracted to a woman. And he wanted to get to know her better. "So what really brings you to the city?"

She hesitated for a moment before saying, "I needed to get away from a man who wanted to continue a relationship with me—when we both knew it was over."

"That's a pretty direct answer."

"I know. But I hate evasions, and I wanted us to start out on the right foot."

Evasions? Like the guy sitting across from you is a vampire?

He lifted the bottle and covered the opening with his tongue, just letting the beer wet his lips, thinking that if he were totally frank with her, she'd run screaming from the premises.

"I checked out some of your work," he said instead.

"How? I presume you didn't make a quick trip to San Francisco or Monterey?"

"Google."

She laughed. "It's hard to keep secrets these days."

"Some people manage it," he answered. "I like your technique and your subject matter."

"In which paintings?" she challenged.

"All of them. You started off experimenting with forms and colors. And you've matured as an artist."

"I've gotten stale," she answered quickly, her slender fingers clenching the stem of the wineglass. Scraping back her chair, she crossed the railing and stood staring out at the dark river.

He followed her. "Why do you think so?"

"I need a change of scenery and some new subject matter."

"In the nightclubs of Sin City?"

She raised her chin. "If you put it that way, yes. New experiences often spark my creativity."

He was thinking of a new experience he could give her when she asked, "Can you tell me a little bit about yourself?"

"Like what?"

"You have a British accent. Were you born there?"

"Yes. But I was lucky enough to get away from that cold climate."

"So the sin attracted you to New Orleans?"

"The heat, actually." He tipped his head to one side, watching her. "If we're going slumming, I need to know we're completely comfortable with each other."

"What do you mean?" she asked, the fine edge of nerves audible in her voice.

He knew from her work that she was an assertive woman who had artistic talent, training, and bold ideas about her own work. But now he sensed the vulnerability that she strove to keep hidden.

He lifted the glass from her hand and set it on the table before turning back to her.

Clasping her hand to his, he led her around a corner, to a small balcony where they were alone in the humid night with only the sounds and smells of the city drifting up toward them.

It could begin and end here, he thought with a mixture of dread and anticipation. But he'd decided that if this wasn't going to work out the way he wanted, then ending it immediately was best.

Silently, he pulled her close, swamped by so many sensations at once that his brain went from anticipation to overcharged in the space of a heartbeat. He could feel the shape of her slender body. The pressure of her high breasts against his chest. The brush of her red curls on his cheek.

And he was captured by that sweet woman's scent that had tantalized him from the first moment she'd walked into the bar.

She stood quietly in his arms, as though debating whether to take the next step.

He held his breath, and slowly, slowly she raised her face, meeting his questioning gaze.

There was only a brief moment of eye contact—but enough for a silent question and answer. With her permission, he lowered his lips to hers.

He had wanted to know if they would be good together. Good was hardly the right word.